# Deadly Pursuer

S. A. Stacy

Farm Girl Publishing

Deadly Pursuer
© by S. A. Stacy. All rights reserved

Published by Farm Girl Publishing
Olympia, WA

ISBN 978-1-7349200-0-0 paperback
ISBN 978-1-7349200-1-7 eBook

Library of Congress Control Number 2020910125

*To Mike, who always believes in me.*

# Acknowledgment

*To April, Joanna, Barb, Maco, Greg, Diane, Sarah, Michele, Jerry, and many others, without whom this book would not have been written.*

*Cover Design by Kerry Ellis*

*Interior Layout by Polgarus Studio*

# PART ONE

# HUNTED

# CHAPTER ONE
## Seattle 5:30 AM

Private investigator Katie Parson shivered in the morning drizzle after having endured a two-hour video stakeout of a fraud target while he pumped away on his elliptical. Her foolish decision at four AM that she needed sleep more than coffee haunted her as her cold body cried out for a hot Americano. Seattle natives thrive on the brown liquid that flowed from shops conveniently nestled in every corner of the city. She hurried toward a nearby shop that shined like a beacon to her coffee-less soul.

Fortunately, Katie's insurance mark had ignored Katie in her homeless disguise as she dragged her plastic bag of stuff. She stood outside his apartment window and crazily waved her funky hat with its hidden camera. The video would be evidence presented later today to her insurance company client, Fidelity State Insurance, who, although they weren't the best in compensation, at least they paid promptly.

Katie needed that check, and she didn't need her morning interrupted, but she saw trouble headed her way.

Between her and a coffee shop haven, two men approached Katie on the street. She recognized Federal officer Matt Dunn, a man she met years ago while training to be a government agent. Both officer's eyes scoured the sidewalks and the homeless woman in front of them.

To Katie's trained eye, they hunted someone, which meant a government operation was in play.

She couldn't afford to get swept up in what they were doing. As Matt glanced in her direction, she muttered, and eccentrically waved her hands at the rain. She ducked into the Pavilion Hotel parking garage. The wrong choice—both men turned into the garage. She slipped behind the empty parking booth and hoped for a quick escape to the sidewalk.

Gunfire shattered the morning. An Asian man in a blood-soaked shirt stumbled from the hotel elevator. Shots erupted from behind a concrete pillar and hit both agents as they dove for cover. Ten feet from Katie, blood spurted from Dunn's inside thigh. Femoral artery? He would bleed out in minutes.

No sign of backup. Katie's jaw tightened. She drew a Kahr 9mm from under her ankle-length skirt, stood, and fired.

Agent Dunn discharged his gun simultaneously, and a bullet hit the gunman in the shoulder and spun him to the ground. Dunn rolled for cover.

Katie saw Dunn's head snap back as he looked for a second shooter. She slid down the concrete wall and prayed he didn't fire on her. In a frantic search for the police app she used for emergencies, she tapped her phone. The sound of sirens echoed in the garage. Maybe this would spook the gunman? A metallic flash near her feet grabbed her attention, and she bent down to recover her brass with one hand and shoved her gun in the holster with the other.

She looked through the Plexiglass of the booth at Dunn's ashen face. He grabbed his phone and spoke intensely for a few seconds and disconnected.

"Hey," she said loud enough for him to hear but not echo in the garage, "I'm coming to help you."

"Identify yourself." The Glock pointed at her indicated he meant it.

"Homeland."

"OP Name?"

Katie knew he would remember a Top-Secret Homeland Security operation that took place five years ago.

"An out-of-date one. Descendant."

As she expected, Dunn looked astonished. He lowered his gun.

"Listen, no one will get here in time to help you. You're in shock—no need to worry about being shot again because you'll bleed to death first. I need your belt," Katie said.

Katie crawled to him, loosened his belt, and dragged it free. She wrangled it around his leg. He grunted and winced when she yanked it tight. The flow decreased.

His green eyes locked on her.

"Do you have any spare change?" Katie asked with a straight face.

"Surprised you didn't check my pockets when you took my belt. Do I know you?"

"Is that your best pickup line? And me sporting my best homeless stink."

"Can't disagree." He gagged.

"Hang on, handsome. Is a Homeland team on the way?"

"Did you *see* the shooter?" He ignored her question.

"I heard a shot. A guy in the middle of the garage went down. What's the ETA on help?" She hoped to distract him from the who-shot-the-gunman question.

He lifted five bloody fingers.

Way too long. Katie didn't like the odds of her rusty shooting skills, along with a critically injured agent against the expertise of a professional killer.

Both heard running footsteps on the far side of the garage. Urgently Dunn said, "Can you see my partner?"

"No. Keep pressure on your leg, I will check on him."

Katie scooted away from him.

Katie had come in on Sixth Avenue, but the shooter seemed headed for the Seneca Street exit. Was he the only gunman? She carried first aid supplies in the garbage bag that she dragged along as her homeless stuff. The hair rose on the back of her neck as she grabbed it and ran to the injured man.

Blood pooled on the concrete under his head as he lay unconscious. She pressed her ear to his chest and heard shallow breaths. He needed skilled medical attention.

Katie inched to a garage pillar and stood behind it for cover as she looked for the shooter. A man ran up the exit ramp across the garage. He looked back for any pursuers, and Katie snapped a picture with her cell phone.

Nothing about his face or attire—a gray sweatshirt, blue jeans, and a ball cap—drew attention. He grimaced as he looked in Dunn's direction and disappeared into the next level.

It had been years since Katie had briefly seen Matt Dunn during the long-ago black-op called Descendent. He had not recognized her just now even though he acknowledged the operation name. In a few minutes, law enforcement and feds would invade the garage. If present, she would be taken into custody for interrogation and maybe even charged for the shooting. If she left immediately, she would avoid involvement in this operation gone wrong. The camera in her garbage bag contained the photos she took this morning, the outcome of two weeks of private investigation work. What if they confiscated her camera? Her chest tightened and her breath came in gulps.

The gunman's quick action when he turned to shoot both agents seemed like part of an ambush plan. Had someone leaked the location of these feds to the shooter? Was the leak supposed to end in their deaths? She shivered—a reminder of why she left government training to become a private investigator.

If she exited the garage, she would break laws, but if she stayed, it could mean publicity. A private investigator lived under the radar, and public exposure could destroy her livelihood. Agent Dunn and his partner would survive until help arrived, the Asian man hadn't moved, and Katie presumed him dead.

A few flies buzzed around her from the stench of rancid grease coming from her clothing. Out of Dunn's line of sight, she squatted and turned off the siren app. She pulled her layered shirts, frazzled hat, wig, and sunglasses over her head and threw them into her bag. The blue hoodie underneath covered her mop of curls. She slid the skirt and boots off to her black leggings. The gloves covered in Matt Dunn's blood she tossed into a smaller plastic bag. Inside the garbage bag was her getaway athletic duffle. Katie grabbed out her tennis shoes and a small umbrella. Everything else she shoved into the duffle and zipped it.

Thirty seconds, a change Katie had practiced many times. Her street alias "Sally" disappeared. Her chances of *not* being recognized as a homeless woman who entered the garage raised a notch. But she still needed to leave the building unseen if she wanted to avoid identification and possible arrest. Her success at this would take all her expertise as an investigator.

Katie looked for an exit on this side of the garage. She saw a door marked "Staff Only." It was not far from the position from which the gunman had fired. Had he entered there? Katie could see the door was held open with a little scrap of wood. Likely done by the gunman and he probably had disabled cameras to prevent recording his presence. Real sirens loudly blasted nearby.

Three black SUVs slammed to a stop before they turned into the garage. Katie kept the pillar as a cover between her and the arriving agents. She tugged her sleeve down over her hand and pulled on the door handle. She saw a long hall, and she needed to choose between two doors, one marked "Stairs," the other "Exit."

Any spying government drone outside or security camera would capture a photo of her as she left the garage, which made the stairs her best hope. The possibility of being hunted by the government or the killer meant she had to evade security cameras. Good PIs always had anonymity in their bag of tricks. Today she would need divine invisibility.

# CHAPTER TWO
## MATT DUNN

Matt watched the woman scuttle toward his partner, Ned York. Nothing in his training taught him to trust people, yet her honest directness and a vague sense of familiarity tugged at him. Matt had called in the attack to his backup team using his government phone. Earlier, when his supervisor told him where the team would be, red flags popped up in his mind about their location being so far away, but he shrugged them off when his boss insisted this was standard procedure.

He took out a different phone from his inside pocket and texted a message.

> Set up. We took fire, Ned is down, condition unknown. Tourniquet on my right femoral. Send someone to ride in an emergency vehicle to the trauma center. Meet there for information control on medical.

His phone vibrated in a returned text.

> Understood. Pluto alerted.

Matt winced as he put pressure on his leg. He heard running footsteps on the far side of the garage—the assassin as he escaped. Both he and his partner left helpless. Whoever had set them up had intended for no witnesses to survive. Anger kept his mind sharp as he tried to work through who knew their position. Who was the woman? Had his handler provided her as a back door in case of an attack? That op name she had used was top secret, and that meant she had to be the second shooter, and yet everything about her appearance suggested she wasn't. If she was the second shooter, she had saved Ned's life and his. He would wait to see what showed up on video surveillance. However, as he considered the intelligence on this possible assassin, likely he would have disabled cameras in the garage. Hard to think. What had the woman said, shock?

Sirens were screaming, and yet agency SUVs were the first to arrive. Men and women hit the ground and ran with weapons at ready to secure the building. The teams searched for him, and he motioned them over. An ambulance arrived with a local hospital logo, and another emergency vehicle that looked to be from the agency pulled in behind.

"Dunn?"

"Here!" He weakly raised his hand as Agent Miller headed his way.

"We found York. Shooter's location?"

"I heard him exit on the upper level of the garage. I returned fire, possible he is wounded."

"You wounded him?" The agent's face was grim as he looked down at Dunn's leg and the blood everywhere. "All units, shooter, the last location believed the second floor of the garage. Possibly wounded," Agent Miller spoke into his phone.

Miller leaned down. "Brown will ride with you,"

Another agent approached, and Matt relaxed. Pete Waters was also undercover on this op with him.

"Agent-in-Charge Thompson sent me to ride with Dunn," Pete said.

Miller looked irritated. "Roger that."

"I leave you for a minute, and you have all the fun." Pete squatted down next to Dunn.

"Pete, get me in the rig with local paramedics."

Pete stood and waved with both arms at the local ambulance team. In a minute, they were all over him.

"Sir, we are moving you now. Stay with us. Keep talking."

"My partner—."

"We got him, sir. Ready to move? One, two, three."

Excruciating pain shot from below the waist. He struggled not to cry out.

Pete was beside him as they loaded him into the ambulance. He stayed out of the paramedic's way as they hooked up the IV and exchanged the belt for a compression bandage.

"Pete?"

"Yeah?"

"There was another shooter. I returned fire, but at the same time, I heard a second shot. There was a homeless woman in the corner of the building when we entered. She applied the tourniquet."

"You let a civilian do that in the middle of a *gunfight*?"

"I know, breaks every rule. She could be a backdoor agent. She went to check on York, and I don't know what happened to her. Find her if you can. Jim arranged for someone to be at the hospital to intercept any agency people on debrief. As soon as you can, get back here and look for her. She might have seen *him*. Don't mention her to anyone."

"We need to check vitals. Step back," one of the medics said.

Dunn felt the edges of his world going gray.

"Sir, sir, stay with us! Who is the President?"

"A good guy, Winston Baxter, my friend."

The paramedic whispered to his co-worker, "He's confused."

Pete leaned in, "Actually, he was in the Secret Service when the President was the Vice President. He's making sense. He knows the President personally."

Matt smiled weakly. He did have friends in high places. He tried to keep his eyes open, but with less success. The ambulance came to a quick stop; daylight streamed into the back end, and hands reached for the gurney. Tired.

"Sir, open your eyes!"

"Gunshot to femoral, stabilize, and get him to OR!"

He drifted. He could see the dirty face of a homeless woman. Wait—did she call him handsome?

*Who are you?*

# CHAPTER THREE
## KATIE

The stairs from the parking garage led up to the second floor of the hotel, skipping the lobby. Katie discovered the door from the stairwell opened to a cleaning station on that floor. It included sheets, uniforms, and supplies. She put on a uniform smock, grabbed a supplies cart, and headed down the hallway. She held a sheet of paper in front of her face to prevent any cameras from identifying her. She needed to find another service exit.

*No way! Dan Beck?*

Halfway down the hallway trying to swipe a card to enter a room, stood her rival in the private investigation business, Dan Beck. The incarnate smug guy who looked like that actor in the Jurassic movies. Of course, he used that whenever it was convenient. Not quite arrogant but annoyingly good-looking, he was an excellent private investigator who irritated her at every point of interaction with him. He always seemed ready for whatever happened as if he studied ahead and were perfectly prepared. He slid right into solving cases as if he had private investigator supernatural power, while a case for her to solve meant plain hard work with some degree of luck.

Bad news. Katie needed to be completely anonymous, and he would recognize her. She held up the paper and scurried forward to pass him. As she got close, she saw the plastic card he was trying to swipe was not from this hotel. The card said "Hilton" which was down the street. Good, that meant he was at work. She could use that. She formulated the lie. Lying seemed an unfortunate aspect of being a private eye, which she only did while on the job, at least mostly.

"Excuse me, are you trying to enter that room with a card, not from our hotel?"

"Oh, just—" he looked up with a smooth smile until he recognized Katie.

"Katie Parson! I'm working. It looks like you found an occupation to help out during the dry times," he chuckled.

"Listen, we are both working here. I can call security, or you can help me. I am following someone and have to get out of the hotel and not get caught on camera. You help me, and I don't turn you in, how's that?"

"Professional courtesy?" He raised an eyebrow.

"Right, like when you asked me to help you with that 'open' case? That was a cold case offering a reward of five grand, the one I solved, and you paid me $500? That kind of courtesy?"

"What's the deal about avoiding cameras?" Dan ignored her accusation.

"I don't want exposure. Same reason you are trying to get into that room without a key?"

"Okay, I can get you out. This is an old hotel, and there is there a dumbwaiter on this floor. You are small enough to fit. It drops you into the kitchen. I know where it is, and all you have to do is pay me $20, and you are out of here in thirty seconds."

Katie glared. "Really? Professional courtesy?"

"That's my Katie Parson discount. If you were an ugly PI, I would charge more."

Showing any tension would only make the price go up. Dan was a sharp negotiator, and his instincts honed.

"One-time offer, $5, or I can find it myself!"

"$20, because you will never find it."

Katie looked at him suspiciously.

Dan put out his hand.

She turned her back to him, reached under her shirt, and slipped out a twenty. Grudgingly she handed it over.

Dan gestured with his head for her to follow him. He stepped in front of Katie as she pushed the cart to the side. Built like a football player, Dan's tee shirt hugged his six-foot-one-inch muscled body, which covered any camera angle of Katie's one hundred twenty-pound frame. She followed close behind as he turned into the ice machine stall. Next to the machine was a door marked "Staff." This time it was a locked door, no card key.

Dan pulled a lock pick set from his pocket and leaned down.

"You're taking all day! Do you need help?"

Dan leaned back with his lazy smile, "We could both do it. How do you like my new cologne?"

"Musk for Manly Men? Good choice for you!"

Dan snorted. He opened the door and found the half-door to the dumbwaiter.

"It's small."

"You fit!" In one move, Dan picked up Katie and her bag and stuffed her in the small space. "They use it for big parties, so it'll hold your weight, I hope." He winked.

"Katie, you might want to invest in some good cologne, girl. Hate to tell you, but you smell like a dirty diaper with a touch of garbage thrown in. I hope the door opens itself when it gets to the kitchen, or you have a problem." Dan grinned and pushed the "K" button.

Katie could hear the mechanical groaning as the old machine started. Crammed in, she closed her eyes and prayed the door would open automatically, as there was no latch on the inside. By now, Homeland Security would have begun to lock down the hotel, and search every person. The gloves covered with Matt Dunn's blood in her athletic bag would be a problem.

Dan would ask her later about why she was there at that time, but she could always pretend she had no idea about the shooting. Just a coincidence to her working her case. Maybe he would buy that, but regardless, there was a code that private eyes followed. No one broke someone's cover. Someday you might need help, and there were times that backup meant the difference between a payday or being hurt. Katie had helped Dan on several cases, and he trusted her. As irritating as Dan could be, he would not reveal her presence.

The dumbwaiter reached the kitchen, and thankfully, the little door opened. Katie tumbled out and hid behind a stack of boxes. She was in a section of the kitchen full of supplies, pans, and pots stacked on shelves. She looked around for an exit sign.

A young man pushed a large garbage can past her. Oblivious, he stopped and yelled back to someone. "Just a sec." He left the can.

She clutched her uniform to her and looked in. Salmon fish heads, barely a third full. Her lucky day. She climbed in with her duffle and pulled the top over her. Fish stink choked her, and her eyes watered.

"Hey, you get the other can, I'll take this one." A different voice from the first guy's, which was good because he would have noticed the difference in weight. The garbage can was moved at a quick pace.

She heard a clanging of a dumpster lid. Must be on a loading dock. The garbage can came to a stop with a thud, and she heard footsteps move away. She cracked the cover to peek out and breathe fresh air.

No one. The worker probably went to get more cans. The dumpster blocked her view of the alley, but all was quiet. No government crowd or its minions sent to check the back of the hotel yet. Early morning dark covered the dock, although bright lights concentrated on the dumpster. The lighting, she knew, discouraged the homeless from scavenging. She climbed out of the can and unfolded the umbrella to shield herself from rain sprinkling and security cameras as she disappeared in the semi-dark of the alley.

She emerged on Seneca and started toward a bus stop half a block away. Sirens screamed from the parking garage, so like other bus travelers, she turned around to look at the commotion behind her.

"Talk to you soon, Agent Dunn," she said under her breath.

She pulled her phone from her pocket and sent the picture of the shooter to a second burner phone in her athletic bag. She wiped the phone of prints, removed the SIM card, and tossed it into the trash. She could hear the loud mechanical noise of the garbage truck coming, so this little bit of evidence would disappear in minutes. She'd toss the phone itself in a different trash can later.

Katie stepped onto the bus and paid for the fare in cash. The driver averted his face as she passed by, and Katie realized he must have caught a whiff of her fish stink. The scene replayed in the garage in her mind like an R-rated movie. To stop her hands from shaking, she sat on them. She remembered being chased before in investigations, and this wasn't the first time she witnessed a crime while dressed as a homeless person.

Criminals committed crimes in front of her with no thought that the crazy lady who begged on the street would report them. Once she had seen a man being attacked and had slipped away to call 911, careful no one saw her break cover.

She was glad she had practiced the last couple of years to quick-change her clothes. She kept that skill fresh so no one would connect as she passed from her undercover to an average person. More than once, the angry subject of her investigations had stood in amazement when they turned a corner to find "she" had vanished.

This morning Katie had worked her private investigator job on an insurance fraud suspect. But to keep bills paid, she did several jobs. Occasionally she made money when she delivered a summons to deadbeat dads regarding child support. The fastest way to make money as a PI was doing background checks, although those jobs didn't pay much, but were plentiful. Her major in college had been in Criminal Investigation, but her minor in Drama gave her an edge in creating street aliases. When she needed an undercover role, she presented to the public as a dog walker, a marathon runner, or a homeless person.

She lived on the streets homeless for a month as her alter ego, "Sally." It had been difficult and dangerous. But it meant she delivered information where other PIs couldn't. With the stiff competition in private investigation, she had an edge.

Years ago, her first choice of career had been to join one of the alphabet agencies, and she spent almost all the required time at FLETC to become a person who worked in intelligence for the government. But a series of things happened at the end of her training that changed her life forever.

So instead of that career, she had become a business owner of a small private investigation agency, which any day of the week hung financially by a case or two. Some months her cash flow rolled, her bills remained paid, and she felt successful with the solid reputation she had built in the business.

The job had opened her twenty-eight-year-old eyes to many people in hard situations. Perhaps she was idealistic because she wanted to find dads who had skipped out on their child support to help single moms or find lost teenagers. In a perfect world, that would seem to be a noble endeavor, but real life meant she took a job because she needed to make a car payment.

Once, in her early naïve days, a furious husband who was the target of an investigation had smashed her camera. After that, she always planned for an escape route when on a case.

She closed her eyes and gripped the seat. This time *she* was the client. A murderer was in the wind and the government on the hunt for the killer.

Had she been seen?

# CHAPTER FOUR
## THE SPEAKER

The Speaker for the United States House of Representatives checked
the text message on his burner cell.

> Completed report on one. Two incompletes. Reporter
> experienced complications, exposure limited.

He cursed with the freedom he felt when alone and the
soundproof window shut between him and his driver.

He responded.

> Reporter comes highly recommended and funded at
> the top of the pay scale. Results unacceptable.
> Payment half.

There was a long pause in the answer coming. He surmised there
was communication going on between the asset and his handler. The
text came through.

> Requests permission to finish the assignment. The
> asset has access to two incompletes. Go ahead?

He stared at the text and forwarded the messages to another
number. Following the forward, he texted a message.

The reporter's completion record is impressive.
Continue with the assignment?

There was a short delay in the response; the Speaker looked outside at the Washington DC gray spring sky.

Go ahead with the assignment—the reporter in the best position to complete the job and briefed. Communicate the need for speed of completion.

This was the best plan instead of a botched assignment the first time. The asset was in place; his reputation among the best in the world. The insane high payment should be the motivating power. He pulled up the first text to respond.

Production must be completed. Use pipeline if needed.

There was another delay as the message relayed to the asset.

Agreed.

The Speaker sighed. Even the best plans can have unexpected consequences. But asserting that payment could be withheld showed authority. Probably this was a simple hitch. It would not affect the outcome of a more critical strategy. He used a cut out between him and the assassin. What bothered him was the familiarity his boss seemed to have with this chosen assassin. Once done, there would be no association at all. The little pieces still needed to fall in place. He was careful to remain disconnected from those small pieces.

He deleted all texts, removed the battery from the phone, and placed it in his pocket to toss in the garbage dumpster of the restaurant during the staff breakfast meeting. He opened his briefcase, pulled out a padded envelope, and slid the burner inside. He pushed the button to open the window to his driver and handed him the phone.

"Robert, can you take care of this while I'm at breakfast?"

"Yes, of course."

His driver would wipe it of prints and dispose of it. He did not need a contact list on any phone because he had an unerring knack to remember numbers. In this town, it was too easy to connect the dots in personal contacts. He avoided technology, which gave him an edge. The blessing and curse of using technology was a trail if you leaned on it. He pretended to rely on staff to "connect" him. No one, especially his personnel staff, would suspect him of any know-how to operate clandestinely.

He trusted his driver Robert, a cousin. His loyalty stemmed from family ties. In his private life, Robert needed occasional help to hide small affairs from his wife. Whatever the congressman required, he did and remained silent about it, grateful for the support with his indiscretions. The Speaker imagined his driver assumed the phones were for government business. In a way, they were, and someday they would lead to the Oval Office, and not just a visit there. He smiled. It had seemed such a long-shot a month ago.

Unrestrained power would soon belong to him.

# CHAPTER FIVE
## KATIE

Katie pulled her hoodie around her face to block her from the bus camera. Setting the athletic duffle beside her, she put her head in her hands. The violence of the past half hour played over in her mind. Her eyes watered from the fish smell and her hands still shook— deep breaths. She reached into the bag to retrieve her second cell phone and tapped her alarm to go off in one hour.

She rubbed her eyes on the back of her sleeve. Work helped her to focus, so she opened her email to start the process of making this an official case. She pulled up her go-to template list, the system she used to investigate cases. Usually, a paying client started that process, but today she opened an investigation with herself as the client. Within the giant government machine, she knew that despite his injuries, Homeland Security would debrief Dunn, identify the Asian man, and Dunn would reveal the presence of a homeless woman. Her identity unknown now, but maybe not in the next few days. Somewhere in the Homeland chain of information, there seemed to be a leak. If those agents were not safe, she wouldn't be either.

She worked her discovery process with a list of the barest of facts.

Who: Murderer, Asian Man, two federal agents, me

What: Asian man killed, agents shot, murderer, wounded by me, escaped.

When: Today, significance?

Where: Downtown Seattle

Why: Unknown plan by an unknown, possible international criminal? Why federal agents involved? The shooter knew agents would be there, indicates intelligence leak. Asian man in Seattle, why?

Katie leaned against the seat and squeezed her eyes shut.

Fred!

The one person she could trust to help her navigate the maze of federal agency communication, and possibly if she needed it, pull strings to prevent prosecution because she left an active crime scene.

Fred Lindley (if that was his real name) was a genuine man of mystery. Years ago, he moved into her family's neighborhood and became her mentor in a criminal investigation. Katie, at fifteen, remembered their first meeting. Her mom had sent her over with a "welcome to the neighborhood" plate of cookies.

She knocked — no sound from inside. When she was just about to leave, the door opened, an old gentleman stood there. She felt he had been on the other side of the door the whole time.

She pointed to the cookies, "Hi. I'm Katie. We live two houses down. My mom wanted to welcome you. She is president of the Neighborhood Watch."

"Of course, thank you. Come in. My name is Fred Lindley. Please tell your mother that I appreciate the cookies. Perhaps you will join me in one? And please tell me a bit about the community."

He seemed like a grandpa. On the way to deposit the cookies in the kitchen, she noticed several framed photographs on the wall with a younger Fred shaking hands with several former Presidents of the United States. She stared at Fred.

"Is that you?"

"Yes. My job with the government meant I occasionally worked with the Secret Service to protect a few of our presidents. I am retired now."

Katie became an instant fan and quizzed him about what he did. Ever courteous, Fred never told her specifics about his work but welcomed her questions about general aspects of criminal investigation. He seemed to take for granted her interest in investigation techniques and encouraged her aptitude to remember and evaluate facts. Later, her mom, ever the matchmaker, had introduced him to a widow at their church, and they married.

As Katie grew up, he became her neighborhood grandpa. He often attended Katie's family functions. However, Katie had observed, although retired, he occasionally connected to some agency. A government vehicle parked near his home testified of his relevant expert skill. He never spoke of that part of his life in more than generalities. But Fred could help her now. She remembered with dismay that he mentioned a week ago he would be going on a short vacation to the San Juan Islands.

The bus deposited her near her car parked on a city street many blocks from the hotel.

She always carried a change of clothes, and today that was needed, fish stink not being a sociable smell. She opened her trunk, grabbed some clothes out, and stuffed the stinky athletic bag in a plastic bag to prevent the permanent smell of fish in her car.

It was just getting light, so she spread a dog blanket on the back seat. She slid down in back to change — the putrid clothes she stashed in a paper sack on the backseat. She rubbed some disinfectant wipes over her hands and sprayed on cologne to finish killing the salmon aroma until she could shower. She wouldn't pass a Dan Beck smell test, but it helped.

This early morning job had caused her to skip a needed Americano, and her body was coffee starved. How could she have thought sleep was more important than coffee?

First coffee, a bathroom, and she would make a phone call to

Fred. She guessed Agent Dunn would be in surgery. Afterward, she would initiate contact. It would involve one more "identity."

Katie tapped a contact on her phone.

"Please leave your message for the Fidelity State Insurance Company."

"This is Katie Parson. I have finished my investigation and will be bringing in my report today."

Katie had two cells, one for business and one for her personal cell phone. She kept the personal one in her car, another precaution because that cell could lead back to her loved ones.

She longed to call the one person whose prayers she felt God always heard, Grandma Betty. Not today, too dangerous. Coffee.

# CHAPTER SIX
## KATIE

Rainy Day Dancing Coffee Shop was always her first choice. She noticed her favorite barista, Aldo, behind the counter. It seemed for baristas, the perennial smell of good coffee contributed to a positive disposition.

"Katie, how's it going? Americano? Breve? Need a slice of pumpkin bread to go with that?"

"Yes, please, Aldo. An egg muffin too, just egg whites, though."

Katie could see by his concerned look that her face revealed her turmoil.

"It's a sad day when the best team in baseball loses," Katie said, letting her emotions spill out, sniffing a bit as she pretended to be upset about last night's baseball game.

Aldo smacked his forehead and rolled his eyes, "Nineteen years since we been to the playoffs, but we believe. Hey, sometime we should go to a game? You down with that?"

"Baseball? Yes, I am always down with that!" she grinned.

His smile dazzled, and she gave him a big tip. He did work his customers, but she liked him anyway. She found the bathroom while she waited for her coffee.

She added extra cream to the steaming cup on the counter and sipped slowly. Coffee perfection needed to be savored. As she drank, a calm seeped into her chaotic morning.

Her eyes drifted to the back of the shop. In the back booth, secluded from the street, Enrique, or "Ricky" to his friends, sat waiting for Katie to spot him. She headed his way.

Ricky dressed in the essence of low key. This shop happened to be one of his "offices" on the street. His hair curled a little around his ears, but his eyes always captured her attention, chocolate brown and framed with long lashes. Whether those brown eyes were because of his Latin heritage, she didn't know, but she tended to forget things when gazing at him.

It had taken a long time to finally meet him because even though she had heard of him on the street, no one met him unless he chose it. He did small services for people for a price. Not into drugs or sex trafficking, two things rampant in the city, he found ways to be useful and make a living, word of mouth being his mode of advertisement. Katie had done favors for a few of his contacts. Their recommendations had admitted her into his exclusive circle of associates.

"Sup, Beautiful?" he said.

She didn't want him to see her hand shake, so she set the coffee on the table and broke the pumpkin bread in two and slid half toward him.

He looked at her face, and the twinkle left his eyes.

"Rough day at the office, girl?"

"Yeah, something like that. Sally saw something."

"Anyone see *her*?"

Katie toyed with her coffee cup.

Ricky took a bite of the bread as he waited for her to get to business.

"I need another burner phone," Katie said.

She pulled out a $50 bill from her jacket pocket. She folded it in the napkin of her drink and slid it across the table to him.

28

Ricky leaned in and looked at her in his mesmerizing way, "You say the word, and we can get married. Then I'll give you a big discount."

He reached inside his hoodie and produced a cell phone from a shirt pocket. He covered it with a napkin and pushed it over.

"I can't marry you, remember, you have to go to church with me first," Katie batted her eyelashes.

"Baby, you are the only one. I don't do the church thing, but we are like cosmically connected." Those liquid brown eyes worked their magic.

Ricky looked at the big screen TV on the wall. It was blaring the latest news of the attack in the hotel parking garage.

"If you have any business up there by Sixth, you should let it go a few days. You need somebody to cover something, let me know, I'll do it," he said.

Ricky knew she had been trying to get a photo near there, and sometimes he helped her on job assignments.

"You and me, girl, today at the courthouse, I got time."

"Sunday, church?"

Ricky shrugged, as his smile dazzled with white teeth against his soft brown skin. He squeezed her shoulder and left.

She gave him five seconds before she turned around. Gone, but the fragrance of his upbeat personality remained.

Katie knew the ladies on the street loved him. It was his persona. Few could equal the way he connected with people.

Those minutes she flirted with him had restored her balance. As usual, she had to check her beyond-friendly feeling for him. The emotion always surprised her, and she never knew if it was mutual.

She looked at the TV screen where reporters covered the breaking news. At least she knew more now than she had before the coverage. The new burner phone went in her pocket, and she headed to her car. When she popped the trunk, fish stink gagged her. She held her breath and got her camera out of the athletic bag.

Thirty minutes later, seated in her Subaru under a tree on a neighborhood street, she set her plan into motion. She rarely took cases where her security was an issue. Her work required attention to her surroundings as it went with the job of being a private investigator. Earlier she had scoped out this residential street to be a safe place to do business.

The alarm on her phone startled her.

As a PI, Katie charged for her time by the hour. She kept track of her progress as she worked through the facts of discovery. In each case, Katie reviewed frequently and gave clients an honest hour of work. Her alarm signaled an hour of work time had elapsed. Clients often approached her with a sense of uncertainty in how she could solve their case. Now that same uncertainty resonated with her as she realized *she* was the client.

She turned up the volume on the radio and listened to details about this morning's violence.

"Breaking news: A Chinese diplomat murdered in downtown Seattle today. U.S. government officials say the diplomat was in the country to meet with Washington State farmers about developing a crop of mint for a specialty tea. Two Homeland Security agents were injured. These are the only details released by Seattle Police at this time."

She pulled up her list of facts and added:

Who: Chinese diplomat, here for agricultural trade? Agency— Homeland Security.

Why: Chinese diplomat killed before he made an agreement with Washington State farmers on a deal to buy mint for new Chinese tea. Significance? Terrorism?

She reset the timer on her phone, this time for two hours.

Her cell in one hand, she grabbed the camera. She almost gagged as the essence of fish guts clung to it.

"Fidelity State Insurance. Can I help you?"

"Hi, Stephanie, Katie Parson. I called earlier and left a message. The assignment on the fraud case is complete. Can I stop by and drop off my report?"

"Yes, Diane is in today until lunch, she can cut you a check if you get here before then."

"I will be there in twenty minutes, depending on traffic. Thanks."

Next, dialed a number that she had memorized years ago, as she expected, a click, and a soundless recording followed.

"Fred, stopped by the grocery store early this morning around 5:30, had to get band-aids. I saw my friend John there. He wanted me to say hi and ask a favor." She ended the call. The message went to a cell that he kept in his gardening shed.

Fred and Katie long ago had developed a code language. Fred told her it was a good experience, and Katie just thought it was mysterious and fun. Today, that language would communicate an important message. Fred would understand that something happened at 5:30 AM in public (grocery store reference). He would check the local news and find that several agents were wounded, and a Chinese diplomat killed. He would understand Katie knew something about the incident, and her reference to "John," an anonymous name from long ago, meant he might surmise it indicated her time at FLETC. The part about the favor meant she was in trouble. If he was not in town, she did not know if he had taken the cell with him. She could only wait for his call back.

After the visit to the insurance office, she would head over to her current dog-sitting job, Ellie, a German Shepherd who had an unfortunate bowel problem. Dog-sitting and house-sitting supplemented her income and provided a place to live. Technically homeless, Katie moved from one house sitting/pet sitting job to the next. She usually lined them up consecutively. No rent and no utility bills gave her the ability to pay down her student loans, except for when the dates didn't line up consecutively, and she was without a bed for the night. Her back-up home was the futon in her tiny office.

Closing her eyes again, she wished she could go back a couple of hours ago. Maybe she would have never dodged into the garage. Her appearance as a homeless person wandering the streets during that operation would not have revealed a private detective. But if she had not intervened, Matt Dunn would be dead and probably his partner, too.

"Katie, we all have divine appointments in life. There is some reason things happen the way they do." Her mom's advice at dinner last Sunday came unbidden to her mind.

Her mind swirled, a divine appointment this morning? Or were the familiar knots in her stomach caused by her natural penchant to find trouble?

She remembered something her Grandma Betty used to say, "God says He is our hiding place, and some days we need that."

Grandma had nailed that one.

Katie's phone rang. It was the same number that had called twice this morning. Hopefully, a new client?

"K. R. Parson Investigations, Katie speaking. Can I help you?"

"Yes, my name is Beckie Clark. I have a missing person, my mother, and the police have refused to look for her for a forty-eight-hour period. Are you able to help me find her? My drug-addicted nephew and his girlfriend came to visit her last week, probably to try and get money from her." Beckie finally took a breath as she rattled all the details to Katie. "She is eighty-one, and now her apartment is empty, and she is gone. Can you help?"

"Yes. I'm available this afternoon. Would you like to meet at my office in south Seattle, actually Kent?"

"Yes, please, I got your office address from your website. Is three o'clock okay?"

Katie looked at the time on her car clock, only 10:30. Somehow it felt like late afternoon.

"Yes, that's perfect. See you at three."

Her training in this job had taught her clients like Beckie, who worried about the location of a loved one, were often right when it came to their safety. She knew police policy was to make sure the person was missing forty-eight hours before using agency resources for a search. But in this instance, all her instincts as an investigator told her Beckie's mom needed help, and Katie's bank account could use help too. Katie felt Beckie's fear as she wiped the sweat from her forehead. From one mess—to another mess—a typical day, only today, her trouble squeezed her heart as she prepared to hunt to find one person, while another person stalked her. She gripped her coffee cup hard with both hands.

Her other client, Ellie, the German Shepherd, would have to settle for a quick in-and-out pit stop because of this case, and this could mean trouble for Katie later. Katie pulled out the cell phone with the shooter's photo. She studied the picture and felt a cold finger down her back. This man seemed familiar to her, and that creeped her out.

Katie looked out at the rain now pouring down. Fingers poised on her phone, finally she googled a number.

"Channel Five News?"

"I have some news of the shooting today, actually a picture of someone running in that area. Not sure if it's important," Katie said.

"Someone will be *right* with you. Please hold on."

# CHAPTER SEVEN
## MATT

He heard voices miles away.

"Hey, Bubba, you awake? You're snoring and keeping all the rest of us awake!"

"Dad?"

"Open your eyes, Matt."

"Uh, the blurry look is good on you. I'd swear you're ten years younger."

"Remind me if you want to come back to work for me, you can have a raise for flattery."

"Mr. Dunn, we are going to have to debrief Agent Dunn and will need to ask you to leave the room," another man said.

Matt turned to that voice, not one he recognized but one that must belong to someone from the agency.

"I didn't catch your name?" Matt's dad asked.

"Agent Redman, I was sent in to debrief your son."

Matt focused on this man. He had never seen him before. Why would Homeland send an agent unknown to him to debrief in a situation with two men down and an assassination? Something seemed off. He was about 50 years old, 5' 10", glasses, sort of dark brown hair, unremarkable in his appearance.

"Agent Redman, I am a licensed contractor for the U.S.

government, with a security clearance that I guarantee is higher than yours. If you need to debrief my son, I stay. And before you call someone, as Agent Dunn's father, I have medical power of attorney. Besides, it's clear, my son and his partner took fire because your agency has information leaks the size of Niagara Falls. The shooter knew they were coming. Everyone on the planet can figure it out."

"Mr. Dunn, we cannot confirm that information, and we must contain communication while we are investigating this incident. I am going to have to ask you to leave the room, and if you don't, I have agents outside who will escort you."

"You sure about that? Maybe you should ask them in?"

Redman pulled out his phone and tapped the screen. He put the phone up to listen.

Redman's jaw went rigid.

"Agent Redman, I own the foremost security company in the U.S. When the safety of my son is on the line, I have resources and contacts that rival any government agency. The only men outside work for my security agency. When my son has recovered from the anesthetic, you are free to investigate."

"Your son works for the U.S. government, and he's a part of this investigation. While his partner is critical and still in surgery, we must debrief him as soon as possible."

"Who is your superior, Agent Redman? Because my good friend, Assistant Director Fitzgerald, assured me a little while ago that any debriefing can wait until Matt has recovered from the influence of anesthesia. Unless you have some higher authority, I suggest you follow your leads on this case somewhere else."

Everyone's cell phones started going off. Matt's dad looked at a text on his phone and grabbed for the TV remote on the nightstand. He clicked it, and the news blared.

"We have breaking news on the attack in a local downtown hotel this morning. This cell phone photo of a man believed to be part of the attack this morning was taken by a commuter. We have exclusive coverage of this. The Seattle Police Department is working with the Department of Homeland Security. If you have seen this man, please contact the Seattle Police Department immediately," the news anchor announced.

Matt could see a photo that caught a man looking back as he was moving up an auto ramp. From the background, it was the same parking garage, with a man running. He had sandy colored hair, sweatshirt, jeans. It could be anyone.

Instantly Agent Redman was on his phone. "Shut it down! Get the picture."

The news station cut to a commercial break.

"Agent Redman?" An agent poked his head in the room.

Redman nodded curtly to both Dunns' and exited.

"Way to go, Jim Dunn, you terrified him!" Matt grinned at his dad.

"He will be back. He'll talk to someone who will tell Assistant Director Fitzgerald to stand down. Might last an hour, maybe more considering the magnitude of this leak. Any idea where the picture came from?"

"Sure, you heard the news guy, some bystander snapped a picture and sent it in."

Both men looked at each other. Jim made a sweeping motion with his hand and shook his head. As unclear as his thinking was, Matt understood. The room could have listening devices.

"Where are my pain meds?" he growled.

His hospital phone went off, and he looked at it warily.

"Go ahead and take it, Matt, it's probably just the hospital staff calling to see if you want dinner or meds. By the way, your team ordered liver and onions for your dinner. You might want to change that." Matt's dad chuckled and started channel surfing for more news.

"Hello?"

"Good to hear your voice Agent Dunn, glad you made it. Sorry I couldn't stay to help."

Matt paused a beat, "I heard my team ordered liver and onions for my first hospital dinner. Who in the kitchen do I have the privilege of speaking with?"

"The smelly woman who saved your behind this morning. And yes, before you try and ask in code how I know your name, I heard the guys coming to get you yelling for Dunn. But now that we have our introductions over, did you catch the Channel Five News just now and the picture of the bad guy who shot you?"

"I'm assuming you are responsible? That you can change my menu, right?" Matt continued as though he was ordering his meal but cleared his throat. His dad looked at him.

"Can I order steak and prawns? Listen, nurse. If you can get me steak and prawns, I will buy you dinner at the Sea Star Restaurant on the Pier. I can send my dad to buy you dinner tonight, at 8:00 PM if you are off work."

"News crews that filmed at the hospital identified a 'James Dunn' who entered the hospital, the same James Dunn who owns Premier Security, the most well-known security company in the U.S. Not a stretch to imagine who your dad is. No, I'm not going to dinner and be swept up in a sting by Homeland Security. I wish I could chat, but soon someone is going to get wise to this conversation. Do *not* expect me to come in as I have no desire to be a target. This morning when your mission turned into a shootout in the OK garage, I did the good Samaritan thing. I helped. And I took a picture. Once you know my name, the shooter will too. This guy is probably on your Top Ten list—"

"Steak and prawns on my top ten, yes, absolutely, I would say number five on my list. No Jell-O."

"I like you, Agent Dunn. Do your job. Find the guy. If you want to talk again? Put an ad on Craigslist that you want Great Dane puppies, and include a phone number. You owe me more than dinner."

"Great, thanks for changing that menu," Matt said as he heard a click.

"The dietician nurse called you from the kitchen? You're getting steak and prawns?"

"Yep. I wish I could thank that nurse personally. But these lines are untraceable. She could be one of the four thousand staff members here, impossible to find in that crowd," Matt shrugged.

Jim looked at him thoughtfully and made a note on his cell.

"My people say an assassin known by the name of Terrell Huff is the kind of guy who could have this pulled off."

Matt caught the question in his dad's statement. He could not comment, despite his dad's security clearance.

"He is number five on the FBI's ten most wanted list. I have a contact, actually here in Seattle, who retired years ago. He is the only man who ever pinned down any details about Terrell Huff as an assassin for hire," Jim said.

"Are you talking about—"

"Yeah. Legend at the Agency," his dad interrupted.

Matt looked on his nightstand for some water and took a sip.

"The shooter knew we would be there surveilling the Chinese diplomat."

"Yeah. That part is easy to figure out. Matt, get some rest, I will check in on you tonight. Tyrone Johnsen is here to stay with you, Andrew and Sam will be outside keeping an eye out for trouble." He patted his son on the shoulder and left the room.

A nurse came in and asked Matt, "Can we give you something for the pain?"

"Yes, ma'am."

Matt lay back, closed his eyes, and smiled. Tyrone, as he recalled, was a man with no sense of humor. The intimidating part about him included his height at six-four, and he weighed in at two hundred ten pounds, all bulging muscles. A great comfort to have that guy at his bedside.

Something tugged at his memory. He felt again like he was drifting, trying to catch a vapor that was blowing away from him— Operation Descendant.

Like many in the intelligence community, he practiced memory retention. But the events of the past few hours weren't the ones replayed in his mind. Memories from five years ago slid slowly across his mind like a video.

After his transfer from the SEALs to Naval Intelligence, and his subsequent assignment to protect Admiral Westington, he had received a call from an old friend in Homeland. The friend had recommended him for the Secret Service detail assigned to one of the Vice-Presidential candidates. He applied and was accepted. His new job with the Secret Service eventually placed him on the Vice President's detail. One night while he was guarding the Vice President, something went wrong with the Secret Service team assigned to the VPOTUS's teenaged daughter.

Late at night on a typical teen dance, she slipped her Secret Security detail with a lot of help from her girlfriend. With no protection detail, a local sex trafficking gang abducted them. In the first minutes, it became apparent they did not know who they had scooped up with the original girl they had been grooming. There was no ransom or demand for the VP's daughter. Just a twofer as far as the gang was concerned. Minutes counted in this kind of situation.

She could be overseas or in Mexico in a matter of a few hours.

Principals met and decided to seek a trained agent who could pass for sixteen. One of the men in the room thought he might know of someone. A tense phone call brought a young woman to the meeting room within the hour. This assignment was at the highest security level.

The VP talked to her privately. Dunn had stepped back to the door, but he overheard the conversation.

"You understand this is a life or death assignment? You are still a trainee, but we understand you are near the top of your class. If you cannot find my daughter in the next couple of hours, we may never find her. If she slips and says who she is, she'll be tortured, and our nation held hostage," the VP said.

His voice broke. "Why would you take this assignment?"

"My grandmother says trouble comes to us because we're meant to go through it. You asked me here because I can look the part for this operation. Maybe I was meant to help. Mr. Vice President, I do not know if it will be enough, but I will give you my *all* to get her back."

He saw the Vice President reach out a hand, and the young woman shook it. She went to a location FBI intelligence had set up to be another snatch and grab event.

Six hours later, after being beaten, that probie agent escaped the gang with the VPOTUS's daughter. In a secret ceremony, she received the Presidential Medal of Freedom.

After the formality, the VP had another private conversation with her. Again, Matt stepped away, yet he overheard the conversation.

"Mr. Vice President, this was not an accident. The gang had someone asking about her. I think there was a plan by someone to reach her," she had explained.

Was his head still fuzzy, or was the voice he heard five years ago the same as the woman on the phone a few minutes ago? Only she could have known the name of Operation Descendant.

He remembered about a month after the operation, he had heard through the intelligence grapevine, this same young woman had left the FLETC training program early. No explanation why. But if anyone in the U.S. had a "get-out-of-jail-free" card, it was that young woman because the man whose daughter she rescued was no longer the Vice President, he was the President.

Matt did not have the security clearance to tell anyone, including his dad, about his current operation. His top-secret assignment focused on finding how information was being released covertly from Homeland. What was the source of information leaks? Who was responsible?

His mind wandered. Was he supposed to die today? Either he used up one of his nine lives or coincidence put a gutsy woman in the line of fire. He had allowed the woman to approach him because he believed she was a backdoor agent sent to observe and report. Or was she? If not, he had broken protocol, a grave mistake—one that could end his career. Did someone know his real assignment, and was making sure he did not complete it? Dunn knew he could trust his life to his hand-picked team. Beyond that, he could not trust Washington to keep its secrets.

His priority was to identify a "homeless nurse" before anyone else did and keep her safe. He owed her that, her country owed her that. However, he could not go through the usual channels. He knew Redman's search would be relentless to find the photographer. Who was Redman? He would need to ask Agent Thompson about him.

An ad for Great Dane puppies. Did that have something to do with her smell? Five years ago, he recalled he thought she was rather cute. What did she say, handsome? He smiled and closed his eyes.

The sound of the door opening caused him to open his eyes. He expected his guard, the unsmiling and always intimidating Tyrone, to check-in. Not Tyrone. A nurse.

This nurse did have a name tag, but it was not the nurse's name listed on his whiteboard on the wall. Odd, she wasn't with one of his dad's security team. She approached the bed.

# CHAPTER EIGHT

Katie hung up the phone in the hospital volunteer/employee lounge area. It had taken a few calls to discover Matt Dunn's room, but she had finagled it. She was not a nurse, but a registered volunteer at Harbor Point Medical Center and had been for several years. HIPAA laws being what they were, information about a person's medical condition was nearly impossible to uncover, unless of course, you worked or volunteered at the hospital. So, there had been times in following a case she needed to unearth medical facts. Once a client had wanted her to follow her husband because the client suspected him of having an affair. It turned out he was undergoing cancer treatment but did not tell his wife, afraid she would leave him. Katie had only told the wife that he was going to the hospital. A happy-ever-after, it turned out the wife wanted to help her husband, not leave him.

Careful to avoid greeting anyone, she straightened magazines, organized a bookshelf to legitimize her reason for being at the hospital today, and slipped out. She checked her phone and prayed for good traffic. She had just enough time to get to her dog-sitting job and her office for her appointment with the new client.

Fred had not called or texted.

Katie took a moment to snap a picture of her check and

electronically deposit it to her account. She noticed the deposit got in before any automatic withdrawals, no overdrafts. Whew, a relieved sigh. She chose to work for this insurance company because they settled promptly, even if they did not pay well. It was better than waiting two months for the accounting department to catch up to her billing. The way her work ebbed and flowed, it seemed she needed the money sooner rather than later.

Dog-sitting Ellie, the former police dog, had been a job Katie had landed on and off over the last year when her retired handler left town for his condo in Hawaii. Ellie was mostly a one-person dog. When her person was gone, Ellie tolerated her as a substitute.

"Ellie, Elllllie." Ellie did not bound into the room, but she padded in to investigate Katie. She sniffed in a circle around Katie. The fish aroma would not escape *this* nose.

"Sorry I couldn't bring you some, girl," Katie said. She went to get Ellie's food, and another smell assaulted her. Ellie had hung behind.

"Really?" Katie looked sternly at the dog.

A few minutes after the cleanup, Katie fed Ellie, who daintily consumed the food. Then she put her in the back yard and stood on the patio as she waited to see if Ellie would take care of her business.

"Good girl!" Katie said.

A brief shower removed all fish smell. Katie dressed in clean clothes and felt normal again.

Katie felt her phone vibrate in her pocket. A text from her mom.

I got a call from Fred's wife, Marilyn, to tell me that Fred had a stomach bug, and they came back from the San Juan Islands early. She wondered if you were coming to our home soon? Something about Fred heard of a job for you. She said you could call from our house. I

don't know why you couldn't just call them on your
phone. He tends to be a strange man. Let me know if
you are coming. Love you, Mom

Fred!

Mom, I will be at your place at six, let Fred know I
would love the details and will call from your house.

Two things: Fred moved fast on this, speed being something he
avoided. Next, he relayed his message subtly through her mom. That
also not his MO, unusual and not good.

# CHAPTER NINE
## KATIE

Pulling into the Storage Solutions lot, Katie was thankful for an office that was secure even if a bit small. Lots of security cameras here, plus the motion lights and alarms, every storage facility utilized.

Katie traded work for the use of a tiny extra office located at the storage facility lot. Every other month she worked a shift at the storage office, taking new rentals, recording payments, and showing the facilities to potential clients. In exchange, she received free rent for the office. Sometimes the owners asked her to locate deadbeat storage customers and paid her a small fee.

A glance at her phone showed an hour before her client arrived. Opening the door, she grimaced at the stale smell. Katie often ran from one place to the next in field investigations, and rarely stopped at her tiny workspace.

She opened the front door and opened a window to let in the fresh air. Her compact office consisted of a desk with a laptop, two chairs, a filing cabinet, and a futon against the wall. A wall separated the office area from a bathroom with a stand-up shower, toilet, and sink. Katie got some wet paper towels from the bathroom to clean off the dusty desk, chairs, and futon. She set up her diffuser with some relaxing lavender essential oil. Her sister preached to her that essential oils had a scientific basis for helping people to relax. Katie breathed in the aroma. She needed a peaceful moment.

Atop the filing cabinet was an espresso machine, a necessity for coffee snobs. She went back out to the car for the fresh half and half and donuts she had grabbed at the Quick Stop convenience store down the street. Opening the small refrigerator by the futon, she gagged at the sour milk smell. She delivered the spoiled creamer to the dumpster by the storage office. The pungent smell would not entice a new client.

Katie started the coffee, taking deep breaths of the lavender and coffee aroma filling her office. Lavender to calm her down, coffee to make her brain work faster. She searched her supplies in the bathroom and found paper cups. She added a plate for the donuts and set them on the corner of the desk. The donuts were for clients only. Such carbs would find their way to her hips.

Her stomach growled. Katie's breakfast at the coffee shop seemed a distant memory. She was glad for the burrito truck parked next to Quick Stop. Coffee and burritos, her basic food pyramid. She began consuming the burrito as she logged into her laptop. Her espresso maker pinged, and she gratefully sipped a cup of good coffee, while she checked the news—no new reports on the shooting.

Her email revealed the usual advertisements, and one inquiry from a potential client, a relief to find some possible business that could pay bills. She wished today she could lose an hour on Instagram or Facebook, but that distraction was a luxury she could not afford.

All she smelled now was coffee and lavender, so she quickly closed the door and window and turned on the heat. The rain had stopped, but with a Washington spring, the weather could change in ten minutes.

A car approached her office and parked. It was early, which usually marked an anxious client.

"Hi, come on in," she greeted the middle-aged woman who knocked. "I'm Katie Parson."

"I'm Beckie Clark. I called earlier?"

"Yes, can I get you coffee?"

"Thanks, that would be great."

Katie grabbed a paper cup and headed toward the espresso machine. "Cream?"

"Yes, thanks."

Katie pushed the button to brew the coffee and waited as it spat out a cup. She added cream and gave the coffee to Beckie, who had found the chair in front of her desk.

"I know you told me a little on the phone. There is no charge for a consultation. We can decide after you tell me some more details about your mom, whether you'd want to hire me."

"Thanks. The police say they cannot help me. My mom could have gone with my useless nephew willingly. She doesn't think right sometimes. She might be in early Alzheimer's."

"Elder abuse is a serious matter. When did you notice she was missing, and why do you think it's your nephew?"

"Mom said they were coming to visit last week. I knew better than to let them come without me being there. My nephew, Jay, is a liar. Drugs wrecked his life. Sad, but everyone in the family knows we can't trust him."

"When Mom told me they were coming, I asked her to call me after they left. But she didn't call. She lives at an assisted living apartment complex. So, I went over there after a couple of hours. She didn't answer the door, but I have a key and let myself in. No one was there, but there were some clothes on her bed. Kind of like she was putting clothes out to take with her. She always tells her apartment manager Rachel where she is going. I went to find Rachel, who said she saw her leaving a few hours before with a sketchy-looking couple. She waved and seemed happy, so Rachel did not think much of it."

"When did that happen?"

"Friday. I tried calling constantly. I called my sister, Karen, to get my nephew's cell, but she said he doesn't have a phone anymore because he can't pay for it. Karen doesn't do anything with Mom, and she said her son just wanted to see his grandma."

"She's in denial that he has a drug problem. When I called the police, they questioned Karen, and she told them some story about Jay taking his grandma to the beach for a few days because Karen didn't want to get him in trouble. She never mentioned that Mom has a memory issue."

"Mom has been gone for almost two days. The police seem to think it's just a family issue, and they are not going to get involved yet. But I know Jay and his girlfriend want money, and my mom would give it to them. I am worried about what would happen to mom if they got high and left her somewhere? I don't know what to do." Her voice broke.

"Any truth to the beach story?"

"Could be. Karen and her ex-husband used to take their kids to Ocean Shores years ago."

"Beckie, I think I can help. My fee is $75 an hour plus expenses. For this case, I would need a $750 retainer. If I can get results for you quickly, I will return any retainer not used. With my clients, I usually send you a text or an email once a day and let you know what I know. Does that work for you?"

"Yes, I am too afraid to let this go longer because something could be happening to mom now, and I can't wait for the police to decide if this is life-threatening."

"Great. I have a PayPal account if you want to pay that way?"

"Yes. When will you start?"

"I can start this afternoon for a couple of hours doing some preliminary calling. Any idea where your sister used to stay in Ocean

Shores when they went there? I have some connections in the area."

"I think they stayed a couple of places. The Sandy Shores motel and they liked the Hawaiian motel too, but that is a little pricey for Jay unless, of course, he persuades my Mom to pay."

"Does she have a credit card?"

"Yes, but I have access to her accounts, and I haven't seen any charges. That was the other reason the police did not take it seriously because no money was going out."

"What kind of car does Jay drive? Or does your mom have a car?"

"Mom doesn't drive anymore. I sold her car because she wasn't safe on the road. Jay doesn't have a car, but Karen said his girlfriend does, but she wasn't sure what it was, maybe a blue Honda?"

"Do you have a picture of your mom?"

"Yes, on my phone. Can I text it to you?" She tapped her phone.

Katie studied the photo for a minute.

"Um—"

"I can see you noticed. She has a deformity. Her right arm only has a partial hand," Beckie explained.

"That's important. People will remember her because it's significant. What's her name?"

"Irene Wells."

"Okay. Let me know right away if you hear from your mom or see any unusual credit card withdrawals from her bank account."

"Thank you so much." Beckie stood to go.

Katie shook her hand and gave her a reassuring smile.

"I will be in touch later tonight or tomorrow when I have more information."

Beckie nodded, tears shining in her eyes.

As she drove away, Katie decided to check Craigslist. If she saw a message for Great Dane puppies, she *might* talk to Dunn. She wanted to know what he knew and wondered if he remembered her.

She sat down at her laptop and hit her search engine for Craigslist, Pets Wanted.

Labradoodle puppies.

Wanted: A Boa Constrictor, prefer about two years old. Also, I need frozen mice.

Gross.

ISO Russian Gray kittens, please respond to the link.

Then.

ISO Great Dane puppies. Matt. 360-475-8250.

*Not good.* She hadn't talked to Fred. There was one person who could help. Katie texted her mom.

> Mom, can you pray, I'm working on a hard case.

Ping

> I am praying. You know, if you didn't just livestream church on your phone, you might have some friends there. You could call for prayer too. Just saying.

Katie smiled. Her mom always had to get in a word. She texted back.

> I think that is not "just saying" but "just nagging." No worries, I'll go to church someday. I pray too, but God must listen to you more because you don't live stream church! See you tonight at six. Got to go, love you, Mom.

A string of heart emojis appeared. Her mom loved her emojis. Her mom would pray because she prayed about everything. For the first time in a long time, Katie felt like she did want to go to church. She knew one or two women there, and whenever she stepped into the building, it made her feel safe. Katie had grown up in the church.

Somewhere after high school graduation, when there was no longer a youth group, she found other things to fill her Sunday mornings. Katie went to a group called Bible and Brews occasionally at a trendy bar. Sometimes she exchanged Instagram info with a few people there. The sad truth was she interacted more with people on Instagram than in real life these days. In the light of her mom's comments, these relationships seemed shallow and transient. Who knew anyone anymore?

Grandma Betty would have a Bible verse right about now, but Katie didn't.

*God, I need that hiding place.*

# CHAPTER TEN

## MATT DUNN

"Hi, are you the new nurse?"

"Mr. Dunn, we have so many people here to make you better. My job is to make sure your IV is functioning and that you have all the right medications."

"Right, Nurse Lynette? So, what are you—"

The nurse was reaching for the IV port with the needle.

The door banged open, and Tyrone Johnsen steamed into the room like a black locomotive.

"Hey—"

The nurse ignored him and pushed the needle into the IV port, and hit the plunger.

In one motion, Tyrone swept her aside and grabbed the IV tube, and cut it in two with a wicked-looking knife.

Tyrone had one end of the tube in his hand, a knife in the other, and jumped between Matt and the nurse.

"What are you doing?" she hissed as she moved instantly toward the door. "You're crazy."

"You know what I am doing. Stop!"

IV liquid was squirting everywhere, and Tyrone threw down the severed tube.

Nurse Lynette moved fast, and she was out the door before

Tyrone could grab her.

"*Security,* he has a knife," she screamed.

Tyrone charged. At the door, he secured his knife behind his back.

"*Tyrone,* let her go. Call it in," Matt yelled from the bed, trying to grab the end of the dripping IV tube.

Tyrone slowed his pace and disappeared out of the room.

Matt clutched for the phone on the bed stand and furiously tapped a text.

**PLUTO, Attempt here. Protect York. Tyrone on point.**

The door opened, and Matt tensed until he saw an unsmiling Tyrone.

"She was good. Some other nurse told me I needed a badge or something to stay in the room with you, and when I turned my head, that nurse Lynette came in here, only no one out there knows her, and she isn't an employee. It seems she came to send you down the long dark path."

"I get that. Somebody thinks I know something, and whatever that is, I'm *persona non-grata* right now. No fingerprints as that fake nurse took her syringe with her."

"Yeah, a smart lady. Jim is going to take me apart. I should have been here! Can't believe I fell for that."

"Tyrone, these people are professionals."

"Yeah, Matt, but so am *I.* That should've never happened."

"Okay, so she got in here, but she didn't succeed, thanks to you. Thanks. Listen, you and I both know stuff goes off. We are not supermen with powers that see everything, know everything. I believe that is the Big Guy in the Sky, or so my Aunt Joyce tells me. Look at me. Look at my leg. Did I see this coming? No, I didn't. I wish I had for Ned and me both. He has a family. I was leading that search. I should've protected him."

"Yeah, well, your boss? He is not your dad. Your dad *is* my boss, and he makes the devil look like a wimp."

"Trust me, Tyrone, he'll ream you out, but he will not fire you."

"Yeah, as long as my learning curve doesn't mean you die."

"I like that part about me, not dying. Hey, who is watching Ned? They might try and do this to him."

Tyrone's face told a story.

"Ned didn't make it through surgery. Either from his injuries, or they had someone in there. But he is gone."

Matt grabbed his plastic plate and threw it against the wall. Tyrone didn't move.

"We are going to hunt them, and hurt every one of them," Matt said.

Sam and Andrew burst into the room, looking from Matt to Tyrone to the still spinning plate.

"Ned," Tyrone explained.

Matt's phone rang.

Matt stared at the ID on the call.

"Good to know you are still there."

"Dad, Ned's death. Was he helped?"

"Matt. We are looking into it. But your government buddies are all over it. No one can know until there is an autopsy, and they aren't going to tell anyone. I don't know, son. Ask your boss. He will know, but he might not tell you."

"I want in on this, Dad. I want to find them. I don't care what path that is either."

"Understood."

"I need to stay in Seattle. They will want to send me back to DC to recover. I'm not going. Can you pull some strings to keep me here?"

"I can, but I'm not God, so it might not work."

"You're not God, but when the owner of Premier Security calls, people listen. Just make the call, thanks. Tyrone pulled me out of a fire today. Don't fire him. I need him."

"Yeah, about that. Tell Tyrone to leave the room, have Sam and Andrew stay there with you. I need to have a chat with him."

"Sure." He ended the call with his dad. Matt signaled to Tyrone, and then he pointed to his phone, to Tyrone, and the door. Tyrone scowled more than usual and left.

Matt leaned back, his phone in hand.

He hit the search button and googled Craigslist. In a minute, he had searched for Pet's Wanted and checked to see if he had a message from his Great Dane Puppies ad.

Was his mind processing her voice? Did she sound like another woman at another time? He had to hear her again. But there wasn't a response to the ad.

He placed a call.

"Miller here. You ready to be debriefed?"

"Yeah, is Redman doing it?"

"No, he got called back to DC. They sent him out special to handle this case, but they called him back. I never met him before. I will be in soon."

"I might need the video of the area to help figure everything out. Everything got hazy after I took a bullet."

"You are the only video. Someone disabled all the cameras in the place. Nothing, even our drones outside, didn't record anyone that we can recognize. The State Department is all over me. They want an explanation of what happened to the Chinese diplomat because the Chinese are all over them. I need everything. I will be in there soon."

Matt processed the comment about the Chinese diplomat. That naturally would have provided a great cover story for attacking him and Ned. So maybe the whole storyline sent to the agency about there being a Chinese spy was a plant to do something else? But what?

Tyrone entered the room grim. He motioned for Sam and Andrew to head outside. Matt figured if he was still here that his dad saw the benefit in keeping him employed. Matt's dad was a fearsome employer, but fair and a good judge of character.

"Tyrone, my boss, Ted Miller, will be in here soon, so you know."

Tyrone nodded, his unsmiling persona on alert.

Matt had decisions to make. They murdered Ned. If he revealed the woman's presence in the garage, the cowards would kill her too. He just needed to plan his story.

He could only hope the smelly nurse could hide.

# CHAPTER ELEVEN
## KATIE

She had two hours, maybe, until dinner at her mom's. Katie remembered she had a friend in Ocean Shores who worked at the only grocery store in town. Everyone who needed groceries shopped there. If Beckie's mom was in Ocean Shores, odds are her drug-addicted nephew and girlfriend would come in for food. She had another friend who worked at the library, but it was doubtful that Beckie's nephew would go there. She would call her friend there too and see if someone matching Beckie's mom's description had come in.

Might as well try the library first. Voicemail. Katie disconnected. She didn't want to leave a message. She'd try back later.

She scrolled through her contacts again and called her friend Lisa who worked at the grocery store.

"Hey, Lisa, Katie, here. How're you doing?

"I'm great, but since it's you, Katie, I'm assuming you need a place to crash for the weekend?"

"Oh, yeah, usually, that would be why I'm calling. But this time I'm working and hoping you can help me out. I wanted to ask you if you have seen someone, maybe at the store? An older lady, looks like in her seventies or so, and she has a deformed arm, one hand has a few fingers on it. She would have been with a couple. Maybe the couple was sketchy-looking?"

"I did see a lady like that yesterday, but she was by herself. She looked lost, but she bought a candy bar and some potato chips. I remembered her because she asked me if there was a bathroom in the store. Someone she was with had told her they were going to the bathroom, but now she couldn't find them."

"Interesting, did she find them?"

"I felt bad for her, but I got busy, and I didn't see her after that. It was about noon."

"Hey, let me text you a picture. I want to make sure it's the same woman."

"Yes, that's her! What's up, is she missing or something?"

"Maybe. The woman's family is concerned about her whereabouts. Can I ask you, did she have a purse/? How did she pay for the food?"

"I think she just pulled the money from her coat pocket, but she had several twenties, and I think she wasn't sure how much she needed. I hope no one cheated her out of any money because she looked confused."

"Lisa, any idea at all where she might go?"

"I'm sorry, no. You could call some motels and show them a picture?"

"Thanks, Lisa, you helped a bunch. Save me your couch sometime soon, I feel like a run on the beach. I am dog-sitting for Ellie again, and I think she would love that."

"Sure, girlfriend, you are always welcome. I appreciate all you did for me in getting my inheritance back. I owe you."

"Hey, you paid me, right? You don't owe me, but I still will take that couch! Thanks."

Katie had struck gold with the information on Beckie's mom. She loved it when things happened that way. Her clients thought she was the bomb, when in fact, she got lucky. Most of the time, she did not have a contact where she needed one, and things became sticky. On those occasions, she turned into "Sally."

Once Katie had panhandled on the corner of a small-town street because her insurance company client had sent her to investigate a "staged" accident. After three days with nothing to show for it, a woman she recognized as a principle in the case came out of a building. The woman ignored Katie in her homeless attire, which made an opportunity Katie didn't miss as she had turned on her video app.

"Hey, my lawyer says the insurance company is about to settle. Their maximum payout is $150,000. The lawyer says they will settle most likely at $75,000, and if we pay Cynthia about $5,000, we are home free with seventy grand. Looking good, Dalton."

Dalton was the name of the man in the suit against the insurance company, and their witness was named Cynthia. Jackpot.

Katie got Cynthia to roll over on her friends with the tape on her phone and the threat of prosecution for fraud from the insurance company. With no witnesses, the couple disappeared to peddle their kind of fraud in a different state.

Undercover as her homeless persona Sally, occasionally, Katie felt the sting of disgust from people who viewed her as a street beggar. The life of the homeless was beyond sad, often complicated by addiction. Even worse, many who passed them scorned them, assuming homelessness was a choice they could have avoided. Katie wondered if, in some way, the homeless population was the new disadvantaged group in the world, and experiencing discrimination for them was a way of life.

She needed to get to Ocean Shores, but it was crucial to talk to Fred in case some government agency had tracked her. He wouldn't know, but he could find out. Katie didn't want jail to be her future. She would make a few more calls, and maybe head down to the beach tonight. It was only an hour away, so a quick trip might mean she could find Beckie's missing mom.

Luckily her mom liked Ellie, so she would feed the dog and take her along tonight to dinner at her mom's house.

If only traffic co-operated, she would be on time — one more call to Ocean Shores, the obligatory call to the local police.

"Ocean Shores Police Department, can I help you?"

"Yes, my great aunt went to the ocean a few days ago, but we haven't heard from her. Do you have any information? She is disabled. Have you had any reports of someone who is lost or confused? Sometimes she has memory issues, just not all the time."

"Your name, please, and where are you calling from?"

This was the protocol. The local police would not give Katie any information unless they thought she was family. When Beckie Clark had been in her office, Katie had casually noticed when they exchanged phone numbers that Beckie listed Kylie Clark under family contacts. A decent chance she was a daughter, making her the right contact name to use. Sometimes as a private eye, she fudged a little on how she was able to open the door to get information. It wasn't a significant ethical breach. She hoped.

"Kylie Clark and I'm calling from (Katie quickly pulled up the contact Beckie had signed and got her address) Des Moines, Washington."

"Just a minute, please."

They would verify the address and check a license number for a Kylie Clark. In a minute, she came back on the line.

"A disabled woman fitting that description was found wandering on the beach. She is in the local hospital. We don't have any ID. I would suggest you come down as the hospital won't give out medical information."

"Thank you so much. We'll do that right away."

Several bills were due in two days, and this case could pay them. If Katie called Beckie and said her mom might be in the hospital, Beckie would race to the beach to see if it was her mom. But if it wasn't Irene Wells, Katie could lose her as a client. "Disabled" could mean a lot of things, and it might not be Beckie's mom. It did make sense she might have walked from the grocery store to the beach. It was just a few blocks away.

If she waited until tomorrow, more payable hours would accrue and the cost of the bills covered. Katie hated "gray areas," where maybe she should call the client, but if she waited, she made a little more money. Katie did need to verify if the woman in the hospital was Irene Wells. So technically, she couldn't tell Beckie she had found her mom until she was sure.

Ping. Another text from her mom.

> Katie, I just heard from Fred's wife, Marilyn. I tried to call you, but your phone just went to message. They rushed Fred to the hospital. It could be a heart attack. Headed over there now. Don't come yet. Let me find out how he is doing. I will keep you posted. I am praying. You pray too. Love you, mom.

Katie stared at the screen. Her hand shook as she texted back.

> Mom, I'm praying too. Please let me know as soon as you can—hug Marilyn for me.

*Fred. Please, God, help him.*

Katie shivered, a heart attack was terrible, but was this something else entirely? Some years ago, when she was taking criminology classes, she had been sitting in Fred's house, and they talked about how criminals ended up on the FBI's top ten list. In the course of the conversation, Fred mentioned he had worked on a few cases involving people on the list, one in particular. He gave no details at all, but she had pulled up the file on her phone. Using her finger, she stopped at each name on the list and looked at him. Finally, when she got to number five, a Terrell Huff, Fred had nodded briefly. All Fred would tell her at the time was he was a specialist in studying government assassinations, both foreign and domestic.

The Chinese diplomat.

Over the years, Katie knew that Fred consulted in his retirement. His outward personality, an unassuming older man, was a cover for an astute man who paid attention to detail, brilliant at times in helping her in her criminology classes at the University of Washington. In her job as a PI, whenever she felt stumped on a case, she had shared coffee and cookies with Fred to pick his brain. Like clockwork, he often pointed to the one detail that changed her perspective, that detail that made her dig deeper and find answers. He was phenomenal. He often said you had to think like a criminal to know what they would do.

In his old gardening shed, there was a locked closet. Once, when he was getting some tools, Katie had glimpsed some clippings and notes of assassinations over the years. Occasionally a government car parked near his house gave testimony that Fred still consulted as a resource from some agencies in the government.

Who knew that? Did Fred have a real heart attack? Would Matt Dunn know?

*That hiding place, God? Can you make it big enough for Fred too?*

# CHAPTER TWELVE

Katie picked up Ellie to accompany her. Ellie loved to go places in the car. It came from her years as a police service dog.

She needed to do one small errand on the way to Ocean Shores. She scrolled in her phone contacts for Aunt April and put through a call.

"Hello to my favorite niece, Katie!"

"Hey, Aunt April, I am headed down to the coast, but I was wondering if I could stop by and do a pit-stop run for my daycare dog, Ellie?"

"No problem, but I am leaving in about a half-hour. You know your way around, help yourself to anything you need. Does that work?"

"Yes, that works. Thanks so much. I'll stay longer next time for your amazing coffee!"

"Next time come for the weekend. We started going to this small church with a young pastor. His name is Andy. His wife is about your age, and I think you would love to hear him, he brings the Bible to life."

"I would love to do that. I'll call you soon."

Katie needed to have a place for Ellie to do her duty, but she needed something else that Aunt April had on her farm in Puyallup.

She had a farm burn barrel, and Katie needed to burn her bloodied gloves and her homeless clothes. Fortunately, this early in the spring, there was no burn ban, and they often burned old corn stalks and rotted fence posts.

Traffic was light, and Katie found her way to her aunt's farm quickly. Aunt April and Uncle Dennis raised pumpkins in the fall, often had a petting zoo and farm produce they sold at a roadside stand. In the spring, they were busy plowing, planting, and fertilizing. Katie let Ellie run and remake her acquaintance with the ancient farm dog. An Australian shepherd named Buck. After they made friends, Katie strolled to the back of the barn, letting Ellie do her business as she watched the evidence of her presence in the parking garage go up in smoke in the burn barrel.

Most evidence that connected her to the attack in the garage this morning lay in ashes in the burn barrel. But ballistics tests on the bullet that hit the assassin could tie her to the shooting. She needed to figure out that aspect.

Katie played her tunes loudly on the hour-long trip to Ocean Shores as Ellie slept. Well-marked signs led her to the hospital.

Some maneuvering and a few indirect lies enabled her to get into the hospital room.

Problem. According to the picture, the woman there was not Beckie's mom. She was disabled, but more along the lines of mentally disabled with a broken arm in a sling. So much for police having good descriptions of folks.

Where does an eighty-one-year-old hide? What would Fred say?

"If you are looking for an old person, think like an old person."

A senior center?

Katie quickly googled senior centers. Closed now, but they had a satellite one in the community center, which was open until nine PM, and that was just a few blocks away.

Katie drove over and quickly located the area designated for the seniors. Only a couple of people there. It was getting late for older people to be out and about.

"Excuse me. I'm looking for my great aunt, and I forgot to get her phone number before I left Kent today. She does things at the senior center here."

"What's her name?" asked Katie's likeliest candidate for old busybody type.

"It might be easier if I show you her picture. That way, you can know right away. Does this work?" Katie showed her the picture on her phone.

"Oh, she's new. I saw her a little bit ago. Someone brought her here, but she couldn't find them. She was hungry, and we told her that Bill's Seafood a few blocks down had a senior special tonight. She left a while ago. Not sure if she was with someone, but you might catch her there."

As Katie was about to run out, two local firemen walked in the front door. Katie's brother-in-law was a first responder, and she had enormous respect for him.

"Hey, have you guys seen this woman? She might be in trouble." Katie showed them the picture.

"We might have seen her." The one with Jesse stitched on his uniform said, "Are you a relative?" He asked politely, not willing to give more information until he was sure Katie was a safe person.

Katie pulled out her private investigator's license. "My client hired me to find her. She has memory issues."

The tall fireman with "David" on his uniform said, "Jesse and I just came from Bill's Seafood getting takeout, and we saw her go in with a man and a woman. Can we help?"

"Thanks, but I got this."

"Okay, but if you need help, that's what we do," Jesse said.

Katie smiled, "Firemen are the best, thank you. My brother-in-law is a fireman. Be safe."

Katie tried not to sprint to the car. She could see the big sign for Bill's Seafood a few blocks back up the main street. A glance in the back seat at Ellie revealed that she had that *look*.

"Ok, no messing around. Do your business, and we have to go!"

Ellie looked at her like she was offended, and yet she trotted over to the bushes nearby and began the whole sniffing process that would lead to finding a place to make a deposit.

Katie anxiously waited, while Ellie did what she needed, and watched up the road in case she saw a woman who could be Irene.

She felt her phone vibrate. It was Beckie Clark calling her. Should she take the call or wait until she found her mom?

"Hello, Katie, this is Beckie Clark. You asked me to call if I found something out?"

"Yes, Beckie, I did. Did you hear back from your mom?"

"No, I haven't, but I did find something in her apartment, that's important. My mom had a coin collection that was my dad's — some rare coins and things that probably are worth quite a bit. I was looking in her bedroom today, and the case was gone. If my nephew took that, they wouldn't need her credit card as they could get cash for the coins at any coin place or pawn shop."

"Beckie, I think I might have a line on your mom. I'm in Ocean Shores now, if I find her in the next hour, what do you want me to do? Bring her back?"

"Yes, and please call me if there is a problem with my nephew. I don't know what they think they are doing, but robbing my mom of her coins and taking her somewhere when she doesn't know what is going on *is* what you said, elder abuse. I will have him prosecuted for that. My sister might ignore this, but I won't. Especially if they took her coins."

"Okay, give me a half-hour, and I will get back to you."

Katie called Ellie, who bounded over, wagging her tail as if to report she accomplished her duty. Katie noticed her deposit was far off the path in the bushes, so she crossed her fingers and didn't clean up the mess. Fortunately, there was no little old lady around to shame her on this.

"Good girl, Ellie!" Katie opened the door, and Ellie jumped in the backseat. Katie quickly tossed her a doggie bone, as Ellie needed positive reinforcement when she got that aspect of daily living right.

Katie pulled in the parking lot in front of the restaurant. She opened the car door, and before she could tell her to stay, Ellie hopped out to investigate a tall young man walking a dog. Ellie went straight to the other dog.

"Oh, sorry. She *is* friendly," Katie apologized.

"That's okay. I'm Sam, and this is Luna. She's friendly too."

Both dogs sniffed and wagged tails. The man smiled, and Katie called Ellie back to her as they returned to their walk.

The restaurant door opened, and Irene and two people who had to be her grandson and girlfriend exited the restaurant.

"Irene, is that you?"

Irene looked over at Katie and smiled blankly.

"Excuse me, but I remember you from meeting you at Beckie's house a week ago? Do you remember? So good to see you," Katie gushed as she dashed up to Irene to engulf her in a hug.

The nephew, Jay, looked uncomfortable. He tugged at his grandma's arm slightly, pushing Katie away.

"I don't know you, and we are just leaving."

A low growl escalating to a louder bark came from Ellie, who now was very concerned as Jay pushed Katie, which was not okay in her book.

Ellie's menacing behavior in full German-Shepherd-police-dog-aggression made Jay step back.

"Hey, get a hold of your dog!"

Katie touched Ellie, and she slowed down her growl to a low rumble.

"Irene needs to talk to her daughter, Beckie." Katie hit redial, and when Beckie picked up, Katie put her on speaker.

"Beckie, I'm here with your mom and Jay. Would you like to talk to Jay?"

"Jay, Mom is coming home with my friend Katie. Do you understand?"

"I don't know what *your* problem is. Grandma is on a little vacation with Selena and me. She wants to stay with us! So, mind your own business."

Katie had inched closer to Irene and was between Jay and his grandmother.

"Jay, send Mom with my friend now, or I will call the police. And if you have mom's coin collection, give it to my friend Katie now."

"Grandma, come on," Jay grabbed for his grandmother's arm.

Ellie saw this as hostility toward Katie and instantly went on full snarling and vicious barking. Jay sprang back. Sam, with his dog Luna had turned around at the commotion and was watching Jay suspiciously. He pulled out his cell phone.

Jay exchanged a glance with his girlfriend Selena, and both edged toward a car parked a few stalls over.

"I don't know what you are talking about, Aunt Beckie, but I can send Grandma with your friend. You need to chill, and I am going to call the cops on your friend and her crazy dog. We were having fun with Grandma. This is stupid!"

Both Jay and his girlfriend hopped in their car and pulled out.

Katie gently took Irene's arm with a smile and petted Ellie. She said, "Come!"

"You guys, okay?" Sam called out.

"Yes, thanks so much." Good Samaritans were everywhere today. Katie turned to Irene. "Can you talk to Beckie as we drive?" and handed her the phone.

A half-hour later, they had stopped for a bathroom break in Aberdeen at a large strip mall. Irene pointed out a place.

"That's where we took Bill's coins."

It was a coin and a baseball card shop. The "Closed" sign showed on the door.

She called Beckie back and named the shop and passed on the phone number printed on the door.

Beckie thanked her over and over when they met in Kent and said she sent Katie's payment over PayPal, adding extra for the whole hassle with her nephew and locating the coins. Katie sighed inwardly in relief as this payment would cover all her outstanding bills.

This morning seemed like a week ago when she got home. She stumbled into her pajamas and fell into bed.

She checked her phone and read her mom's text.

> Fred is doing better. The medics were able to stabilize
> him, but he is in ICU. I wasn't able to see him, but
> Marilyn won't leave him, so I am headed home and
> plan to go back tomorrow. I will let you know if anything
> else goes on—no need to come tonight.

Later Ellie seemed to think Katie needed close observation, so she lay asleep on the floor next to Katie's bed. Katie was surprised at Ellie's protection, but she had been a police dog for eight years, but now too old for the force. One thing Katie knew, no one was getting past Ellie tonight.

"Good dog,"

Katie pulled up the covers and started counting. She had learned that counting sometimes kept the nightmares from coming. Always the same one, the feeling of being smothered. Five years seemed so long ago, yet the memory was painful, and the nightmares real.

Matt Dunn seemed to be a key to finding what she needed to know, but maybe, she didn't need to call him. What if she called his father, the head of Premier Security? She could always ask about a job, and maybe that would get her past the gatekeepers? What was his name, Jim?

One, two, three.

# CHAPTER THIRTEEN
## MATT

Matt was still waiting to be interviewed by the agency. Yesterday Agent Doug Miller texted Matt that Agent in Charge Riker Thompson would debrief him this morning. After he read the message, he slept the rest of the day and night, thanks to medication.

That gave him some time to absorb that Ned York, who had been with him through the Secret Service and his partner at Homeland— was gone— killed in the line of duty.

Tyrone Johnsen had the previous night off but checked in this morning. Kicked back in the recliner, he seemed relaxed, but Matt knew he was fully alert.

Another attempt on his life had missed. Why kill him? He was on an undercover mission within Homeland Security to find anyone who had leaked classified information from the agency. His undercover assignment was a need-to-know basis for those directly above him in the agency. However, his regular job had indicated intelligence from a reliable source there might be an imminent attack on a Chinese diplomat. Even perhaps, that he was a spy here on trade issues. The fact that the shooter knew their location indicated there was more to that intelligence. He would have classified the attack on himself and Ned as a casualty of the job, except for the second attempt and possibly, Ned's death.

His phone vibrated—text from dad.

I can't attend the debrief. Informed is on a need-to-
know basis. I have interviews today for people to run an
expansion office here in Seattle. Offer still stands for
you to head it up.

There was a sharp rap on the door, and Agent Thompson came through the door, giving a curt nod to the grim Tyrone Johnsen.

"Dunn, are you up to debrief?" More a statement than a question, no time spent on formal greetings.

"Yes, sir."

Agent Thompson placed a recording device on the rolling table next to Dunn. He looked over at Tyrone. "I'm sorry, classified info, so you'll have to wait outside."

Tyrone stood unsmiling and gave a slight nod.

"Start with entrance to the location, and I will ask questions as you give your summary."

Dunn recounted their entrance into the garage and the immediate gunshots that resulted in the death of the Chinese Diplomat, the wounding of Ned and himself. When he got to his returning fire, Thompson stopped him.

"Could you see the shooter from your position?"

"Partially. But I could see where he was firing from, so I laid down covering fire for Ned as he was in the line of fire. The gunfire ceased, and I thought I heard someone fall. I heard footsteps toward the upper entrance of the garage."

"Your report is consistent with what we know. That is what Agent Miller said you recounted at the scene. No blood at the site, and no brass. If this was Huff, and he was wounded, he could have a clean-up kit. We have no video surveillance of the event. Anything else you want to add?" Thompson leaned in.

"Yes, a question. Why was the support team location set farther from our location?"

"Not my call. Just before everyone left to investigate the intel, a call came in for additional locations that needed a team. We responded by spreading the teams out a bit. Headquarters didn't get that right."

Dunn finished the report, leaving all mention of the homeless nurse out of his retelling.

"Question, your service weapon, a Glock? Did you have a second weapon?"

"No. The agency team took my Glock at the scene, Miller, I believe."

"Yes, we have it, just checking for a back-up."

"I need you to recount yesterday's incident with the nurse who attacked you in the hospital."

"I have a question first. Ned York? Did he die from his injuries, or was there evidence of interference in the surgery?"

Thompson reached over and turned off the recorder.

"The autopsy is complete. The report says Ned died from a bullet wound to the head." His expression softened. "I am sorry for your loss. I understand you knew each other for several years and were on the same Secret Service detail before transferring to Operations. He was an excellent agent and will be missed. FYI, in addition to your dad's security, we posted a man outside your room and in the building."

"Thanks. I am requesting to stay in the Seattle area for my recovery time. My father is opening an office for his company here, and I will be staying with him. Please keep me updated on the operation. As soon as I'm cleared medically, I want to get back to work. Ned was a good friend."

"Understood. However, until you are released by the doctor to go back to work, we can't have you in the field. If you remember anything else or we have additional questions, we'll be in touch. We all want justice when one of our own is killed in the line of duty. We will do everything we can to find the person responsible."

He reached over and turned on the recorder. "Can you report on the incident in the hospital yesterday?"

Matt complied, and Thompson turned off the recorder and pocketed it.

"Without any video of the incident, we are operating at a loss."

"The picture on the news?"

"We shut that story down. Without corroborating testimony, from you or York, that this man was the shooter, we cannot say it was him. We are continuing to follow up on leads and the person who released this photo to the news. So far, nothing there, as it was an anonymous tip. The person calling it in used a disposable phone, so we have no ID on the caller."

"Does that seem odd to you?"

"The world seems odd to me. Lots of people today don't have a phone contract. They use a disposable phone. It could mean something, but no way of knowing. We'll continue to investigate and see what turns up." He stood up and reached out his hand to shake with Matt.

"We will find him."

"I would say that's optimistic. Because for the past twenty years, no one has found Huff. But you're right. We'll be looking harder than ever before."

"I'm sending in Dave Wilson, our agent, while I interview your dad's security team."

The new man in the room would mean he would not be able to contact his other boss, the one in charge of the undercover operation. He closed his eyes. Funny how a gunshot could slow a person down.

It seemed like only a few minutes, and Tyrone was waking him up.

"Hey man, the doc is here to tell you how bad you're doing."

One more day in the hospital and he could stay with his dad at his temporary home base, an Airbnb. Fortunately, there were no complications with his wound, and despite the constant ache, all had gone well with the surgery. The stern lecture from the doctor to stay off his feet did not fall on deaf ears. To be useful in the coming days, he would follow medical procedures so he would heal. Being sidelined physically didn't mean he would stop investigating.

He desperately wanted to find out more about the woman who had saved his life and attempted to save Ned's. Never in his professional career had he withheld information from the government. But in this situation, he had the whole army of agents and his dad's security team to protect him from further attacks. She had none of that, and it was clear from the two attacks on his life he had a target on his back. Why? Had he ticked off someone in the agency? Was the true nature of his assignment known, and those who had leaked information found it easier to remove the investigator than to be exposed?

If the woman's presence were known, she would be hunted and killed. The photo of the man in the garage immediately disappeared from the news, and the misinformation regarding its authenticity could only point to the Deep State and control at a high level. If he had trusted that the information given in the debriefing would have been kept secure, he would have told of her presence. But the very reason he was here, intelligence leaks, prevented him from disclosing it.

He kept replaying that last question Thompson asked him in his mind regarding the attack. Why did he ask him about his service weapon? Using his service weapon at the scene was a non-question, of course, he would have used it. So why did Thompson ask about it?

Unless the shooter was wounded and the bullet recovered wasn't from a Glock. In that case, who was the person who shot Huff? He would know then there was a second shooter besides the agents. And if that was the case, someone had a line into Homeland Security. If the bullet did not come from Matt's gun, there was a second shooter and a second witness. Someone who probably also took the picture. That being the case, and the leak being real, then Huff would hunt for the second shooter. Matt wondered if they knew he left that out of his report. Maybe they thought he didn't see the second shooter? His life expectancy didn't seem to get any better with that knowledge.

He knew Thompson wasn't involved in any corruption regarding information leaks. He was a straight shooter. The thousand-dollar question? Who did the asking about his service weapon? He doubted anyone had seen the woman hidden behind the parking booth. There was no video—or none yet, as Homeland's investigation included combing local business's street cameras.

Should he make contact? It could be difficult because of agents who watched him, but not impossible.

He grabbed the only phone he had, as the government techs had taken his agency phone to search it. His cell showed no service, typical to most hospitals. That post on Craigslist needed to be deleted. He sat up and looked over at Tyrone.

Tyrone ambled over his nonchalance deceiving. Matt grabbed a napkin and scribbled on it what he needed.

He handed over the napkin, and Tyrone glanced at it, folded it and put it in his pocket, and for the record said out loud, "Taking a personal break, I'm sending Sam in here."

He hoped the woman wouldn't call right away. If he were a praying person, he would pray she didn't call. His mom would have smiled at that. She'd been the one to pray in the family before cancer took her two years ago. While he did not understand why all her prayers couldn't keep her here, she was a rock to her final breath. Her last moments peaceful, she had said to him she was going to her Savior and asked Matt to take care of his dad.

*If you are looking down, Mom, send an angel to look after the nurse. I owe her one.*

# CHAPTER FOURTEEN

The Speaker of the House tapped on the window that separated him from his driver. As the window slid open, the driver passed him a Ziplock bag with a new burner phone.

He quickly unpackaged it and texted the number from memory.

Status Update.

He waited and could see the repeating dots, which indicated a response.

One completed. Unfortunate, information to media. Contained. Opportunity to complete. Needs extension due to unexpected security from an outside source. Recommend a slower schedule temporarily to avoid notice. Assurance completion is accident-related. Pipeline acknowledged weapon used by the incomplete target was Glock 17. Further investigation needed.

He swore and banged his fist on the seat. He had waited until this convenient window in time, and he did not need delays. He would have to report this. He texted another number from memory.

One complete, other complications. Suggestion from

asset to slow schedule temporarily. Still, a go on the
asset?

He nervously looked over his schedule for the day on his tablet as
he waited. He had a three PM meeting with the Director of the Secret
Service. At least that was on schedule. His cell pinged.

Unfortunate, information leaks. Asset best source
currently, recommendation accepted. Some delays built
into the schedule. Stick to plan on others. Status report
on Dir. SS when complete.

He deleted the text thread and texted back the on the first text.

Recommendation accepted. Go ahead on the pipeline
to access any further information on incomplete target's
weapon info.

He made a mental note. The asset had made no excuses, only a
concise explanation. At least he could count on this connection to
see the importance of commitment to the assignment. Perhaps it was
vital to have some useful contacts. This person would be worthy of
future consideration.

The plan continued forward. But after completion? They would
muzzle those who asked questions. Years of granting interviews and
leaking information to trusted sources meant that these sources
would wittingly or unwittingly publish data to shout down the most
problematic inquiries. There was a system, and most followed along.
It created an atmosphere of belief in any disinformation distributed.

There needed to be a preparation ahead of time also to silence the
unfriendly voices, which would create enough "dust" that there
would be no inquiries to expose the plan.

He licked his lips. Finally, the time had come, and the few

inconsequential lives that could slow the process down would be eliminated next week. A few days from now and he and the team that had propelled him would be in power. Any whistleblowers left after that could be banished using the authority of his new position.

He allowed himself to visualize sitting in the Oval Office, calling other world leaders. The country and the world would see him as a rescuer and hail him as a hero. Absolute power, and while he would have to share it, he could find ways to remove those who had helped him. After all, he would be the President, and after that, what required him to continue his allegiance? He had, in every way, been the team player, never giving any indication of anything other than complete obedience to the plan. That would change.

But from the beginning, he had his backup plan. Ruthlessness was the name of this game, and those who thought they were running him had no idea of his cunning and ultimate goal. He played his card of subservience, and his cloak of technological ineptness played well into that. Those working with him, although always suspicious of anyone, had no clue to his extended plan. The thought of the power available at his fingertips sent a shiver of delight through him.

Soon.

# CHAPTER FIFTEEN
## KATIE

Ping. A text from an unknown number, not unusual but now unnerving.

> Katie Parson, we received your resume for a job
> opening with Premier Security in our new Seattle office.
> I am conducting interviews at a temporary location.
> Please call to receive a time and place, 206-586-2179.

Katie had emailed her resume to Jim Dunn's administrative assistant three hours ago. Either Jim Dunn liked what he saw, or he was ready to hire, and she was one of the first to respond to an ad on the agency's website.

"Yes, I'm calling for a time and location for an interview with Jim Dunn this afternoon?"

"Thank you. I will text you an address. Please arrive in thirty minutes. Knock and enter into the house when you arrive. It's a temporary location while we are looking for space for a new office. Mr. Dunn is at the location, and if he does not come out to greet you, have a seat. Thanks for applying."

"Thank you."

Katie's phone pinged with a text message address. She hit her map app and put her phone on its magnetic holder.

She leaned her head on the steering wheel. What was she going to do? How would she bring up the situation in the garage? Bad ideas seemed more common than good ones lately.

She found Grandma Betty's contact number.

"Grandma? How're you doing today?"

"Katie, girl? You don't sound like yourself."

"Yeah, I got some things going on and need you to pray. I'm worried I'm not going to make the right decision."

"Let's pray, honey. God, Katie needs your strength, your power, and your wisdom today. You say in your Word, 'God is our refuge and strength, a very present help in trouble. Therefore, we will not fear.' Help Katie not to be afraid. We give you this day knowing your limits are infinite and your love inexhaustible. Help her make the right decisions. Protect, her Lord."

"Grandma, thank you, I needed that. I love you. How's Potty Dog doing?" Grandma Betty's ancient Yorkshire Terrier often had accidents, and her name described her behavior.

"She's been good lately. She bit the UPS man again, but he didn't notice much because she only has a few teeth left."

"Well, she has her spunk." Katie chuckled.

"I love you, Katie. You come over for some tater tot casserole this weekend, OK?"

"Grandma, I'll try and get over for the casserole soon, but not this weekend. I love you too."

Katie felt better but still didn't know how she would approach Jim Dunn with her information.

A soft ping—she had a notification on Facebook.

"Sometimes, the only transportation you have is a leap of faith." It was a meme, and her mom had sent it. Katie looked skyward and smiled. "Okay, definitely not going to livestream church the next time, God," she whispered. There was a warmth that spread through her, and the anxiousness seemed to melt a little bit. She put a "like" on her mom's meme.

Katie hit the GPS map on the phone and headed off to the interview.

Should she reveal to Jim Dunn the entire incident? Fred was still in intensive care.

The location was a house in a residential area in the Ravenna area of North Seattle. Katie knocked and did not hear an answer, but the door was unlocked, so she entered the living room. She took a seat on the couch.

Jim Dunn came out of a room to the right, where she caught a glimpse of a desk and a chair. Katie recognized him from his brief appearance on TV when he entered the hospital for his son. Jim was a little shorter than his son, about five-foot-ten or so, she would guess. In his late fifties, but fit, and he gave off an aura of confidence and calm. His company provided personal security to people, and perhaps he made it his business to offer a soothing professional presence. At least Katie felt reassured this man seemed trustworthy.

"Afternoon. I'm Jim Dunn. Are you Katie Parson?"

"Yes, happy to meet you."

"Katie, Come on in." He gestured for Katie to follow him into the office area. "I do have someone here who, I understand, you know?"

Katie felt a cold sweat trickle down her back. Who knew she would be here? No one.

Katie looked into the room made into an office, a large desk, and two comfortable chairs situated in front. An older man was seated in one of the chairs. Katie stopped in shock.

She gasped out, "Fred? But you are—"

"Katie, my dear, sorry for the deception, but it was necessary. I will explain in a little bit."

Fred stood and opened his arms. Katie went to him immediately and received a hug, which was the most comforting thing she had experienced in the past few days.

Katie looked into Fred's eyes, and she could see he was troubled. She experienced tightness in her chest, and it seemed hard to breathe.

"Katie, please have a seat. You are probably confused a bit as to why Fred is here," said Jim Dunn.

"Fred and I go way back to years ago in the FBI. Fred was my mentor and boss. I learned more from him than from anyone in my career. Because of the nature of the assassination of the Chinese diplomat a few days ago in downtown Seattle, I reached out to Fred immediately, because I knew he lived nearby. He said he might have more information on the incident, and we set up today for our meeting. When he arrived, I told him I would have limited time this morning based on my interviews for people to staff my new Seattle office. He asked if I was interviewing any local private eyes, and I said yes. When he asked who, I told him about you, and he said he would need to stay for your interview as we both might learn more about the incident a few days ago. I have to say that made me curious."

Katie looked at Fred, and he gave a small nod.

"Mr. Dunn—"

"Please call me Jim."

"Jim, I am sorry I have used this interview as an opportunity to speak to you about what happened a couple of days ago. I didn't know what to do, and I heard Fred—she looked over at him for a moment, anxiously—was in the hospital. So, I took a chance on contacting you on the pretense of a job."

Jim leaned back in his chair. "Go on."

"Two days ago, around 5:30 AM, I was coming back from the investigation on an insurance case. One of my disguises for doing undercover work is being a homeless person. It was dark, raining a bit when I noticed two men approach up the hill. I recognized your son, Matt Dunn. I knew him because years ago, I trained at FLETC, and he was on some training webinars we were required to watch for security protocol." Katie crossed her fingers as this man would be someone who could spot a lie a mile away. It was true that she had seen some training videos on aspects of security protocol that listed Matt Dunn's name while at FLETC, but she had never watched them.

"When I saw him, I figured that he was there for some government operation. I decided to stay out of their way and slipped into a parking garage nearby."

"Unfortunately, they entered the garage too, and then there was a lot of gunfire. An Asian man was murdered as he exited the hotel elevator to the parking garage. Next, the shooter turned and fired at both agents."

"You say he shot them immediately? Would you say that he acted because he expected them to be there?" Jim Dunn leaned forward.

"I saw his gun swivel from the first target to both agents. There was almost no stopping in his motion. Like I said, either he saw them enter, or he was waiting for them to enter to begin his attack."

"Where were you?" Dunn asked.

"I was behind the parking booth near the entrance to the garage. The gunman could not see me from his vantage point, although I could see him. I could see through the Plexiglass of the booth your son was bleeding in spurts from what looked like a femoral artery wound. The shooter was advancing on the other agent, probably to finish him. I took out my weapon and fired. Your son started firing at the same time, probably to cover his partner."

"Did either of you hit the gunman?"

"I think so. I watched him go down and dodge behind some cars. I knew your son needed a tourniquet on his wound, so I crawled to him and convinced him not to shoot me. I used his belt for a tourniquet. When he was secure, I checked his partner, took a picture of the attacker on his way out, and made my escape. I still don't know if I was seen on any video by local police or Homeland's team."

"Do you have medical training?"

"Yes, I studied to be an EMT, something that comes in handy as a PI."

Dunn had a puzzled look on his face. "My son, let you approach him in the middle of a shootout? Did he know you from FLETC?"

This man put his finger on the one piece of information Katie could not tell him. How was she going to get around this?

Jim Dunn's phone on the desk vibrated, and he looked down. "Please excuse me a moment. My next interview is here." Jim went to the door, but stopped, "Katie, since you are a local PI, and this person who is waiting outside is also one, have you ever heard of a Dan Beck?"

Not again? The man who always looked ready, who smelled good and always gave his best movie star imitation, was *here?* Yet, could this be one of those divine appointments her mom always talked about because Dan Beck was the one person who could verify that Katie was in the hotel.

"Actually, yes. I have worked on a few cases with Dan, and he's probably the best in Seattle. There is one reason you might want to let him in here, though. He saw me at the hotel that day."

Jim Dunn stared at her, and Fred coughed.

"When I said no one saw me, no police or Homeland agents did, but Dan was working at the hotel upstairs, and he helped me get out of the hotel. He didn't know why I needed help getting out without being recognized on camera or what happened in the garage."

Jim looked over at Fred.

"From my sources, he is a man who is tight-lipped and excellent at investigation," Fred said.

Katie turned to Fred and raised an eyebrow.

"Do you trust this man?" Dunn asked Katie.

"Yes, I do," Katie said immediately, surprising herself. Well, he was *good* at what he did.

Dunn left the room for a few minutes, and Katie looked over at Fred.

"What is going on?" she whispered.

"I got your message, and when Jim asked me about the incident, I knew that you knew about it or you were there. I was going to call you, but I couldn't break the cover created. I will explain in a minute. Jim knows."

Dan came into the room, nodded at Katie, and offered his hand to Fred.

"Good to see you, sir," he said. Dan pulled an extra chair from near the desk.

Great, Fred and Dan *knew* each other?

There, in person, sat Dan Beck, giving her his star-studded smile from the other chair. He looked like he belonged there, utterly relaxed and irritating.

"Katie, Dan told me you are well acquainted and have worked together?"

"Yes, we collaborated on a case last year." Katie forced a smile.

"Dan, normally I would conduct an interview, and we will get to that. But there is a development regarding my son who was shot in a government operation a few days ago."

"Yes, I heard about that," Dan said guardedly.

"Katie explained something to us about being in the hotel. She said you were there too?"

Dan looked at Katie. She nodded.

"Yeah, I was there working a job and ran into Katie on the second floor. She said she was on a case."

Katie appreciated his careful response.

"For the moment, I am going to dispense with the interviews and go right to what Katie has shared and why I particularly need help in the next few days. I had no idea that both of you were involved in this situation. Dan, I will let Katie bring you up to speed about what we are talking about because I need to check in with my security team at the hospital."

Katie leaned closer to him and looked into his blue-gray eyes. A minute ago, Dan had looked relaxed, but now he seemed on edge.

"I was in the shootout in the garage. I saw it all and helped Jim's son, who is a Homeland Security agent, with his wound. The shooting seemed to be a setup, and I chose to leave when both agents were safe. I raced upstairs and ran into you."

"So, you didn't tell anyone you were there?" Dan's tone was neutral, but she understood he was politely trying to find out what she had said so far and how he figured into it.

Jim Dunn ended his phone call. The mood in the room seemed awkward to Katie.

"I need to say here, this is a difficult situation. At this point, Dan, you are not implicated. Beyond your knowledge of Katie being in the hotel, you are uninvolved in what happened. And you can leave if you choose not to go any further with this." Jim said.

"If I may, I would like to stay. I don't know how much time I can give. I have a full slate of cases. But I do want to be a part of a start-up for your agency here in Seattle." Dan said.

Jim broke into a smile, "That seals the deal for me, I would like to hire you. Whatever you do going forward in this is salaried, and I appreciate your willingness to help before you knew what's at stake here. Loyalty is my key factor in everyone who works for me. We are going to need professional skills in the next few days, and looking over your resume, I like your Army Ranger special ops background.

Let me fill you in on what we are doing here."

"Perhaps Katie and I can adjourn to the kitchen for coffee while you bring Dan up to speed?"

Katie threw a relieved look at Fred, and they exited to the kitchen. Katie put in a decaf pod for Fred and found cream in the fridge. Better than drip coffee, at least.

"So, were you in the hospital at all?"

Fred smiled at her. She knew that look, the same one in past years when he had given her a crime puzzle to do and was pleased with her progress.

"Do you remember a few years ago, meeting my brother Tod?"

"Yeah, you two could have been twins. He also worked for the government?"

"Yes, well in the last year, Tod developed congestive heart failure. He is very ill. Tod was visiting with Marilyn and me when I took the call from a contact in Homeland that they believed Terrell Huff to be in the area, and he possibly was involved in the attack in the Seattle parking garage. He asked if I would be available to consult. I said I might not be available due to family constraints but that I would get back to him. Naturally, I discussed this with Tod, and he feared if Huff was in the area, he might try to harm me. It's always a risk when you know information about dangerous men."

"Tod has very little time left. We had a long discussion. About this time, Jim had contacted me and Tod, Jim, and I then conducted a three-way discussion. Tod wanted to enter the hospital under my name. He said he could do something for his country and me. I fought against this idea, but finally, we decided to go ahead with the plan. Marilyn informed my contact at the agency that I had entered the hospital with a heart attack. We knew that if Huff tried something, Homeland would have leaked the information. Marilyn went with him to make the cover complete."

"But who is watching over him? Couldn't Huff get to him?"

"Every medical professional near Tod is an agent working with Matt Dunn and his dad to uncover the information leak in the Department of Homeland Security. This operation is as tight as any operation can be because the prize is a criminal of international reputation, a man wanted by every intelligence agency in the U.S. as well as Interpol. It would be the ultimate capture. Matt only knows the basics as we cannot get much information to him without compromising the operation. I'm sorry, I would have told you sooner if I could."

Katie passed Fred his decaf cup and grabbed a pod for her.

"You do know that a couple of times, I peeked at your information about Huff in the shed, right?"

Fred smiled but did not comment.

"When I called Matt Dunn at the hospital, he told me via a little coded info that the person who shot him was on the Top Ten list, number Five. I looked that up, that would be Terrell Huff. I realized this was the same man you had hunted in your career. On another note, so, what's the deal, how do you and Dan Beck know each other?"

"Small world, dear. Dan's mother is Marilyn's cousin."

"Is there anyone in this town you don't know?"

Fred's eyes twinkled.

Jim poked his head in the kitchen. "Can you both join us?"

"Katie, please fill us in a little more, if you can, on what happened Monday."

"Something more than the killing of the Asian diplomat was going down. I also know from my experience at FLETC, that the government screws up. If those agents were in danger, staying would put a target on my back. There had to be a leak in information, or why were both agents shot instantly? I knew the government wouldn't protect my identity or might try to blame me for a whole operation gone bad. I didn't want to be a scapegoat."

Fred coughed politely, "Katie reached out to me in a phone message." Looking at Dan, he went on, "Katie is a close neighbor and has been my friend for many years. She is aware that before I retired from the Agency, my specialty was working on investigations involving the Top Ten Most Wanted list. From that experience, I am aware of a man whose MO matched the killing in the garage. He is currently number five on the list, a Terrell Huff, as we suppose his name.

"Additionally, Jim was an associate at the Agency during my tenure there and aware of my specialty. That said, I was made aware by my contacts that Terrell Huff was in the area, and that I should be more alert than usual in my daily activities. A man who kills for a living isn't fond of people who know anything about him or his methods. There is always caution when a person like this occupies the same local vicinity.

"At this time, a plan was put into place. I have a brother, although not my twin, one who looks very much like me. He is in the later stages of congestive heart failure. He knew of my situation with Huff and offered to go into the hospital, under my name, to see if his presence there could lure Huff out and let us capture him. My brother's time is short and his sacrifice for me beyond words. I refused at first, but he told me it was the one last operation he could do, and asked me to please let him. Both he and I served in the Agency together.

"A plan is in place with Homeland regarding anyone who would approach him. My wife has been there but is now home and an agent look-alike in her place. We don't expect there to be any danger, but if we could get close to Huff, it would be the first time it's ever happened. He has been virtually untouchable."

Jim leaned forward, "Someone attacked Matt and attempted to kill him. My security team stopped the person. His partner Ned has died. We do not know if he died from his wound and or there was some foul play."

"Why would anyone in the agency set Matt up? Was he involved in some agency shakedown? A whistleblower? I know from the training videos back then he was in the Secret Service at that time. Now it seems he is in another branch of Homeland?" Katie asked.

"He was given a promotion to transfer to Homeland Operations. The Secret Service has management problems, and he was frustrated with all that. His partner, Ned York, was also with the Secret Service, and they both took the assignment to this new agency."

"My original purpose in opening an office here was partially a cover to work closely with Matt. We are paid consultants on this operation. But what happened to Matt has changed all that. I decided, for now, I would hire people here to add to my crew in protecting Matt and let them be a part of my agency going forward. Everything you all have just told me confirms my need to hire additional security and get to the bottom of who is running this operation against my son."

Dan leaned forward, "Just listening to all this, I'm trying not to be a conspiracy theorist, but it is obvious there are leaks from the department and almost a plan surrounding these events."

"I agree. I need to ask you something, Katie. Did you call Matt in the hospital? Are you also a nurse?" Jim said.

"Yes, I called him. I am not a nurse, but I volunteer at the hospital. I wanted to find out if he was okay. And I wanted to find out if when he debriefed, he told them about me. Because if he did, people are going to start looking for a homeless woman. But there was no way to find that out in the conversation. I left him a message to contact me, but I have not had any contact with him since."

Jim leaned back in his chair and was quiet for a moment. "I was not at his debrief, so I do not know what he told them. The doctor said Matt could leave the hospital soon. I need to have an exit strategy and location here where he will be safe. Can you help us get him out of the hospital without being seen? Oh, Katie, you are hired, by the way. I assume you and Dan can work together again?"

"No problem," Dan said.

"Sure." He was not her favorite person, but if she had to rely on someone, Dan was excellent at what he did.

"I can get Matt out of the hospital without anyone noticing. When is he due for release?" Katie asked.

"Tomorrow morning."

"Good, tomorrow starts at midnight tonight, so let's aim for a three AM dismissal. It's when nurses are changing half-shifts. The hospital is trying to make fewer twelve-hour shifts, so nurses are more alert while working."

"I have a couple more interviews scheduled soon. Let's go over a few details and meet back here at eleven PM," Jim said.

PART TWO

# DANCING WITH DRAGONS

# CHAPTER SIXTEEN

"I have a tentative plan." All eyes turned to Katie.

"We can get Matt out through the laundry exit. We'll get a laundry cart in there to strip the bed. Someone can cover the camera in the room. He gets in the cart. We'll cover him with sheets and get him down the service elevator to the laundry. After we get him out, we say he moved to another facility for security by Homeland. The hospital will be good with that explanation. I have a friend in the laundry department. I will distract him. You guys can move Matt to the exit. We can have him out in about twenty minutes." Katie said.

"That could work. I will work on the Homeland detail by letting Matt know my people will take over late evening. We won't tell them until the last minute, in case there is a leak in info. I will work on things from this end." Jim Dunn said.

"I can drive tonight. I have an old car I inherited from my step-grandmother. If someone runs the license plate, it goes back to her, and she died a few months back. The tabs are still good, and the plates lead to a dead-end," Dan offered.

"Sounds good, bring that vehicle tonight. Thank you both."

Dan reached across the desk and shook Jim's hand. Jim came around to Katie. "Can you stay for a moment?"

Dan shook Fred's hand and stepped out of the office.

"Katie, thank you for helping Matt. He is the most resourceful man I know, but I have never known my son to be a trusting man. He'd been critically wounded, yet he *let* you approach him and put a tourniquet on him? Is there something you aren't telling me? Did you know him at FLETC?"

"Jim, I believe your son was in shock. He had lost a considerable amount of blood, and I can't explain *why* he let me help him. I knew I had to help, or he would bleed out. Maybe I convinced him, maybe he felt I meant him no harm." Katie stopped and looked at Jim searchingly before going on.

"Maybe I was meant to be there. Sometimes in life, we have coincidences. Why was I passing that garage that day? I saw your son. He was critically injured, and I helped him. My mom has a name for that. She calls it a divine appointment."

Jim's face softened. "I suppose Matt's mom would have called it that too. Thank you, it took courage to do what you did. I have two sons, and I'm glad I didn't lose one. You will always have a job with me if you need it."

Katie was glad he did not press the matter as she couldn't tell him because of national security how Matt might have known her. Matt hadn't recognized her in the garage. However, without her homeless disguise, he would recognize her tonight, and both of them would have to act as if there was no other explanation than the one Katie provided.

Katie was surprised when she left the house to see Dan Beck leaning against her car.

"Hey, how about coffee?"

"As long as you are buying! I have a dog to walk but can squeeze in a coffee break. There are two coffee places in about a quarter-mile. Not sure the name, but I passed them on the way here."

Dan pulled out his phone and searched. "Looks like Heavenly

Bean is close, see you in five."

"Okay, that works."

On the way there, Katie was uncomfortable. It was one thing pretending to like Dan, another to have a sit down with him. That discomfort came from the way she felt about payment on the case she'd solved for him. He'd paid her what he promised, the $500, but it still stung that the client had paid $5,000 for her work. For all the professional courtesy he claimed, he could have easily shared half the reward since she did the job. It wasn't so much that is was unusual; it just felt to her as if he could have handled it differently.

Katie would have done it differently. Although when she talked it over with her dad, he said that any business deal needs lines of clear-cut communication. Dan had communicated the job paid $500, and that is what he gave her. He didn't indicate that it paid him ten times more. Her dad told her to let it go. Next time she should work on a contingency basis where she got a percentage of the payment. She had not said Dan's name because technically, he hadn't done anything wrong. It wasn't the first time her dad had advised her in business, and he always seemed to shed wisdom.

Katie parked and pulled up her hood to run into the coffee shop as in typical Seattle fashion, it torrentially rained. Dan was at the counter. Katie walked up in time to hear the barista gush over Dan.

"Did anyone ever tell you that you look like that actor—"

"The Star Trek guy?" Katie quickly added.

"Yeah, that guy, you look just like him!"

"More people tell me I look like the Guardian of the Galaxy guy."

"Um," she turns her head and looked confused, "Maybe, but the Star Trek guy for sure."

"Thanks. Katie, you got a coffee preference?"

"Americano, with room please and whip?"

"Find us a seat?" Dan said.

"Sure."

Katie looked around and found a table in a corner, as she assumed Dan wanted a little privacy. Not sure why, because he had not explained, so part of her was curious as to this spontaneous coffee date.

Dan set the coffee down in front of Katie and slid into the seat across from her. Always that good-looking, confident guy, but he appeared slightly nervous.

"I need to ask you something. Are you going to stick with the Premier Security thing after we do this job for Dunn?" Dan asked.

"I don't know. I took the interview because I needed to talk to Jim Dunn. If I had just seen it in the paper, maybe I would have checked it out. Why?"

"I need the job, and I hope you will stick because it would mean that he probably will open an office here, and we both would be in on that."

"Is there some big reason you need this gig Jim Dunn is offering? Because I have clients that tell me they tried to get you, but you were too busy. I was one of the referrals that you gave. So, if you have lots of work, what's up with this job?"

Katie took a sip of coffee and looked at Dan expectantly.

"So, you're still mad that I didn't pay you more for that job a few months back?"

Katie looked down and took another sip of coffee.

"I get it. I could have shared the fee." He leaned forward.

"I'm sorry, I couldn't. My mom was diagnosed with early-onset Alzheimer's a year ago, and she is in a facility that costs over $8,000 a month. She had no income other than her job, which she lost when she started forgetting things. I need about $11,000 a month to keep her there and pay bills. I was short that month. A few clients were slow in paying, and one even stiffed me. You solved the case so I could pay the bill that month. I was already over my credit limit. I'm sorry, I needed the money, and this job with Premier means I have something to fall back on."

"You did tell me the job paid $500, and you paid me that. I feel bad now I was mad about it. Wow, that's how much Alzheimer's care costs? That's like buying a used car every month."

"There are lots of places that cost less. But either the level of care is scary, or the place is dirty. I have visited lots of them. Some patients are strapped to a chair, given Lorazepam, and drugged until it's time to change their diaper or go to bed. It's disgusting. I could not put her in one of those places. She still is aware of her surroundings, and I can't put her in a place where they would drug her to oblivion. This place she can walk around, be safe and the staff are nice. But the cost is relentless. She gets almost a thousand in Social Security, but that's it as far as to help financially."

"I'm sorry about your mom. That's a tough decision to have to make. Hey, Fred told me his wife is your mom's cousin? That's how you know him?"

"Yeah, Marilyn came and sat with my mom a couple of times before I got her into the place. Mom was wandering, and I needed people to look in on her, Marilyn was wonderful, Fred came with her a couple of times. I would appreciate it if you keep that confidential about my mom. My business."

"We all have secrets, Dan. That's why you and I have jobs."

"Speaking of secrets, is there something more to you and Matt Dunn? None of my business unless it's going to get me shot. What gives? You list on your resume you trained at FLETC with Homeland Security, but you did not serve. Is that something to do with him?"

"You *read* my resume?"

"Yeah, and don't tell me you didn't read mine at my website just like I read yours. We have to know our competition in this town.

You are a good private investigator. But quit changing the subject, why didn't you serve as an agent for Homeland Security?"

Katie looked at Dan, the devastation of five years ago flooded her mind.

The look on Katie's face must have warned him.

"I don't *need* to know. I just don't want to get shot tonight if it's something I should have known."

"It has nothing to do with Matt Dunn," Katie looked out the window. The rain was coming down in buckets, the coffee shop's lighting dim, and the gas fireplace on the wall comforting. Any other day sitting with a cute guy, having coffee in the middle of the day, safe out of the rain would have been pleasant as long as she never had to relive that night five years ago like she did in her nightmares.

There was a long moment. Dan didn't press her, and she knew that her counselor had told her that sharing helped ease the trauma. Only a few times had she been able to do that. She took a deep breath.

"One night, coming back from a training class, I was assaulted by someone who hit me on the head from behind. As I was passing out, I must have hit the alarm button on my car keys because my keys were in my hand. I seem to remember hearing an alarm go off nearby. Someone pushed me down and was holding me there. I wanted to scream but I couldn't. It's all fuzzy. He probably had a hand over my mouth. Finally, the noise of the car attracted some people and the person left. I must have called out for help. I don't remember anything after that but waking up in the hospital with a concussion. Later I found out other women had been attacked similarly at night and sexually assaulted. The person responsible might have been identified but never charged. I never knew if he was one of a few folks who left training at FLETC early to go on special assignments."

"They just sent this degenerate person off to serve the government?" Dan said incredulously.

"There was a shortage of people needed for intelligence work around the world. I don't know, and I didn't want to know. I left and decided I wanted to be in business for myself. My degree in criminology and training at FLETC gave me what I needed to get my PI license. I think sooner or later, I wouldn't have liked doing what you have to do when you work for the government, so I'm happy to be doing what we do. I knew of Matt Dunn just from training video's he had produced for trainees to watch on Security Protocol. I had not met him personally." Katie hoped that lying did not become a part of her character, but she had to this time because of national security.

"Sorry I didn't know. I only wanted to make sure nothing was going to affect tonight. I am sorry, Katie, that is ugly."

"We all have things that have changed us. I like to think when I am helping a woman to get away from someone who is abusing her, I know how she feels, I am a little bit more driven than others in getting her to safety. It matters to me more. Whatever. I like it when my job means I can also help someone." A tiny smile tugged at the corners of her mouth.

"I know that feeling, not as you know it, but I like helping people too. Sometimes I help a guy to remember what it's like to feel pain, so he decides that he should leave an ex-girlfriend who's hired me to protect her, alone. Mostly a guy thing, I guess." Maybe his movie star smile was not fake. She liked him. He wasn't a bad guy, at least not today.

"Back to business. Dunn did not mention salary. I am going to ask $75 an hour plus a retainer for being available. I would like us both to offer the same, not undercut each other. Okay, with you?"

"I'm sure he might offer even more than that. He knows what we charge. His company is large. He'll offer us a contract, I'm sure, but it's good to be on the same page."

"Why do I feel like there is something else I don't know about?"

"There is. We don't know who's going to shoot at us tonight — no big deal. You are former Army Ranger, special ops? I didn't know that. That helps us to get Dunn out. We need to miss the bad guy and win."

"Yep, no big deal." Dan looked like he didn't believe her.

At least she didn't have to tell him she could not tell him more. He was relentless. He would have hounded her regardless of the confidential nature of how she knew Matt. Maybe the story of her assault lent her vulnerability. Dan gave her a pass on what must be that sixth sense of a good investigator that she was holding out on him. Why did he have to be so good? On the plus side of Dan being on the team, he was a professional, and they needed him.

"See you at Dunn's at 11."

"Try not to shoot anyone else until tonight, okay?" He stood to go.

Katie raised an eyebrow. "Boring..."

She watched him leave and observed that a few of the other ladies in the shop, including the barista, noticed him departing. He must be used to women paying attention because he didn't seem to notice, but when he got to the door, he turned and winked at her. She wrinkled her nose at him. Hmm. She needed a coffee date with her girlfriends Joanna and Naomi so that they could dissect Dan Beck. She put two notes on her phone.

Call the girls—Dan Beck coffee date juicy news.

Live through the day to have coffee with your best friends.

# CHAPTER SEVENTEEN
## TERRELL HUFF

Huff moved his shoulder gingerly, and pain caused anger to surge through him. In the course of his chosen profession, he had taken a bullet once before when he'd been careless. This time the mistake rested squarely on his handlers.

The risk analysis of this operation had been low. Huff's intel told him that only two agents would be present in the garage, and his mission was to remove them in addition to the cover target. The target first, to give the impression that was the mission. He had hit both agents with a kill shot. But the second agent Matt Dunn had survived and had returned fire. Assumedly Matt had shot him. But the bullet removed from the flesh wound in his shoulder was from a 9mm, not a government issue Glock. Additionally, Dunn's survival had been improbable as his femoral artery wound would have required immediate attention. It would have prevented Dunn from an accurate aim.

Terrell had focused on finishing the first agent since he was outside Dunn's line of fire. While focused on the first agent, someone else had shot him.

Dunn had help. The pipeline he was referred to for intel on Dunn, and the shooting said there was no second agency team. But that was not true.

He always disabled surveillance cameras in the areas he was working. In this instance, that hindered his quest to find a second shooter. He was waiting on satellite images from the street to see if someone entered the garage, but knowing the rain cloud cover that day, he did not expect any help there.

It was likely that Dunn had help from outside the agency, or he was undercover on a different assignment. He had someone to research that, and information would be coming soon. If his help came from outside the agency, that help would have been from his father's security agency, a person watching. Dunn's agency would have the gun, and he would have to pull favors but could find it. He would find the person, and they would die painfully.

First things first, kill Dunn tonight before his release. A shift change by the staff occurred at three AM. He would be in place for that time frame as there is always less security and attention as nurses wrote reports, and brought oncoming staff up to date.

While he was in Seattle, he also decided it was time to dispatch an old thorn in his side, Fred Lindley, a retired Secret Service and FBI agent who had started the file on him at the agency. Through his connection, he found that Fred had suffered a heart attack, not uncommon at his age. He was also in the same hospital as Dunn, so before he did Dunn, he would make sure Fred had another heart attack. While Fred was not involved, he knew that occasionally he was consulted on background information on him, as he was considered an expert.

He laughed. Expert? Fred had nothing but crumbs from all his hits over the years. The agency had nothing but a supposed name, "Terrell Huff," the name they called him an alias used once. But it only lent to his mystery, as no one knew his name or his history.

Since he was in Seattle, and Fred did live here, he might as well remove all links or information Fred might have. Sometimes he wondered if the old man knew more than he let on or had told the agency? He would handle him now and not worry about him again.

The plan was moving ahead, and he expected he would be installed at the head of the FBI when the dust settled. He would systematically remove all the competition that would not work for him. After all, he knew them personally. The Top Ten Most Wanted on the FBI list were acquaintances. Occasionally they would refer jobs to each other. It was a professional alliance that worked when necessary. When he became the Director, he would access them to remove or threaten Heads of State, who blocked their plans for world power. NATO and every other alliance would come together under their leadership. No one realized how those fragile alliances could be manipulated.

The first step in a broader strategy, he assured those guiding the plan his part was unique, and he could accomplish all asked of him. After all, he had his man uniquely in place in the Secret Service. To proceed, they needed someone who could act on a moment's notice, experienced, and excellent in all methods. He had trained this one himself, so there would be no mistakes. He moved his shoulder, and his anger flared. When he found the person responsible for this stupid mistake in intel, they would never make it again.

He looked forward to doing the old fool, the current Speaker of the House. That would be easy, and their plan would advance. Just days now, not months as before. He would have liked to have been the President, but he would not be able to do what he enjoyed most, killing. The director of the FBI gave him the best of both worlds, prestige, and power to do as he wished. After all, previous Directors had used their power to alter elections, and he would also do that. There was a pattern to control, and he would follow it.

The new President would eventually be the man behind all the changes. The man who had paid him enormous sums to come alongside him, and who would give him incredible power. The temporary man, the current Speaker of the House, would step into power and have his dreadful accident, which would enable his boss to succeed in his position. After instilling those loyal to them in the Cabinet, he would give up his role as FBI Director, to move to the world stage. He would become the assassin to the Leader of the known world.

He smiled. A little killing tonight was the beginning of many who would disappear because of their little bits of knowledge. Individually their knowledge was scattered, and most likely, they would not be able to connect any series of events to an organized attack. But nothing was being left to chance. By removing those scattered with their individual information, they could ensure complete surprise and move quickly to fill any vacuums of information with planned news releases and interviews from planted sources. The only narrative released would be theirs.

His part was simple, remove all those who had any account to tell. His status was known worldwide as deadly at what he did. But this was different, and he would receive the recognition that what he did was valuable. He was not just killing for profit. He was surgically removing people who stood in the way of progress. His eyes glittered in anticipation.

He moved his shoulder in pain again deliberately, to raise his level of hate for those who would try and stop him. Their pain would be so much more significant.

Looking at his phone, he tapped in a number.

"Harbor Pointe Employee Services, can I help you?"

"I am with National Employment Services. I will be working tonight at the hospital. Is your office open for me to pick up my Employment ID for work tonight?"

"Yes, what is your name please so I can verify we have an ID for you?"

"Jim Thompson."

"Yes, Jim, there is a pass set aside for you. Please arrive one-half hour before your shift to pick up your pass and get a short tour of the area you will be working."

"Of course, thank you."

At least the people who were employed by his employer were good at paperwork. He suspected that the mystery shooter at the garage was someone placed there unknown to his immediate pipeline. Perhaps not a mistake but the hideous "unexpected" that can happen even to the best plans. The fact is, someone other than Matt Dunn shot him. It was deliberate and stupid on their part. He would find them, he always did.

He began the selection process for his elimination needs tonight. First, obtain the specimen he needed to dispatch Lindley. Dunn's departure did not need to be as subtle as that, as the bungled attempt by an associate had elevated the security.

He would watch to see if they would remove him from the hospital sometime tonight. He was sure they would, as it was something he would do. He planned to quickly dispatch Dunn and any with him in a car accident. A young assistant who was excellent at cutting brake lines to make them looked frayed was ready to act. In case they departed from a different exit than the main one, he would station a chase car with a drone so they would not lose the follower. Either way, he would find and dispatch Dunn. He clasped his hands together, the hunt glorious. He would schedule Lindley first and get Dunn after he left the hospital. There would be some effort at getting him out unnoticed, but these people were amateurs, he would easily track Dunn's departure.

# CHAPTER EIGHTEEN

Katie checked her phone and saw she had a voicemail. She had expected a voicemail from an email client inquiry.

She needed to check on Ellie, and get ready for tonight's operation. She clipped her phone on the dash, hit the speaker for voicemail.

"Hello, we are calling for Katie Parson Investigations. We have an unusual job we are asking you to complete. Our history class of home-educated students would like you to solve a local Tumwater historical mystery. We have earned money as a class for your retainer, and I look forward to meeting with you to discuss this matter. Please contact our teacher, Mr. Ted Wendle, at twendle@gmail.com."

Odd that they didn't leave a phone number, the person calling sounded like a teenager. Interesting. Solving a historical mystery? Not her everyday skip trace. She sent the email asking for background information on the case and almost immediately got a response. She would read it later.

Any other time, she would have jumped at this. That is, depending on if she wasn't in federal jail, or being hunted by an international assassin as she might be in the next few days. Looking up at the gray, rainy sky, she murmured, "God, kind of need you to weigh in today. Be with Matt, Jim, Fred, and Dan too. And protect Fred's brother Tod."

She caught sight of a beautiful rainbow making its way across the sky. A rainbow was a promise, according to the old Sunday School story. Katie smiled. It was something to hang on to when the night ahead seemed full of uncertainty.

Katie pulled onto her street and slammed on her brakes, barely missing a running cat. Unfortunately, the car in the opposite lane couldn't avoid it. Too late, the driver slammed on her brakes.

The driver stepped out of the car as Katie pulled into her driveway.

"I'm so sorry. I tried to stop."

The young woman looked pale. "I don't know what to do." She said.

"It's okay. It's not my cat. I think it's a feral one. I am staying here. I can put it in a bag and call the animal control to see how to dispose of it. Maybe the city does it? I don't think it belongs to anyone. Most cats here are indoor cats, and I rarely see any wandering around. I will ask around the neighborhood first, though."

"Thank you so much! I'm an Uber driver, and I need to get to my pick up. I'm new, and I can't stop to take care of it."

"It wasn't your fault, no way you could have stopped in time."

"I feel terrible about it." She looked relieved and sad too.

She backed up and left, and Katie went inside the house to get a garbage bag. There were lots of feral cats around, and Ellie loved to bark at them when they came near the fence. She took her guard dog persona seriously and wanted her people to know she knew "stuff" by barking ferociously.

"Ellie? Here El."

Ellie didn't look guilty, a good sign, as Katie breathed deep. Ah, fresh air. She fed Ellie and let her out in the backyard. She went out front to get the mail and deal with the dead cat.

Would she get in trouble if she called the garbage service about the dead kitty? It might seem a little convenient to say "someone" hit it. She decided to double bag and put it in the garbage can.

Thankful for almost no blood, she scooped up the dead kitty. Katie had seen enough blood this week. It looked like a female that might be nursing kittens. Katie enjoyed the companionship of one or two beloved cats growing up, and she felt sad for this kitty. She wished today there could be some good news.

Ellie barked loudly out in the back yard, so she hurried as she tied up the bag and deposited it in the garbage can. She did have another almost full sack in the house she would put on top before she left today, so hopefully, nothing would be amiss to send the remains of the cat to the dump.

Katie opened the slider and could see Ellie barking energetically in the corner of the yard.

"Ellie, quiet." When Ellie stopped, she heard a faint sound. She went to the fence and listened. Was that a cat cry on the other side of the board fence? She'd need to go around to the green belt in back to locate the animal.

"Come on, girl, let's go see." Ellie jumped up eagerly.

Katie entered the green belt from a community gate and followed the mowed trail around the outside of the planned greenbelt. The cleared path kept brush from growing over people's fences. She headed toward her client's yard and began to look around. Ellie didn't wait. She ran to a small maintenance shed situated for grounds keeper's equipment. As much as Katie could tell from this side of the high fence, it was just opposite of her client's backyard. The nearby shed sat on concrete blocks, and Ellie barked as she tried to get her head into the small space under the shed.

"Ellie, quiet!" Katie got on her hands and knees and looked underneath, but it was too dark to see anything. She pulled out her cell, switched on the flashlight to look under the shed. Two little eyes about midway under the shed looked back at her. A kitten hissed at her and Ellie, spunky, but unreachable. Ellie's loud barking would soon irritate the neighbors. Katie headed back to the house to put her inside, Which was a little hard as Ellie was reluctant to leave the kitten. She went to the garage and looked for some tool to get the kitten from under the shed.

A small hoe with a long handle leaned against the wall, perfect for her needs. Katie pulled a box with a lid from the recycle stack, added a little tuna from the cupboard. Her kitten rescue kit was complete.

Katie walked back and laid flat on the ground beside the shed and shined her cell phone light underneath. A lively hissing noise and two glowing eyes helped her locate the little one. She put the handle of the hoe behind the kitten and pushed it to the edge of the shed. It kept trying to crawl under and back, but finally, she got it within her reach, and she grabbed the kitten by the scruff of the neck and pulled it out.

It tried hard to curl up and scratch her, hissing bravely. Quickly Katie put the kitten in the box, next to the little pile of tuna. She shut the flaps and carried it back into the house. Ellie began jumping around her as soon as she entered, she sniffed eagerly and wagged her tail. Carefully Katie opened one end of the box. More hissing, but the kitty had flecks of tuna on its whiskers, so the food was being consumed. Katie wetted one finger at the sink and gently stroked the little kitty as though she was licking it. A tiny purr escaped the black kitten. Undoubtedly this young kitten came from the cat that died this morning.

Katie was interested to see what Ellie would do, so she let her look in the box, with one hand on her collar. She began immediately licking the kitten, who accepted this large animal's attention as if it expected it. Ellie had never had puppies, but she seemed to know what to do.

The kitten seemed safe with her, so Katie put the box down on the floor, and watched as Ellie continued to lick the kitten. Katie located a little bowl for water and put it in the box. She would probably have to buy some kitten milk, although the kitten was eating the tuna. It looked to be about six to eight weeks old, hard to tell at this age.

"I'm going to name you Lucky because you're lucky Ellie heard you, or some big bad animal might have eaten you tonight!"

Katie always had mismatched socks, so she found two, tied them together, and put them in the corner of the box for the kitten. She would get some kitty litter and kitten food later. Being a kitty mommy was not on her to-do list today. Her dog-sitter clients wouldn't take on a kitten or appreciate one left for them, so after her world was back to normal, she would find a home for Lucky. Ellie lay down beside the box, her one purpose in life to guard the kitten. Katie smiled. Lucky was safe and now had a substitute seventy-five-pound protector-mother.

Looking at her phone, she had just enough time to grab something to eat, get her hospital uniform on, and be at Dunn's temporary office at eleven PM as long as there was minimal traffic. Most of the time, Seattle experienced gridlock, and planning for it meant you figured on an hour of extra time to get anywhere.

But she had a little bit of time, so she sat cross-legged on the floor next to Ellie, and peeked in the box at Lucky. At first, he hissed as she stroked him with one finger, but soon he began to purr. Katie lifted him out and set him on her lap. Ellie immediately started licking, and Lucky continued to purr. As she stroked the kitten, she felt the tension leave her shoulders. As an orphaned kitten snuggled against her, Katie felt a blissful minute in a day full of chaos and tragedy.

# CHAPTER NINETEEN

Katie's phone vibrated with a text.

> Just letting you know that Fred is still in the hospital,
> but Marilyn says no visitors yet. I hope your schedule
> slows down, and you can come to dinner soon. We
> miss you, and I have someone for you to meet. Love
> mom

On top of personal danger, her mom was interjecting emotional vulnerability in her life. Occasionally she would invite some "nice young man" to dinner for Katie to meet, always from her church. Usually, it was a disaster, and Katie avoided the dinners that included potential suitors whenever she could.

> Hey Mom, I am sorry. I have two cases that are right on
> top of each other and can't make dinner. I hope to see
> Fred soon too. I am sure he will be okay. He had
> pneumonia and beat that. I miss you all too, will come
> before long. Love you.

A second text pinged. Hmm, Dan Beck.

> Hey, I don't think we all should be bringing cars tonight.

**I can pick you up in my step-grandma's car to minimize the crowd at the hospital. That work?**

He was probably right. It would look better to have fewer cars and fewer people together. Best to blend in by not arriving in a herd of cars.

**Yes. I will text you the address of where I am housesitting.**

He did not respond right away, and Katie realized she should probably get some dinner for Ellie, the kitten, and herself. Her phone pinged.

**Can I bring pizza in an hour?**

That gave them two hours to get to Dunn's to plan the operation. Maybe he still felt a little guilty about that work deal, and the pizza was a peace offering.

**Sure. Thanks.**

Katie got busy with Ellie's food and more tuna for the kitten. He seemed to be eating it all, and with no problems. Maybe he was past the milk stage? That was good because she had no time to find some for him. She would share her half and half, as long as there was enough left for coffee in the morning.

She put Ellie out after her eating. She whined and looked at the kitten, reluctant to leave her new charge.

"It's okay, Mama Ellie. I got him. Do your business," Katie said sternly.

She had noticed there were no little kitty messes but knew that Ellie probably had seen to that. Gross, but most dogs did get into the cat litter box if they could. At this point, it was a help. With Ellie out, Katie dressed in her hospital outfit. It would seem odd for her to be volunteering at night. She should call.

"Hi Trudy, this is Katie Parson. I was wondering if there are any volunteer things I can do tonight? I'm thinking about interning as a nurse, and I want to see what the night shift does."

"Yes. We'd love to have you. I have a few things you can do. Thanks, what a great idea."

"You're welcome. I'll be in tonight at about 2 AM."

All she had to do is get those things done first and be ready to get Matt Dunn out next. For their plan to work, this would have to be a God thing, full of miracles and a lot of hard work.

Right after she got Ellie in, the doorbell went off. Katie looked through the peephole and saw Dan with a pizza box in one hand.

"Hey, thanks for the pizza."

Ellie immediately presented herself, positioning herself between Dan and Katie.

Dan looked down, "Nice doggie, I hope?"

"This is Ellie, she is a retired police dog, and she thinks she needs to protect me."

Katie took the pizza box and led the way to the kitchen dining bar. A curious kitten bounced out of the box and ran after them.

Dan bent down and scooped up the kitten. "Cat sitting too?"

"Nope, his momma got hit by a car this morning, and Ellie found him in the green belt behind the house. Not sure what to do with him, but I couldn't leave him out there to die. Ellie seems to have adopted him. His name is Lucky."

Dan stroked the little purring kitty, and this gentle side of Dan surprised her. She knew he took on jobs that required some physical push back to protect female clients, from being threatened by violent ex-boyfriends. Those threats that came from violent men vanished after a visit from Dan.

"So, what happens to this little guy when your house-sitting job is over?"

"I usually plan one house or pet-sitting gig right after each other, so I will have to find a home for the orphan. He loves you." Katie suggested with a lift of her eyebrow.

Dan scratched Lucky under the chin, and the kitten purred. He smiled.

"I have two roommates, and both have cat allergies. But I might know someone who would take him."

That reminded Katie that her parents had lost their longtime family dog a few months back, maybe they would take Lucky? Best way to get back into her mom's good graces for being gone so long, a kitten. Might work.

"I think I might have someone too."

Katie put out two Selzer drinks of water to have as they munched on the pizza.

Dan looked at his phone, grabbed one more piece of pizza, and said, "Ready to go?"

"Yep, let me put Ellie out for about five minutes, and we can go." Ellie looked up at Katie like she was unsure about leaving her with Dan.

"Come on, girl, time for your business!" Ellie looked back at Dan and slunk out the back door.

"She doesn't trust me."

"Ellie doesn't trust anyone, and she tolerates me. Well, she has gotten better lately about that. Her owners live in Hawaii for several months of the year, and I am their designated dog sitter. But they will be coming back in a few weeks, so she will be happy to see her former dog handler. He was with the Seattle Police Canine Division. Hey, before we get to Jim Dunn's, question for you?"

"Shoot, not literally, I hope," that movie star grin distracting.

118

"When we head off to the hospital, could you drop me off at the entrance to the hospital, and drive around to the service laundry entrance? I think I can get you a uniform from the laundry supply closet. We'll get a laundry cart to get Matt Dunn out."

"I think Jim would appreciate the pre-planning. Yeah, I can do that, unless they have a better idea."

Katie got Ellie in, gave the kitten a little bit more tuna, and dumped him back in his box under Ellie's watchful eye.

Following Dan out to the car, she couldn't resist, "Chick magnet?"

The old Honda Accord looked like it barely ran. Rusty, paint peeling, the kind of sedan that smacked of "old person."

"Free is good."

"Right."

Dan raised his eyebrows, "My other rig is a truck."

"Ah, manly."

Dan opened the door with a loud creak, "Your chariot madam."

Katie pinched her nose, "Smells like old socks from the attic."

# CHAPTER TWENTY

"Do you know why Fred wasn't at the meeting?" Dan asked as they were on the way to the hospital.

"Oh, he'll be at the hospital, but you won't recognize him. I probably won't either. He's a master at being the person in the room you don't see. "

"We didn't talk about confronting Terrell Huff. Think we will run into him?"

"If you were an international assassin, who had failed at killing Matt Dunn twice, where would you be? I think it's a foregone conclusion he'll be at the hospital, but will we see him? I saw him once in the parking garage, but I wouldn't recognize him again, because he, like Fred, will be the person in the room you least think is him. We can hope our schedule is different than his, and that he goes for Fred's brother Tod, and all the agencies swoop in for the grab. In that case, we miss him while we are getting Matt out. He's good at what he does, so trust no one."

"I'm glad Jim gave us all clean weapons and disposable phones. The tricky part will be figuring out the good guys versus Terrell's associates."

"Friends are praying for us that all goes well."

"Good to hear." Dan's noncommittal response.

Dan pulled up in the parking lot. "It's 1:30 now. Meet at the laundry service entrance at 2:15. Bring the uniform. I'll head back and change in the car. We'll grab the cart and head to Dunn's room."

"I will text you if there's a change."

Katie had changed her appearance too. Glasses and a short blonde wig and some fake freckles finished her look of a young volunteer. Katie had always had a face that looked younger than her years. Often at twenty-eight, she was carded in bars and the grocery store if she bought wine. Her look of inexperienced volunteer would give her a pass on anyone seeking help or information. Most people looked for an older person for answers.

Katie finished the tasks the head of volunteer services left for her to complete. After she straightened piles of magazines and cleaned up the employee lounge, she went in search of her friend in the laundry department. Her phone clocked the time at 2:05.

"Jake, how about them Mariners?"

"Katie, girl, you changed your hair. It's a good look on you. What are you doing here in the middle of the night? Can't sleep because the boys of summer are going to miss the playoffs if they don't start winning?"

"That and I am thinking of doing the whole nursing program, so I'm checking out what they do at night. Hey, can you check if you have any magazines down here for the rooms? I know you sometimes pick them up when you get the bedsheets. I need to sift through them and recycle what's old. If it's okay with you, I will put some of these in the supply closet and put out the ones you have."

"Sure, go for it, I'll see what I have."

Katie went into the supply closet, left the stack of magazines she had brought, and grabbed a uniform top and bottom that she hoped fit Dan. She grabbed a plastic sack and shoved the uniform inside. There was a stack of disposable paper hats like the doctors wore, and masks for entering infectious rooms, she stuffed both in her tote. Jake was coming out of his office with a big stack of magazines.

"Hey, can I borrow a cart to take the magazines with me? I'll take up some clean sheets too on my way up to the waiting area on the second floor."

"Sure, get it back as I only have about three carts left, everyone keeps borrowing them. A temporary employee was just here about ten minutes ago, and he borrowed one. He said the nurses were going to have him stripping beds for a while. You gotta know the nurses put those temps on the worst jobs."

"The nurses have earned it. Hey if I see the guy on my rounds, I'll bring that cart back too, what did he look like?"

Jake looked puzzled. "Can't say really, he had short hair, umm I think he was about five-ten. But the cart he took was number five."

"Great, if I see him, I'll bring it back when I bring this one back. Go, Mariners!"

Katie felt like sprinting to the laundry exit. Terrell Huff was here, and he had cart number five.

Dan was waiting outside the back door, leaning on the wall, smoking a cigarette.

"You smoke?" Katie asked as she handed him the bag with the uniform inside.

"Sometimes. It's cover to stand out here." He ground out the cigarette.

"Hurry, some temp employee borrowed a cart ten minutes ago, cart number five. I think it was probably Huff. We need to get to Dunn's room now. You can change in the bathroom around the corner."

Katie texted Jim Dunn on a group text that went to Fred also.

**Likely Huff is approaching Matt's room dressed as a**

hospital employee pushing a cart with number five on it.
Heads up, everyone.

In less than a minute, Dan emerged from the restroom, looking like a hospital employee complete with a paper face mask. He threw the bag with his clothes in the cart and covered it with the sheets. Katie grabbed out the stack of magazines.

"You push the cart ahead of me. I will follow about twenty steps behind when we get close to Dunn's room." Katie said as they entered the elevator.

Katie watched the elevator numbers. The tenth floor arrived.

"Showtime," Dan muttered.

# CHAPTER TWENTY-ONE

Terrell felt his phone vibrate. A text came through.

> We sent satellite images to your email. Cloud cover
> obscured the view. Few individuals near the garage
> at the target time. A possible homeless woman
> nearby.

A woman. It wouldn't have been his first choice, but the government might have sent a backup agent. With his network, he would know in a few hours if that was the case. He needed to check in with his drone operator Greg.

> You in place at the entrance? Watch for a woman.
> Might be accompanied. Tag vehicle and follow with a
> drone if sudden departure.

A response came.

> In place, I will follow any car in a hurry to leave.

His plan for old man Lindley would go after Dunn. It would seem like an accident. This hunt seemed more satisfying. He liked it when his quarry tried to escape, they never could, but it made for stimulating work.

He found it tiresome to check in with both sets of contacts to confirm a hit. He looked forward to dispatching the unnecessary contact. Perhaps he could lobby for payment on this one too?

# CHAPTER TWENTY-TWO

Katie walked fast to keep within twenty feet of an unrecognizable Dan Beck with his protective mask, as he pushed the laundry cart to Matt Dunn's room. Katie had also snagged for Dan an off-duty laundry attendant's name badge in the laundry supply cabinet. Claire Butson, even if Dan didn't look like a "Claire," Katie figured no one would look close at 3:00 AM. Interestingly, no one pushing another cart. Maybe she was mistaken that Huff was in the building.

At the far end of the hall, Katie noticed an older woman parked in a wheelchair. It seemed odd that she was left napping there with no hospital staff nearby.

Katie went to the nurse's station to check in as Dan proceeded to Matt's room.

"I have some magazines, could I put them in a few rooms? I know people are sleeping, but I'm trying to get them out as I'm on duty tonight."

"Let me check," as she reached for a phone. In Katie's peripheral vision, she noticed Dan had negotiated the agent outside of Matt's room and entered. The older woman had *moved* closer to Matt's room.

"Okay, thanks. My supervisor said it's okay if the room door is open or if you see the light on you can knock. Some people are up in the night, and wouldn't mind a magazine."

"Thanks a lot. I will do that."

Katie started walking toward Matt's room and saw an open door. She popped her head in, and the patient was sleeping, but she quickly put a magazine on her bed stand.

As she came out of the room, she could see the wheelchair woman had moved again, only about six rooms from Matt's.

Matt's door opened, and Dan exited with the cart piled high with dirty linens.

The woman was on the move, just slowly rolling toward Dan. Katie had to act fast.

She smiled at Dan as he passed by her going toward the elevator. She stepped in front of the wheelchair and blocked her path.

"Oh, hi there, would you like a magazine? Can I help you?" The back of the hair on Katie's head stood up as the woman's cold dead eyes stared.

She or "he" shook her head, violently no.

"Oh, no magazine? Let me help you back to your room," Katie said brightly.

Before he/she could figure out what Katie was doing, she leaped behind the wheelchair and expertly put on the rear brake. She stepped away from the chair, stood in front of it, carefully staying out of reach.

"Oh sorry, just a minute, let me ask at the nurse's station where you go," Katie said as with the best fake smile she could muster.

She almost ran to the nurse's station. Dan had arrived at the service elevator, and he pushed in the cart. Katie sucked in a deep breath as the elevator closed.

"Oh, I was wondering about the little old lady in the hall down there, can I help get her back to her room?" Katie asked almost out of breath to the nurse at the station as she pointed down the hallway.

"What woman?" the nurse asked.

Katie turned to look, the wheelchair was in front of Matt's room, and the agent who was standing there a minute ago was slumped over in it. The room door slid shut.

Katie ran to the elevator and punched the fifth floor. It opened with no wait but seemed to advance anciently. She jumped out on the fifth floor and ran to the stairs. Katie slid on the railing to get to each landing, exiting on the third floor. From the stairwell, she ran to the service elevator and hit the button for the basement laundry. Huff would be only a minute behind her. She also prayed that the men in the room from Premier Security were alerted and were ready for an assassin.

The door opened, but no Dan. Katie ran to the exit and noticed the cart off to the side, laundry still piled high. She ran out the sliding doors just as Dan was pulling up to the door in the Honda. She jumped in.

"Go!"

Dan slowly drove away.

"Calm down, girl. We can't look like we are in a hurry."

A voice from the backseat chimed in, "Would you happen to know a homeless nurse? I think I owe her a big thank you?"

Katie turned around and could see that Matt was on the floor.

"Yeah, I do. I will pass that on. Hey, Huff's right behind me, he went into your room about two minutes after you left in the cart. He disabled the agent outside the door, but I don't know what happened to your dad's man inside the room."

"He got a text from dad and left the room about ten minutes ago, and told me to go with a laundry guy. So, I don't think Huff would've seen him. The only thing in the room was a couple of pillows under a blanket. It would have taken him about 10 seconds to uncover that and get out. Did he see you leave?"

"No, but if he ran to the elevator, he would have seen it emptied on the fifth floor. I got off there and took the stairs to the third floor and back to the service elevator. I hope that slowed him down."

Dan had exited the parking lot and was looking to find the entrance to the I-5 when Katie's phone vibrated with a text from Jim Dunn. Dan looked over at her, and she was sure his cell phone had vibrated too. She read it out loud.

Decoy in the main parking lot worked too well. Brake line cut, discovered when we braked for a person who had to jump out of the way. Hospital security came immediately, held us until the police arrived. They called it an accident and called for a tow and cab. Our visibility is high. We are going to a hotel from here, not to the rendezvous. A tail is present on our end. Go to the second rendezvous.

Katie immediately texted back and spoke out loud.

"In the clear, will proceed. The second target at risk, beware."

Dan put on a ball cap and attempted to slip on a jacket over the uniform top. Katie reached over and helped him pull it on. She pulled off her wig and glasses and stuffed them in the bag at her feet. Like Dan, Katie covered her uniform with a jacket and pulled on a beanie. She saw Dan's eyes shift back and forth as he checked the rearview mirror.

"I'm sliding down in the seat, so it looks like there's one person is in the car. Do you think he's behind us?"

"A car exited the parking lot behind us and since there are only a few cars on the road, he looks like he's headed our way."

Dan took the entrance ramp to I-5, and before the car behind him could see, he exited the freeway.

Katie tried to read his face as he was staring at the rearview mirror.

"Does anyone have a weapon? I'm naked back here."

"Woman present, keep it clean." Dan quipped.

"Look in the bag on the floor to the right," Katie instructed.

Dan quickly took a right turn and headed north. Light traffic made them an easy target to track. Two more quick right turns, and Dan slipped into a hotel parking lot, up the ramp, and pulled into a spot next to a large van, which covered their car like a tent. He turned off the car and slid down from view behind the wheel.

Katie spoke first, "Did you lose him?"

"I don't know yet," Dan shrugged as he pulled his gun from a bag in the front seat. Five tense minutes passed.

"We'll need to wait for at least a half-hour to let morning traffic pick up. It's 3:30. Around four we'll go if we see more traffic," Dan said. Best stay low. The car looks parked with no occupants."

The quiet seemed loud.

"Knock, Knock."

"Who's there?" Katie asked.

"Will."

"Will Who?"

"Will, someone give me gum or a mint? I have hospital mouth."

Katie smiled, and after she rustled in her kitbag, tossed a piece of gum in the backseat to Matt. Dan looked over and put out his hand, which prompted Katie to drop gum in his palm. The mood lightened.

Katie texted Jim Dunn again on the group text that she believed Fred would see. She read it for the men to hear.

"Any word on the second target? Believed Huff followed us, and we lost him, we hope. Waiting for traffic to pick up before we move to the rendezvous point."

No word. All is quiet on that front. Perhaps word leaked
of our presence.

"Would either of you care to fill me in? Now that I have a weapon,
I'm not naked, but I'm lost."

"Sure, should I start with Great Dane puppies? Or are we past
that?"

Matt chuckled. "Past that. I don't smell any bad smells, so I
assume you haven't resumed your normal homeless cologne. Who
are you, and why are we here?"

"Let's see, Terrell Huff, we think that's his name, tried to kill you
in the garage, sent a nurse to try and kill you in the hospital, and just
tried again to kill you. We'd like to understand why, but we prefer
not to use the term, 'dying to know.'" Katie answered.

"I'm Katie Parson, a private investigator. I recognized you from a
video years ago at FLETC training for Homeland. I'm not with
Homeland now. I was in the garage because I saw you and figured
you must be on some government operation, so I decided to hide in
there. Unfortunately, Mr. Huff ruined that idea when he killed the
Chinese diplomat and shot you and your friend. I stayed to help.

"I didn't want to get swept up into the investigation. There seems
to be a leak in your system and could be why you got shot. I didn't
want to be next, so I left. Hopefully, without a trace, thanks to Dan
Beck here, another PI, in the front seat with me. We are now both
employed by your dad, by the way, who helped plan your exit
tonight."

"What I don't know, and need to know, is when they debriefed
you, did you tell them about me?" Katie asked.

"No, I did not. As far as I know, there is no video of you as the
camera's in the garage were disabled, and because of the cloud cover,
there was no satellite video either. Why did you tell me you were

Homeland in the garage?"

"Would you have shot me if I said anything else?"

"Maybe, especially since you smelled bad."

"Hey, you noticed that too? Katie here needs a personal assistant for hygiene," Dan chimed in.

"I get a lot of investigative work done as a homeless woman. No one notices me. So being stinky pays bills. I am not stinky today!"

Dan leaned over and breathes deep. "Check. She smells kind of good right now."

"Good to know," Matt piped in.

Katie gave Dan a death glare. He shrugged.

Headlights flashed the car, and all heard that car pull to a stop just past their vehicle. Katie reached for her weapon.

# CHAPTER TWENTY-THREE

Someone slowly got out of the vehicle parked just past theirs. Katie tensed at the approaching footsteps, and then a flashlight flickered over the front seat.

"Hey, it's a security guard, probably for the parking garage. Stand down. Dan, sit up and put your arm around me, he'll think we're parked here."

Dan reached for Katie. No way he intended to plant one on her? The guard tapped his window with his flashlight. Dan turned to be blinded by the light in his face. He unrolled his window.

"Hey, you can't park here, this is by permit only. Move on, or I'll call the police."

"No problem, sir," Dan replied and started the car and rolled up his window.

"It's a wonder he believed we were parking in this "chick magnet."" Katie raised an eyebrow as she slid back to the safety of her passenger space.

"This car smells like old people. Is this the best you can do on a PI salary?" Matt complained from the back.

"Hey, we go for anonymity, old cars are like gold," Dan said as he backed out and took the long way out of the garage. Katie checked her phone, almost 4:00 AM.

Matt popped up in the back seat, and all of them scanned the traffic. Dan took surface streets and blended into traffic. A steady hard rain began to batter the windshield, cutting visibility. Katie, as well as the men, continued to watch the cars around them.

"Hey, what do you guys think? Can we head to homeport?" Matt asked.

"I have been checking for a tail for the past fifteen minutes. I have changed direction and slowed down and sped up. I don't see a tail anywhere. Katie, you see anything?"

"I think we are good."

Katie's phone vibrated. This time, it was an incoming phone call from Jim Dunn.

"Katie, can you hand the phone over to Matt?"

Matt took the phone offered by Katie and listened quietly for a few minutes.

"Were any others injured?" Matt asked.

He ended the call. "Katie, I need to use this phone for a few minutes."

He immediately started dialing before Katie could ask what happened about injuries. She waited, anxiously.

Dan was exiting the freeway. "Katie, can you pull up on my phone the GPS to the safe house?"

She put the GPS on the speaker.

"Five minutes to destination."

Matt had turned away and was talking in low tones with his back to the front seat. She could not make out his conversation.

"Arrived at the destination." Dan pulled into the driveway of a rambler type house.

"Hey, before we go in, you guys need to know a few things," Matt said.

"Dad said that Huff got to Tod. I'm not sure who that is but said to tell you, Katie. Someone dressed as an old lady in a wheelchair came to the room and said she was a cousin, and no one could verify it. She got into the room, escorted by two agents. Tod was asleep. She went up to the bottom of the bed, touched his feet, and said she'd come back. The woman left the room. It seemed with no incident. But in about twenty minutes after she left, Tod went into seizures. She had released a small poisonous snake that bit Tod. The hospital staff tried to save him, but they didn't know what started the seizures. About ten minutes later, the snake fell out of his bed onto the floor. One of the agents killed it. It took a few minutes for the agents to connect the dots, and because it didn't seem the woman had done anything. She got away."

Katie clenched her fists.

"How long ago?"

"Fifteen minutes."

"It wasn't Huff who followed us from the parking lot. He must have had an associate there."

"Did your dad say where Fred was?"

"Fred Lindley, the legend at the Agency and Secret Service? Is he what this is about?"

"Partially. Tod was his seriously ill brother, pretending to be Fred in the hospital with a heart attack. The plan by several agencies was to draw Huff in and capture him. *How* could they have missed this? An old lady in the middle of the night, and no one saw that as odd? Especially when they expected Huff to make an appearance? Where is Fred?"

"Dad didn't say."

Katie held her hand out for the phone and hit redial.

"Sir, Matt told me about Tod. Where is Fred?"

"Katie, we don't know."

"You don't, or you can't tell me?" Katie said with an edge to her voice.

"I don't know, but you know him. Where do you think he is?" Jim Dunn's voice was gentle.

"I don't want to think where he is. Because I think he's chasing Huff alone, and he can't do that! He's too old. He'll die too!" Her voice rose.

"That old man is the most intelligent man I know. He's probably the only man who could run Huff to ground. But because he is *that* man, he will ask for help when he needs it."

"If he's able to ask for help," Katie paused. "As long as you don't need us, I have a few cases to follow up."

"Don't go looking for Fred. He'll call me. And we'll send an army, which will include you. Just wait. Do you *trust* Fred?"

"Yes," Katie said quietly.

"Give him time. He can do more than ten men in this."

"Thanks. Please call me if you hear *anything*."

Katie ended the call.

"Hey, if you don't mind, I'm not going in. I have to take care of my dog, and I'm going to catch some sleep. Dan, can you get me home?"

"Sure, no problem."

"Hey Katie, I want to say thanks for what you did in the garage and tonight. Not sure why you would save someone you don't know, but thanks."

Matt was looking at her, and he winked. Well, that was that. He did recognize her from five years ago and was corroborating her story. At least both of them knew the information they couldn't reveal was secure.

"Next time I ask you for spare change, pony up!"

"I usually give homeless people a dollar, but if they stink, I leave it near them."

Katie narrowed her eyes, trying not to smile.

"Although even if they stink, cute homeless women get more. I owe you girl, and I always pay up," Matt grinned. "Dan, thanks too, both of you will be great employees for dad, and I will tell him."

"Thanks, Matt, I'll be available tomorrow if needed."

Dan hit the remote for the garage to open and slid inside, shutting the garage door. Dan handed Matt the remote as he got out. He gave both of them a parting wave from inside the garage.

"Home, James, please," Katie said as she checked the time on her phone, 5:00 AM.

"Yes, ma'am. I have cases waiting too. Hope to snooze an hour or two before that all hits."

"Hmm..." Katie's eyes closed as she leaned back.

"So, what's up with the wink?"

"A girl can't get a wink? Please! You don't sometimes wink at women?"

"Yeah, I do wink, but usually, it means something."

Irritated, Katie sat up, "A guy winks at me because I saved his life, and you want to know all the juicy details?"

"Fine, but don't think I believe for one minute the story you didn't know him at FLETC, there is more to that Katie Parson."

Katie glared at him, she hoped convincingly.

She closed her eyes, never thinking to look up.

# CHAPTER TWENTY-FOUR
## TERRELL HUFF

Terrell's phone vibrated. He received a text from Greg, his drone operator.

> I followed a car that left the hospital entrance at 3:30. A woman is in the car. They arrived at a residence and pulled inside the garage after utilizing some evasive driving that would indicate they thought someone might follow them. The car is leaving with the same two occupants that arrived. Do I continue to track with the drone and monitor?

Terrell responded.

> Send the address of residence, and also the license plate of the car. Follow the vehicle to a new destination utilizing the drone. Send that address when you have it.

Terrell made a note of the address and license plate on his phone. Although he doubted anyone would be there when he arrived at the location, he would find Dunn quickly. The house probably was a temporary location, but he would check it out and proceed to Jim Dunn. Another drone operator had the elder Dunn's position.

He felt elated. Despite the high security, he had dispatched Fred Lindley, and he would request payment for him too. His old woman disguise worked convincingly, and no one had suspected the method he used to kill Lindley—stupid agents, easy to deceive.

Dunn's temporary escape didn't concern him. He knew his location, which meant he would end him soon.

The woman interested him. A woman was at the garage, and now a young woman in the hallway near Dunn's room. Something about her, the way she looked at him? Her action to stop him in the hall seemed intentional, and the man pushing the laundry cart had to be involved as well because he believed Dunn left the room in it. These two were together, and he would find them. Was she the one who shot him? He moved his shoulder, and the pain was instant. Her pain would be infinitely more intense. Of that, he would make sure.

Another text.

Status update on incompletes.

He could not ignore this one, as it was not from the buffoon Speaker of the House, but from the other.

Removed Lindley. No problem for me. Payment for him? Have located Dunn, removal is imminent.

Dots indicated a quick response.

Report when complete to me, and pass it on to Speaker. Any info on others present in the garage? Will agree for payment on Lindley when the agency acknowledges his passing.

Huff didn't want to push his luck, but money for eliminating the others needed to be authorized now.

Possible woman and accomplice, have located as well, remove after Dunn. Payment?

There was a pause in reply.

Report elimination status when complete, preference
today. The payment is okay.

Terrell proceeded to put the address in his GPS and saw the
destination was about ten miles away. Traffic at this time of the
morning, 5:00 AM, would be picking up as the city was awake and
moving. He quickly put on a gas employee uniform top over his blue
pants. A ball cap with the emblem of the gas company emphasized
his profession. Glasses and a fake beard altered his look significantly.

He felt exhilarated as he hunted Dunn. Again, agents like him
were stupid. They made mistakes and died. The woman and her
friend would be next.

Job satisfaction. He smiled.

# CHAPTER TWENTY-FIVE

The garage was empty, so Matt didn't expect anyone to be in the house. He saw a duffle bag near a side door and hobbled over to it. Inside the duffle were two phones, a stack of cash, a uniform, and an envelope. There was a large umbrella standing up next to the door. Matt tore open the envelope and read the scribbled note from his dad.

"In case of satellite or drone observation, use the umbrella to exit to the alley, follow that one block down. Blue garbage receptacle labeled "Pick Up." Climb in, call. My staff will get to you. You had a call from a friend in Secret Service, Glenn Richter. Suggests you call him at home, says he is retiring, wondering if you can make his retirement luncheon. There seemed to be more to that. Leave right away, call after pick up. Huff will try to track you by association with me. We will distract attention."

Matt changed out of his hospital gown and stuffed it in the duffle. He didn't want to leave any evidence he had entered the garage. Careful not to bump his wound, Matt pulled the uniform pants over the bandaging on his leg. He picked up the umbrella, glad for the cover from drone surveillance and rain. The phone registered the time at 5:15. The alley behind the garage lead him to a sizeable blue garbage container. Normally he would have jumped in, but with his leg wrapped, he could not take a chance on opening the wound. He moved the can under a tree and held it partially down. He slid in and using his weight as a counter popped it back to the upright position. By bending far over, he could stand and keep his leg straight. At least the can was clean. He checked contacts on the phone, one said staff, he texted the number.

Here.

An incoming response.

Five minutes.

Matt felt like his body cramp from the awkward position, but he forced himself to think about the information his dad had passed on about Glenn Richter. They became close friends when they both served on the Vice President's Secret Service detail before he became President. Glenn had stayed on with the new Vice President after the election, not wanting the intense action of following the President as retirement was close for him. Now his call was not unusual, but the invitation to call him at home not standard request. Yes, his dad was right, something more to this invitation than Matt attend his retirement luncheon.

Matt heard the rumble of a truck, garbage truck?

A loud clang and the garbage container lifted into the air. If they dumped it, any rough movement could reinjure Matt's wound. The can dropped upright with a soft landing. He heard a cranking noise like a cover rolled over the top. As uncomfortable as he was, he remained still until the truck started moving. He lifted the lid slightly but could only see a rim of light that came from around the edges of what seemed to be dump truck with a cover.

He heard the sounds of traffic — a stop, presumably a red light, then moving again. The turns almost tipped over the can. After what seemed a long time, but a check of his phone showed twenty minutes, he heard noise and voices outside. The truck stopped. The cranking noise again. The lid popped off the can.

"You okay, Matt?" one of his dad's men asked, he recognized the voice as Nick Gentry.

"Yeah, now that I can stand up, I am. Thanks."

Another man hopped up into the truck, and both men lowered the can and helped Matt to slide out.

"Where are we?"

"Sanitation station. We rented a city truck for a little bit. Just step away and keep moving." Nick said.

"There is a lot of surveillance going on. Your dad figured that we needed a transport that looked like an everyday business in the city. Garbage trucks all over the place, so we found a driver willing to make a little money on the side. We need to get out of this warehouse before someone asks us to move garbage." Nick grinned.

Matt heard a chirp, and a nearby van's lights flashed, that was parked just inside the warehouse roof, protected from electronic eyes.

Matt's phone vibrated with a phone call from his dad.

"Hey, we are calling an audible here. Everyone got out of the house one at a time. We caught buses out and are all on the way to the train station. Go to the station in Federal Way. Buy a ticket for the Centralia station."

"Will do. How long ago did Glenn Richter call?"

"Early this morning, they are a few hours ahead of us, but it's still early on the East Coast."

"I'll give him a call from the train. What's our end destination?

"Lunch at the Casa Aztec food cart four blocks west of the station, there is a city park there, grab something to eat, see you there."

Matt ended the call.

"I'm taking a nap, guys. Let me know when we arrive."

Matt closed his eyes. His leg throbbed from all the movement, and weariness descended on him. He utilized a habit developed in the Secret Service from long duty hours. He imagined the softest bed, a quiet place, and began to drift. Katie's face seemed to float in front of him. Her courage or that sense of strength that flowed from her resonated with him. Her attractiveness and sense of humor only added to her uniqueness. Something about her he couldn't identify. He knew he shouldn't let any emotions in right now, but maybe when this was over, he could connect in a friendly way. Was it a coincidence she entered the garage, or was it something else, or someone else that sent her? His mom had been a praying woman, and she would have been praying if she was still alive. Maybe someone was looking out for him yet. Mom, I miss you. His mom's face replaced Katie's and then faded as he nodded into an uneasy sleep.

"Matt, we're here."

"Right, thanks." Matt shook his head and straightened.

Without a word, one of the men handed Matt a ball cap, sunglasses, and a jacket with a hood, which helped in this rain. Matt trotted into the station.

A train to Centralia arrived in minutes. Matt paid for a ticket and went to the boarding area. He surveilled the area inconspicuously. No one there who seemed out of the ordinary or who ran to buy a ticket. Normal stuff. The train pulled in, and Matt boarded, heading to the last car he sat in the back where he could see everything ahead of him.

Maybe it was a lack of sleep or long years of watching others, but Matt felt like this op had been too easy. Huff was world-class, and he would not stop. He would pick his time, and it would be when their guard was down.

He worried about Katie. Investigators like her were rare. They sensed and searched to find answers, saw things others missed. He knew a few like that in Homeland. They walked to a tune that others didn't hear because what the others heard was "Eight to Five and an hour lunch." The few hunted details like miners, and found solutions. Katie Parson belonged to that club.

Katie's instincts and bravery enabled her to save the President's daughter years ago. He hoped she did not opt for courage against Huff because he cheated. In his study of Huff, Matt believed he never gave his targets a chance. He killed from a safe location and utilized distraction to make a clean removal. His reputation included the description he completed every assignment. Matt saw him as a coward, a killer with the only important thing being his paycheck.

Matt clenched his fists when he thought of his dead partner and his family. Huff would pay for killing a father and a good man. It was either him, Katie, or Huff. Someone would die. Huff was hunting them all, and the showdown would come. Could he out-maneuver the master? Huff didn't know he was chased too by Fred Lindley. Had the assassin been hunted before? Perhaps that changed the balance in this deadly game of pursuit.

He pulled out his phone and dialed Glenn Richter's number.

"Hello?"

"Hey Glenn, its Matt Dunn. You left a message with my dad?"

"Matt, glad you called, wanted to make sure you knew about my retirement luncheon. Will you be in Washington, D.C. next week?"

"I don't know yet, had a little accident, and still recovering. Can I get back to you on that?"

"Yep, not a problem. Talk soon."

Matt waited. He knew Glenn would call him back on a disposable cell as soon as he noted Matt's number. He would also get to a place where no listening devices could pick up the conversation.

His first phone rang, but he didn't answer. He called back on his second phone.

"Hey, what's up?"

"Not sure, but I needed to talk to you. I heard about Ned, I know you can't tell me details, but there is something you have to know. In the last six months, ten former Secret Service agents protecting the President have died, transferred, retired, or disappeared. Ned is just one of the deaths. Was there an attempt on your life too?"

"Two attempts. Terrell Huff's involved. How do you know ten agents are gone?"

"First, what do you know about the line of succession of power if the President dies?"

"That's why we have a Vice President, right?"

"What have you heard about the health of the Vice?"

"He's recovering from some light surgery? He was on the news waving to everyone and giving a thumbs up a few days ago."

"He has a brain tumor, inoperable. He has weeks at best. When he dies, if something were to happen to the President, the next in line to be President is the Speaker of the House of Representatives. Beyond him, the president pro tempore of the Senate would be next, and beyond him, the Secretary of State, then the unthinkable."

"That's a long line, but go on, I have no idea who's next."

"The Secretary of the Treasury, Grigory Volkov."

Matt repressed a shudder. Volkov, a former CIA operative, had been in the Secret Service and guarded the President for a short time when he was the Vice President. While in that position, Volkov supposedly uncovered a plot to assassinate the Vice President from within Ukraine. After his job in the Secret Service, he had transferred to the Department of Treasury. Volkov advanced through the ranks in the Department to Assistant to the Secretary of the Treasury. A calculating, cold man, he had somehow shielded that part of himself from the President by having ingratiated himself so much during the time he served on his detail as the Vice President. Trust had formed.

His mercurial rise up the line in the Treasury Department could be attributed to rumors of those ahead of him in authority dying of heart attacks or mysterious car accidents. Many in the intelligence community viewed him with suspicion and caution.

The President awarded him a cabinet position when he took office. It seemed only natural that he would select someone he knew and who currently served close to the top of the Department. No attempts to dissuade the President had changed his mind.

"But there is a long line ahead of him, and the President is well protected."

"You think so? First, the president pro tempore of the Senate, Bill Webster, is also ill. Mystery illness seems he is coughing and spitting up blood. Doctors are mystified, and it comes and goes. The Secretary of State will be out of the country to conduct talks in South Korea in the next two weeks, while the North Koreans are posturing missile tests. There is always a threat when a head of state is out of the country."

"Consider this scenario. The Vice dies in the next two weeks, and Senator Webster dies either before him or shortly after, and consider the Secretary of State were to be assassinated while overseas. At that time, if the President were to be taken out, it's only the Speaker of the House stopping the Secretary of the Treasury from becoming the President of the United States."

"I get that, and it's a concern, but aren't you counting out the Secret Service?"

"Matt, why did you leave, why am I retiring? Chaos reigns in the department. And you know the agency just changed hands a few months back. The new Director is unknown to everyone. Supposedly suggested to the President by the Secretary of Treasury. Every agent who has served the President in the last six years is gone. Transferred to a different department, dead, or retiring like me. All new men, all positions have been filled by the new Director. Do you understand what I am saying?"

"And you're sure the ten agents that are dead or disappeared did so under suspicious circumstances?"

"Let me ask you something. You were close to the President. You still have a relationship and a line of communication that if you needed to, you could warn the President, as could I. Do you think what happened to you and Ned was routine to the job? Last week instead of retirement, I was offered a cushy position in Hawaii. Unusual, and never given to a person ready to retire. The kind of assignment you never turn down. But two friends of mine accepted positions that were like that, and now one is dead the other is missing. I turned the offer down, and there was pressure to say yes."

Both men were silent.

"He would not see this as a danger," Matt said.

"What if we both speak to him? If something happens to either one of us, he would know the map of power in the world could change dramatically. My daughter is pregnant, and she was reading me meanings of names for the baby. I looked something up in those baby name books the other day. Grigory means "supplanter." Volkov's definition is "wolf." Probably nothing to that."

Matt closed his eyes and leaned on the train window.

"I will come to DC. I will get a flight out today."

"Meet me at Judy's, call on this number."

Matt ended the call and stared out the window as the countryside flashed by. He didn't see any of it.

# CHAPTER TWENTY-SIX
## KATIE

"Hey, wake up, almost home," Dan said.

"In case someone took a picture of your car, can you park around the other side of the green belt area? There is a walkway through it, and if you park a few blocks down, there is no direct link to my place." Katie asked.

"Sure. Hey, I only have a couple of hours before I need to show for a client. Can I crash at your place?"

Katie looked at him.

"Do you practice that "innocent as a babe" look on all the women you ask if it's okay to sleep at their place?"

"No, just the ones who have killer kittens to protect them."

"Okay by me. But remember, I have a police dog who doesn't like you."

"Ellie? I bribed her with dog treats when we first met, and she has not forgotten."

"True, she can be won over with food. We are working on that."

Dan guided the car to the opposite side of the green belt and found a parking place under a huge fir tree. Katie handed Dan one of the umbrellas from the front seat. Seattle rain was in full downpour mode.

"Lead on, girl. You know the way."

Katie picked her way under cover of the tree-lined sidewalk to the covered walkway trail into the green belt. Trying not to get her feet soaked, Katie avoided the river of water running down the path. She headed to the opening on the opposite side. They sloshed into the house, shaking off water in the entry.

"Ellie, Ellie?" Katie called for her as she entered the house.

"Look at that." Katie pointed to Ellie and kitten, snuggled on the couch.

"Ellie knows she is not supposed to be on the couch, but she figures she gets away with it because of Lucky."

Ellie carefully hopped off the couch and wagged her tail at Katie and looked hopefully at Dan.

"Oh, would you look at her, expecting you to pass her a treat! What a mooch!"

Dan grinned. "Here, girl," and he produced a dog biscuit from a pocket for her.

Ellie daintily took it from him and looked at Katie next.

"Okay, I get it. Time for food, then you go out."

Katie headed to the kitchen and fed Ellie in the pantry. She waited a few minutes for Ellie to wolf down her breakfast and opened the backdoor to let her out. Ellie took one look at the pouring rain and balked.

"Girl, you have some business to do. I will let you back in. Go!" Katie gave her a stern look.

Ellie slunk out, giving Katie a dirty look.

She wandered back into the living room, only to see Dan stretched out on the couch, eyes closed with Lucky curled up on his chest. The house was a little chilly, so she grabbed a blanket from the closet and brought it back to Dan.

"I know you're not asleep, but this is in case you get cold."

"Thanks, sister," he mumbled.

Katie smiled.

Ellie was barking on the back porch. She grabbed a towel from the dryer and rubbed Ellie dry.

Ellie immediately ran back into the living room to inspect her new charge. Satisfied that Lucky was in good care, she looked expectantly at Katie.

Katie set the alarm on her cell. She really should get back to the new client soon about the historical case. Solving a cold case that was over one hundred years old would be fascinating and not dangerous, like everything else seemed to be. With all the bad actors dead long ago, no surveillance, and no assassin trying to kill you, that would be a dream job. She could get used to that.

"Ok, Ellie, let's get some shut-eye."

Katie trudged upstairs to her bed, and even though she wanted to fall on it, she changed into pajama pants and a tee-shirt. In a minute, she was under the covers. Usually, there was that time of counting. But maybe because Dan was downstairs, and Ellie was lying beside the bed, for once, she could feel sleep taking over. Something comforting about a big tough man sleeping just a floor away.

Something was pinging. Katie's phone alarm was going off, nine AM. Three hours of sleep. Oh well, it would have to do. She wondered if Dan was still there, but decided to hit the shower first and check after. A hot shower felt like getting an extra hour of sleep, and she needed to be alert for the time ahead.

Getting dressed, Katie picked a pullover maroon sweater, jeans, and warm socks. A quick look out the window showed a gray wall of water. Spring in Seattle was always liquid, but some days more so. She needed coffee. But seeing there was a cute guy in the house, she postponed her trip downstairs to put on some makeup. Her mom would approve of her effort to at least acknowledge a nearby eligible male. Well, she didn't know if Dan had a girlfriend or not, but she felt better with makeup. What did that her pastor say once? "Even an old barn looks good with paint on it." She ran a brush through her curly mop, not that it changed anything, but it seemed to be more in order than before.

Ellie was up and prepared to accompany Katie.

"Why are you looking at me like that? You already approve, he fed you. So, he's safe."

Ellie wagged her tail. Katie could almost swear she understood. There was that website that said that dogs could learn over 5000 words. Ellie probably knew more.

Katie descended downstairs and glanced at the empty couch. She was a little disappointed until Dan appeared in the doorway of the kitchen with a cup of coffee, wafting a pleasant smell her way.

"Hey, thought you were sleeping all day. Found a towel in the bathroom, showered, hope you don't mind."

"All I care about is that you made coffee."

"Coffee is good. Food adds to the mix. I notice you have bacon and eggs, you cooking?"

"I will. You don't know where everything is. Have a seat. Bacon, eggs, and toast are on the menu."

"I happen to love that. Hey, this is good coffee, where do you get your beans?"

"A guy at my mom's church roasts his own. This one is called Genesis, and it's a dark roast. I like that one the best. I'll send you his link."

"You are working on something now? You told Jim Dunn you had a few ongoing cases." Katie asked.

"Got a skip trace. A mom looking for a missing son who probably doesn't want to be found, twenty years old. I have a line on him, but it looks like he is living with a girlfriend to stay under the radar. Not sure if he is into drugs or just hiding."

"Another case I'm doing for a friend, regarding her elderly dad. A person is trying to get him to move from his nursing home into their house. My friend is worried they are after his army pension. She wants me to do a background check on the woman. Her dad thinks she is a nice lady who wants to take care of him. Something not right there."

"I just had as a case like that. If you can't get the person back, you have to go through Adult Protection Services to do the initial investigation to prove if the questionable people are genuine or not. I don't like to get them involved unless the family can't get the people who are predators to back off. But the agency is an option."

"Yeah, I hear you. I think I'm going to shadow the dad, see what I can find out about their methodology to influence him. The best way to end the manipulation is to find out how they access him and cut that off. If they can't talk in his ear most of the time, older folks get back to their routine, and they forget."

"What are you working on?" Dan said.

"Believe it or not, a historical cold case. I just read the email this morning. A group of homeschooling students studied a local community land grab that took place about ninety years ago. They want me to help them solve a robbery of some Tumwater City Council documents that went missing and to see if I can locate the records. Maybe you might want to get in on this if you aren't too busy. That is if we survive past today or tomorrow."

Katie went back to flipping eggs and putting the bacon on a plate to drain as she popped two pieces of bread in the toaster.

"Sounds interesting, I might like to help with that. Changing gears, what is your exposure to this thing with Dunn? Did Huff see you? Did you leave any brass in the garage? My point is, can this guy find you?"

Katie handed Dan a plate filled with food. Ellie was staring intensely at him.

"Please don't feed her. She has a very delicate digestive system, and she has expensive dog food. I know she can look pitiful, but the mess is not worth it.

"I guess I don't know how Huff would know who I am. I picked up my brass, but if my bullet is the one that hit him, he would know it's not a Glock by now, and that's what Matt Dunn used, typical to feds. He would know there was a second shooter, and I can imagine he would use all his resources to find who took his picture in the garage. But Matt said Homeland found no video at all. And when I entered, I was in my homeless persona. When I left, well you saw me, I had a different look. I got out through the kitchen, did not encounter any Homeland people, and had an umbrella that covered me from satellite views walking to the bus. I think I left without getting my face on any camera. Thanks, by the way, for your help."

"Sounds good." He said between bites. "If it was your bullet that wounded him, has your gun been used in any ballistics reports at all?"

Katie stared at Dan.

"I didn't think of that. There was a ballistics report about four and a half years ago."

"Wait a minute. I think I remember hearing about that. Did you shoot a person who was assaulting his girlfriend?"

"How did you hear about that? It wasn't even in the papers."

"My girlfriend was a cop, and she told me about it. When there is news about a private investigator, I want to know about it. Those kinds of things affect all of us in the industry."

"Handy to have a girlfriend who works for law enforcement."

"Former girlfriend. I don't have time for a relationship with my job and making sure my mom gets care. Someday. You seeing anyone?"

"That's on a need to know basis, and you don't need to know."

"No one, huh? Well, the job is demanding."

"I didn't say I *wasn't*!"

"Key is, you didn't say you were, or brag about him. Any good investigator can read between those lines."

"Yeah, well, my mom is always trying to set me up from someone from her church, and so far, I have escaped."

"Maybe she will succeed one of these days."

"I got a better idea. How about I ask her to fix *you* up?"

"No need, I usually am fine in the woman department." Grinning, he handed Katie his empty plate. "Thanks, great breakfast."

"Hey, do you think you could ask your former girlfriend if she knows there is a ballistics record on my gun? I don't have any contacts that I could ask about it."

"Yeah, I can reach out to her. We parted on friendly terms. I have asked her on occasion about a few things so she could check on this for me."

"Thanks, at least I would know if it's out there and if it can be accessed."

"If that's the case, he can find you." Dan looked at her speculatively.

"Yeah, I know."

"Listen, can you put me on speed dial on your phone? I want to have your back on this. You need to tell Jim Dunn right away. If there is a report and someone pulls it, we would want to know who requested it. If Homeland pulls it, there has to be a direct link to Huff through the agency. We should check in with Dunn to see if we are needed."

"Go for it. I will do the dishes."

Katie bolted down her last few bites of bacon. Doing the dishes gave her a moment to focus. Despite all her skill in getting out of the hotel, she had left a trail. If her bullet was the one that hit Huff? But it had to be. She saw the bullet strike him in the shoulder, and she knew she had fired before Matt. A world-class assassin knew how to find her. Not where she lived, as she had no address. But he could locate her office and for a man like that, with his skills? She would be an easy mark. Bacon seemed to find its way back in her throat. She grabbed for her coffee, trying to wash down the fear.

# CHAPTER TWENTY-SEVEN

"Mr. Speaker, I have the Director of the Secret Service on the line for you."

"Put him through."

"Mr. Speaker, we need to discuss the date for the Vice President to address the Agency."

"Of course, Director Anderson, I believe the plan was for next week at the Agency conference?"

"I checked with the Vice President's Chief of Staff, and he indicated that he might not be able to attend due to his recent illness. Can POTUS replace him?"

"We will send out the request immediately to his Chief of Staff. He has been willing to replace VPOTUS if needed."

"That was our plan. Please follow up with an email on specifics, and we will do an agency-wide notice. With the weather heating up, it might be nice to utilize the new outside training facility here. It included a stage and podium for addresses. Will that work?"

"I will run that by POTUS's Chief of Staff and get back to you on specifics. Can I trust you will be up to speed on security?"

There was a pause.

"Mr. Speaker, we will be completely ready at that time to receive the President of the United States."

"Good, I know we have spoken of this momentous occasion, and so I think that this is a time for the Secret Service to step to the plate and show that the reorganization under your leadership has been a tremendous step forward."

"Thank you, Mr. Speaker, I know we will not disappoint you."

"Many people are counting on your execution of a great day for the Agency. Thank you for planning this, and if there is anything else I can help with, please contact me."

"Thank you, Mr. Speaker."

Perfect.

He needed an update on the status of his asset's targets.

The slowness of the progress in taking down the targets seemed off. So far, this asset had never missed and completed every assignment, a perfect record.

He beeped his driver so he could talk away from the office and any prying electronic eyes.

A half-hour later, he was on his way to a meeting that did not start for an hour. He sent a text.

I have an update on the possible second weapon used.

He was pleased to see someone typing a response.

What information have you found based on the bullet we sent?

We believe the weapon was a 9mm Kahr.

There was a pause. The Speaker waited to see if there were further questions.

Can we rely on you to utilize your resources to find ballistics information on this weapon?

What? Why was there a need for a search?

What is the need to know?

A pause.

A possible second agent involved. Need a ballistics
search to confirm. Also, process a request to utilize
pipeline for local ballistics in the area.

The hair on his arm raised. He hated any trail that led to him. He
shifted in his seat, leaned forward, and texted each word with force.

I will check for authorization for this search.

He didn't want to do this. He almost handed the phone to his
driver to dump it. But he hesitated. This asset asked for something
he could get in a few calls. He breathed deeply because so far, the
plan moved forward. He would at least ask the man. The answer
would probably be what he believed, a no, and a proceed to target.
This was a rabbit trail.

He texted the number from heart, tapped in a question mark, and
waited for a response. Five minutes passed.

Is there a question?

The asset is requesting ballistics information on the
gun, including local searches in the area. I feel this is
unnecessary and will only lead to more time lost before
the assignment is complete. How would you like to
proceed?

His contact was typing immediately. A good sign, he would say
no.

Find out, go through your pipeline, and search for any

> ballistics within the system or locally. Put a rush on it,
> so our timeline goes forward. As soon as information is
> available, send it to the asset. Ask for an update on
> completion. Report when complete.

The Secretary swore. There would be a trail back to him. Why would his boss choose this outcome? Perhaps he believed that when the asset had completed the assignment, there would be nothing to investigate. The Speaker had survived in this town a long time, and it rested on never having his name or finger on anything that could come back to bite him. He would be cautious who he asked to get the information, and he would parcel it out — no need to leave a visible trail if he had to leave one.

He typed in the number for the assassin.

> Authorization is a go-ahead on ballistics information. I
> will secure the information and send it as soon as
> possible. Update on completion?

He didn't respond right away, which irritated the Secretary.

> Expect completion shortly. Need ballistics to clean up
> tasks.

The Speaker went through his usual protocol with the phone and handed it in a plastic bag to his driver. His jaw set, he made a call to a friend in Homeland.

"Jim, this is Ted. Yeah, doing great, you? Hey, you know that mess in Seattle? I need a favor."

# CHAPTER TWENTY-EIGHT
## TERRELL HUFF

He arrived near the destination, where he believed that Matt Dunn had been dropped off. Pulling a device out of his bag, he aimed it at the house. No infrared heat signature came from inside. There seemed to be a residual signature in the garage. He moved the device and saw where the remaining heat signal emptied into the alley behind the house and disappeared. It seemed odd knowing Dunn needed rest. He needed satellite images. But this had to be off the grid from his paying benefactors. No need for them to realize he had temporarily lost the target. It didn't matter, he had eyes on Jim Dunn, and Matt would go home to daddy. No way Dunn could hide. He texted his contact.

> Need a favor. Satellite images from 0500 to 0700, will send coordinates next.

Now he had time to burn while he waited on info. He wanted to find where the woman and her accomplice went. He needed to see her connection to this. He texted his employee, operating the drone.

> Location?

Someone typed back right away, at least this person was doing his job.

South Seattle, near a green belt in a residential
neighborhood. They parked the car and entered a
covered walkway and tree line, so the drone could not
follow to a destination. They are in a nearby
community, and I'm sure they will return to the car,
watching it. Plates go back to a deceased person.
Seems would be a good cover vehicle, presumed the
right vehicle to transport Dunn. No ID on the occupants,
they carried umbrellas and covered their faces.

Terrell swore. Professionals. But even so, he was better, and they
would find that out.

Report when you have eyes on them. Follow and send
location.

He would get with his person tailing Jim Dunn. Wherever daddy
was, these people would show up, they had moved Matt, so they
connected to daddy Dunn too. He would remove them all at once.
He liked the massacre idea as it removed the idea that Matt Dunn
was a lone target.

Unless, of course, his client got information to him on the gun
used to shoot him, which would result in a delightful side job.
Whoever shot him would die, and it would be excruciating. He
found the side jobs he did satisfying. Sometimes he just killed because
he could. He practiced his craft to confuse local police. He kept sharp
at what he did, and he found it exhilarating.

Besides, any targets he missed would show up at Matt's funeral.
He would follow them and take them out too. People were too
predictable because emotions were the best way to lure people. Grief
blinded them from danger.

Next, he texted his tail on Jim Dunn.

Location?

An immediate response.

The train headed south. Unknown destination, to
Olympia or farther south, not sure. Might be traveling
alone, or others in different cars. No apparent contact.
Will advise when he leaves the train.

Hmm. He would go to the location of the woman and her
accomplice and locate them. He needed to extract information and
eliminate any help they would be to the Dunn's. At least he could
redeem his time this morning.

# CHAPTER TWENTY-NINE

"So, if you don't mind me asking, you told Jim Dunn you had a backlog of cases, and if that's true, are you sure you have time to consult with me on the Olympia case?"

"I have to make about $11,000 a month to take care of my mom. It's like a grind. I have to make that money to keep my mom at her place and pay bills. Yes, I have cases, but I need that steady income that Jim Dunn's gig could provide. And yes, if you don't mind letting me in on that case, I would love to help. It's one of those things that isn't the usual thing we do. I help you, and maybe other things like that turn-up. Who knows? Where are you at with it?"

"Ready to meet with them and find out the details of the case. You are welcome to come, I'm not sure what it pays, but I want to find out more about it. Tell you what, I will share it fifty-fifty with you. One of those cases that come along once in a career, but could also mean some good PR if we solve it. I would be glad to have you along on this one, not sure I can crack it myself. One condition."

"What?"

"We are not driving that piece of junk car."

"Deal. I will leave it there, you drive, or better yet, I drive your car as someone might be looking for a woman, not a guy. You ride in the back until we get out of the neighborhood. I probably drive better than you."

Katie practiced her death glare in his direction.

Suddenly a black streak entered the kitchen and, in a flash, tried climbing Dan's leg.

"Hey, little guy," Dan chuckled as he picked Lucky off his leg.

Katie came around the counter. "I have to feed him and figure out a kitty litter box. Eventually, Ellie is not going to eat all his you-know-what's."

"I like this little guy. Maybe you should keep him?"

"Can't, I don't live here, and the people are coming back soon. I have an idea, though, for a home for him. I think he will be fine." She reached for him.

Katie snuggled the little kitten, who immediately started purring.

"Time to get you some tuna, and for you to sleep on Ellie."

Ellie looked at Katie expectantly, like she understood completely.

"Take care of Lucky until I get back. Don't set a bad example for him, right?" Katie sternly said to the dog.

"If you can get ahold of Jim Dunn, please check-in for us, I will call my client/contact for the historical case, and we can get it set up for today."

Katie carried Lucky off to the pantry and located a can of tuna. She opened it and watched him wolf some of it down.

That done, she headed to the den to send some emails. She sent one to the teacher, hoping to get a quick response. She paid a few bills, and it felt good to be in the black. As Dan said, the knowledge a payday would come from Jim Dunn's agency relieved her. Having a business meant getting work all the time, or the coffers got thin.

Ping. An email back from the history teacher about the place to meet for the consultation.

Katie poked her head back in the kitchen, but Dan was still on the phone.

She formulated a quick email reply.

"Ted, my associate Dan Beck and I will come. Please send any materials that we might be able to look over beforehand. We can go over simple detective practices with the students, and we will discuss our costs with the class. Katie Parson."

She peeked into the kitchen to see Dan held Lucky and petted Ellie. Kind of a Hallmark moment, certainly redeeming qualities as she upped her Dan-opinion a bit.

"Hey, we have an appointment in Olympia at two, does that work for you?"

"Sure," Dan said as he looked at his watch. "I promised mom I would come to visit tonight. I have to pick up some toilet paper, as the nursing home says now they don't provide that. Sheesh, for the kind of money I'm paying, you would think they would provide toilet paper. She won't remember I said I would visit, but I try to think sometimes she does."

"We should be back considering traffic, no later than six. My car is in the garage, so let's head out. I can catch up with a friend I have at the Tumwater Historical Society on the way. He will know the background story, and that will give us some information on the case."

Katie grabbed her purse and keys. Dan held up his hand to catch the keys.

"I drive."

Katie made a face at him but tossed them to him. He pulled on a beanie and a pair of sunglasses. Katie took his cue on changing her appearance and grabbed glasses out of her purse and a Mariner's ballcap.

"What did Jim Dunn say?" Katie asked.

"Just a sec on that info. First, I got ahold of my former girlfriend at the Renton Police Department, and she is going to pull that old file on your case and see if there are any ballistics evidence that is still there. If she can get to it, she'll get back to me today."

"Back to Jim. He had a lot to say, and I guess Matt left for Washington, DC. They were going to meet up in Centralia, but Matt got a call from an old buddy in the Secret Service, and he needed to check something out. Jim said Matt told him he might require you to use some influence you have with a "big guy" in DC. What's that about?"

"Have no idea. But since Matt was so spy-like with it, I'm sure he will explain. I need to let Ellie out before we leave, and we can talk on the way to the meeting with our clients. Can you do me a favor? It's garbage day, and I need to put the garbage out. It goes in the alley outside the back gate."

"Sure, no problem. I used to be a garbageman in college."

Katie raised an eyebrow. "You have that look about you."

Dan shrugged, "At least I don't have that smell about me, like some people."

Katie narrowed her eyes, withering him with her specialized scowl.

She noticed that Ellie seemed eager to do her business. Maybe that had to do with the little kitty inside, or perhaps she enjoyed all the attention from Dan. Ellie scratched at the backdoor in just a minute to get back in, and Katie filled her water dish. She also made sure that Lucky had a little water dish too.

"Katie, we've got a problem. I looked up to see if it looked like it was going to keep raining. At first, I thought I saw a big bird, but I realized it was a drone. Probably a couple of streets over, near the Accord. We have a tail, but they don't know our current location. More than likely, they are looking for two of us."

For a moment, neither one of them spoke.

"I noticed there was another car in the garage. Do you have keys for that car?" Dan asked.

"Yes, I do, the owners like me to drive it around the block once a week to keep it charged."

"If we are driving a vehicle registered to this address, it's a good chance that no one pays any attention. You should hunker down in the back seat until we leave the neighborhood."

"So, we talk about this, or just leave?" Katie asked.

"We leave. We share it with Jim, and we figure out what we do next. We know that Huff is one step behind us, and we need a plan."

"You are about the same size as the guy who lives here. Grab a jacket in the hall closet, and one of his hats. I will get the keys to their Ford Explorer. Once we get out of the development, we can head over to your place and get your truck. As long as the drone stays here, and we continue to act as though we live here, we avoid notice."

"Listen, I think until we hear back from my friend at the police department, we need to stick together. If we find out that someone requested your ballistic information, we're going to have to work a little differently. Right now, we need to operate under the radar, especially you. This man is beyond dangerous. Also, he knows there were two of us in the hospital last night. That means he will look for both of us. He also might try and find a way to see who Jim Dunn hired in Seattle. We might have a couple of days before he identifies us. We'll talk to Jim and ask Matt how we proceed from here. Even though the government is trying to capture Huff, we have already seen that they are not very good at that. And we don't know who's leaking information. That must be what your friend Matt is trying to find out.

"Everyone knows there is a leak. I'm sure Matt is working on that. I don't know how much he will be able to tell us, but Huff is looking for us specifically. Full disclosure, this worries me. We need to find a way to put this guy in the crosshairs of the government. That said, our understanding is that they miss sometimes, but he doesn't." Dan said.

"I will get in the backseat of the car, under a blanket, and you will have to keep an eye out to see if the drone follows. I can't leave Ellie or Lucky because I might not be able to get back here. They have to come with us. In my car is my kit bag with wigs, makeup, clothes. I have to grab that and some food for Ellie and Lucky."

She could only hope that they could exit the neighborhood without drawing attention. Their lives depended on it. No matter how professional they acted, fear hovered in every breath, like breathing on a frosty morning.

Hunted.

# CHAPTER THIRTY

"I'm trying not to look, but I think the drone is moving up so it can monitor our exit. I can't see it except that it doesn't seem to be as low as it was. I'm going to head for the grocery store. I have a feeling that it's not going to follow us too far."

Katie rummaged in her small purse for two mirrors that she often used in surveillance. Each had a little sticky piece on the back. She put one high up on the back seat so that she could see forward and one on the end of the front seat so she could see backward. On the floor in the backseat, she could see the mirrors and didn't need to lift her head.

"It's still raining, which cuts down on visibility. Try taking a couple turns on the way to the store, to see if it's following us."

Katie waited as she tried to remain calm. Had they escaped surveillance? Dan made a few extra turns in the housing development. She checked the mirror facing the front and slowly let out a long breath. A man, about five foot ten, hoodie and carrying an umbrella, walked on the sidewalk. He seemed to be out for a morning walk, but Katie recognized him.

"Dan…"

"I see him. Don't show yourself."

Katie's eyes followed the figure in the mirror. When Dan passed him, she turned around and watched him slowly disappear in the other small mirror.

"He has an idea we ditched the car here. He's doing what we'd do, searching. How many times have you looked and found nothing? He is a bad man. But he is not superhuman, and he doesn't know everything. Fear makes people do things that expose them. We do not have to be intimidated by a man. I know you said people were praying for us."

"Yes," Katie said in a small voice.

"Greater is He who is in us than he who is in the world." Right?"

"Um, yes."

A kind of warmth flooded Katie.

Tears overwhelmed Katie. The tension of the past few days spilled out, and Dan's kind words triggered her emotions.

"Stay down until we get to my place. I don't want anyone checking traffic cams or satellite footage to see you in the picture. We have to keep doing our job."

Dan worked his way through some stoplights. It seemed like forever before he was pulling into the grocery store parking lot.

"Katie, I don't see anything following, either a car or a drone."

"Why don't you get gas? We can head to your place and trade vehicles after that."

"Sounds good."

Katie pulled out the phone that Jim Dunn had given them and texted.

It appears we have collected a drone tail. We were able to elude the drone and moved to a safe location. There is a continual leak in information. Homeland? I understand Matt may want to talk to me. Dan and I are following a case. We are available if you need us.

Please update if there is any more information about
Terrell Huff. We had a visual ID, and he is stalking us.

Katie included Dan in the text. There seemed to be no immediate
response. She wished there was more direction on what they should
do. But she understood that Jim didn't know either how this was
going to play out.

As Dan was filling up the car, Katie pulled out her phone and
looked over her discovery notes. Each case represented a puzzle.
People did things for reasons. Her part was not to see and observe
actions so she could tell her client, but to understand the reason.
Sometimes the idea didn't match up to why her client thought the
person was doing what they were doing. Her clients wanted more
than just an observation. They wanted to know the rest of the story,
the why of the person's choice of actions. That was the hardest part
of what she did, learning the why.

As she watched Dan gas up the car, that warm feeling came over
her again. While she didn't think Dan was an angel in disguise, he
was a companion in this storm. For the past five years, a private
investigator's job meant she worked alone and odd hours. That
required extended absences from her caring family. Her sister Tammi
and her kids, her mom and dad, and brother Gary and his family.
The one she missed the most was Grandma Betty. When she visited
with her somehow, Katie always left her grandmother's house filled
with a trust that God could do anything.

It seemed that Dan believed as she did, and it didn't surprise her
God put him into this equation.

"Have you heard from Jim Dunn?" Dan asked as he got into the
car.

"Nothing yet, I reported we are on a case, that Huff was stalking
us, and we are available."

"I live about fifteen minutes from here, and there is a carport outback. I'll have you pull out my truck, put their Explorer in that spot, and we can head to Olympia. You need coffee?"

"Does it rain in Washington?"

"We'll get caffeinated and on the road from there."

Dan turned on country music on the radio.

"Hey, I don't do whiny, "my mama when to jail" music."

Dan's turned up the volume.

Not an angel sent from God.

# CHAPTER THIRTY-ONE

"Hey, if you can turn off that music, I can read you an email I just got from our client," said Katie. Traffic moved at a crawl, typical for Interstate 5.

"Go for it."

"Our client, Mr. Wendall, says his class discovered that back in 1926, there was a break-in at the city hall and documents were taken from the city of Tumwater. There seems to be a mystery surrounding the nature of those documents. One of the homeschoolers in this group found a diary from her great-grandma that seems to indicate she knew why the documents were stolen. At the time, the city was considering putting in a new water system. The land occupying the space the city wanted to for their utility system was owned by this student's great-grandma, a young widow at the time of the theft. Somehow the records of the ownership of this property were stolen in a burglary of city records. The city proceeded to fund the water facility and to seek to purchase the property.

However, there was a question regarding the ownership of the property. The new owner to emerge was a local businessman, Finn Erickson. Some believe the stolen records showed a different owner. The widow (the great-grandmother of the student) claimed her deceased husband to be the valid owner of the property. However, without the records, there was no way to verify this claim. He says to note he attached a document from the early newspaper of the time, The Morning Olympian.

"We look forward to meeting with you today in class." Katie read aloud.

"I'll pull up the document—the *Morning Olympian* headline dated December 30, 1927. **Tumwater City Records Go Missing. Papers and Official Paraphernalia Believed Stolen. Police Detectives Investigating.**

*An outside detective has searched for the missing records from the town of Tumwater, while that community has continued its usual activities minus papers and other official paraphernalia. These documents have been missing from the city safe, located in the municipal hall, for two weeks, it became known Monday."*

"It's not much to go on, but I feel that there might be a lot of money involved if someone stole land records and falsified ownership. It sounds to me like a big dispute for land and money. It could be one of those million-dollar things. What do you think?" Katie asked.

"Sounds like the widow knew the businessman, Finn Erickson, had got wind the Tumwater City Council was going to buy her land for a lot of money. We could be looking at a love triangle that went bad, and there would be no way to prove that. Or, it could be something like you said. But if all we have is a newspaper article and a diary, we might be looking at a mystery that can't be solved. The problem is, we are going to have about 20 junior detectives on our hands teaching them how to detect." Dan said wryly.

"There must be more about this, or they would not be inviting us down and willing to pay money for us to investigate. I was hoping for treasure at the end of this rainbow. Maybe there will be, I guess we could think about doing this on a contingency in case there is a pot of gold, like real estate records that mean a million dollars for someone? What do you think, flat fee, or work for free and hope there's money at the end?"

"Let's hear what they have to say. I never talk money until I know what someone wants me to do. If it looks like there could be a big deal of money for someone, we could work on contingency. Hard to think there would be. Wouldn't all the people be dead by now?"

"The children of the widow are living, and at least the great-grandchild has the diary. Her daughter might be in their late eighties or nineties, with children and grandchildren here. Statistics say that forty percent of the people in the U.S. live their whole lives in the state where they were born, and another interesting fact, twenty-five percent live in the same town in which they were born. There is a good chance they are all living in the area."

"How well do you know Olympia?" Dan asked.

"I have family there."

"Good, that means you will know the places they might want us to check out."

"At least I know where to get good coffee and a great place to eat. Steamboat Betty's has the best hamburgers and shrimp salad in town, and it's on the waterfront. Let's go there, and we'll get coffee at Dorn and Benson's after that."

"That's a good start. I always base information on credibility. The newspaper report is credible. And the diary most likely will be. It's the rest of the story we don't know, and that is where we find who is telling the truth and who isn't." Dan said.

"Changing gears, Terrell Huff. Let's try Jim Dunn again. We need to know if he is still tracking him or what Matt knows."

Katie entered Jim's number on the phone.

"Hi Jim, you are on speakerphone with Dan and me."

"I wish I had news for you. Matt is on a plane right now to DC.

We're in Centralia, and it appears we have a tail. We are going to separate and head in different directions. I have a guy who works for me who looks like me and doubles for me on occasion. He is meeting me on the train, where he will go back to the Airbnb, but I will be heading to a new location. I will let you know when I've arrived and hopefully without anyone following. Matt arrives in DC in two hours, and he will have information after that. I suggest you stay in a safe location until we have some intel on what is going on."

"Thanks, Jim, we working a case for a few hours in Olympia, after that we will head back to Seattle. We appreciate any information or updates on Huff."

Katie disconnected.

The GPS announced it was forty-five minutes to their destination.

"You are trapped in the truck with me for forty-five minutes, and now it's time to spill about you and Matt Dunn," Dan said with a sideways glance at Katie.

"I told you."

"No, you haven't. I noticed when you told Matt in the car you remembered him from FLETC. He said nothing. Like he was hearing that for the first time. It was a cover story, and both of you were utilizing it. My mama didn't raise any ignorant boy. Also, he used to be Secret Service. Almost six years ago, you were at FLETC as far as I can figure out. And if he was Secret Service since he referred to the "big guy" you both know, that could only be the President of the United States, who six years ago was not the President, but the Vice President. Which would mean Matt was on his detail. And somewhere you figure into that. So far, how am I doing?"

"I cannot confirm or deny," Katie said.

"Okay, that tells me more. A Top-Secret assignment. Something that had to do with the President when he was the Vice, or his family."

"Honestly, Dan, I can't talk about it."

"Yes, you can. We're talking about our lives. I have to know what connection you have to Dunn, and how we can out-think a man who is trying to kill us."

Emotion threatened to spill tears down her face. She wouldn't cry in front of Dan. She had to be professional, think through this.

"I should've realized you would figure things out. Yes, there was a top-secret assignment. I did not meet Matt Dunn directly. But I did see him during the job. Not long after this assignment, I left FLETC training for the reason I told you earlier. We never met formally, and I was not sure he would recognize me. We cannot talk about the assignment. You're right, Dan. There's something we're missing here, something that tells the whole story. As soon as I can, I will call Matt Dunn. We need to figure out what's driving Terrell Huff. It can't be just what started in that garage a few days ago. I have a feeling that's why Matt left for Washington DC when he should have been recovering someplace quiet with his gunshot wound. I know you want to know more. Please let me talk to Matt first."

"So, that day in the garage was a coincidence? You were not there for any other reason?"

"I guess that is what you would call a divine appointment or bad timing on my part. I wished that I had never entered the building. But for whatever reason, God allowed me to be there and to help Matt. I have to believe that God will also help us with Terrell Huff. I know how dangerous he is. Somehow God will give us the information we need to figure out the situation." Katie stole a sideways glance at Dan. He nodded.

"I am worried about Fred Lindley. We have not heard from him, and I don't know what part he is playing in this now. Huff did kill his brother. I don't know if Fred is thinking about that, or if he realized that would happen anyway. I think Fred did say that was part of the plan to convince Huff that Fred was no longer a part of the picture. Jim Dunn hasn't said anything about Fred's activity, which leads me to believe he either doesn't know or doesn't want to tell us. From what I know about Fred, he's not sitting around. He knows more about Terrell Huff than anyone on the planet. Huff is dangerous, and after all, Fred is eighty-years old. I want to do whatever it is we're doing without involving him." Katie said.

"Okay, I get that. We'll have to see what Matt gives us and where we go from there. I know you know Ricky. What do you think about asking him to check out your neighborhood, to see if the drone is still there? There isn't anybody I know who is more low-key than he is. Even if he doesn't do it himself, he can have someone who can get what we need without attracting attention. We'll split his fee and bill it back to Jim Dunn."

"Good idea. I'll text Ricky. At least we'll know what the situation is in the neighborhood before we get back."

"Good plan."

"Go ahead and take the 101 toward the ocean. It's the fastest way to get to the Steamboat Betty's. I'll check with my source on local history to see what he knows about the mystery we are researching. Maybe we will get lucky and look like we know what we're talking about when we get there."

"Are you buying lunch at Betty's?"

"I think Jim Dunn's buying, but I'll put it on my tab for now."

Dan switched on the country music.

"At least think about the animals. It's hard for them to endure that noise."

"Hey, this kind of music helps me think. I need my best mojo right now."

Mojo would not be all they needed to stop a killer. *God, that refuge?*

# CHAPTER THIRTY-TWO
## MATT DUNN

Matt saw Glenn Richter approach his table at Judy's diner, a little place with great eats on the outskirts of Alexandria. Back in the day, it was an old hang-out they used when they needed to decompress from a stressful time in the Secret Service.

"Hey, Matt, good to see you. Don't stand, I know you have a bum leg." Glenn extended his hand, and Matt gripped it.

"Thanks, Glenn, I'm still getting used to the fact I can't run a marathon. It looks like this place still doesn't have any cameras."

"Yep, had to lose my tail to get here, it's those drones that will get you every time. It took me a while, but I got rid of them. How about you?"

"No one knows where I am. If anyone did know, I'd probably draw the wrong kind of crowd. Can we order? I'm starving. It's a good thing they still have this back room."

The back room was a place the owner let regulars use for privacy. Just a little room with a back door in case you had to leave unseen. The owner, sensing good business in a town that needed discreet meeting places, had fixed it up as a semi-private room with a double door opening. Outside was a big maple tree, obscuring any exit and entrance from a satellite view.

"Why do you have a tail, that's what I want to know? I mean, you're the guy who puts a tail on everyone else, right?"

"Interesting, isn't it?" Yeah, that means where I go and who I talk to, is significant to someone. The million-dollar question is, why me? But it's probably a billion-dollar question." Both quieted as the waiter approached.

"You know what you want?"

"Judy's deluxe burger with the works. Your house beer. Nothing else is that good!" Matt said.

"Same here, onion rings instead of fries. Thanks." Glenn said.

The waiter disappeared into the kitchen.

"So, I get the death sentence, and you get a tail? Why are *we* that important?" Matt asked.

Glenn leaned forward. "I thought a lot about it on my way here, hoping that we can compare notes. I first started noticing a couple of years ago that the people I worked with were leaving in one way or another. Because I'm retirement age, a lot of people were retiring, and people like yourself were leaving or taking other positions in other agencies. Both of us knew of the problems in the agency, management problems that couldn't be solved because the "old school" thinking of the Secret Service wouldn't change."

"After a few former agents wrote those best-selling books, common knowledge now." Matt agreed.

"It seemed to me there was an exodus that was puzzling to me. Once you have a career in the Secret Service, you don't up and leave. But lots of people began taking "early" retirement, and I found out just recently that people were offered packages like me, some exotic place to spend your last year, and that's the last I heard from them. I tracked a few down, they died in car accidents, had heart attacks, nothing out of the ordinary except that they all died. *That* was out of the ordinary, freaky even."

"People like me don't get to retire. We get bullets." Matt said.

The waiter returned with two plates. The fries and onion rings were heaped high, and the burger was at least five inches tall.

Matt's mouth watered as he took a big bite and washed it down with a gulp from the beer the waiter deposited next to him.

"Got to eat for a minute, haven't had anything this good in days," Matt said.

He noticed Glenn also attacked his burger and grunted in agreement as they both downed juicy bites of burger. For a few minutes, eating was a priority for Matt. He had little real food in a while, and peanuts on the plane didn't count.

"Remember Doug Whitsom?" Glenn asked between bites.

Matt nodded as he chewed.

"He did a lateral transfer to U.S. Customs and Border Protection just about a year ago. He's a supervisor but got called out on a field operation. All of a sudden, everything went sideways, and he got separated from his team. Bullets flew everywhere, but the only person killed was Doug. Interestingly with that many bullets, no one else was hit or injured."

"Doug was on our team when we were assigned to the VPOTUS. Is there anyone else who has disappeared since we were on watch with the VP?"

"I can't go through them all, but trust me, it's an impressive list. Impressive because it's just about everybody who served with us. There are only a few of us left, but I get the impression that the intention is we also should disappear. That's why I think POTUS will listen to us. I'm not sure how we can make that connection. And the other thing, the Vice President will probably die this week. No one knows he's on hospice, but most of us have been relieved of duty as only the family, and a few people know he's at Camp David. The security there is very tight, and they're waiting."

"There is one more interesting thing that you need to know.

There is a long-standing appointment on the VP's calendar for next week. He was supposed to speak at the annual conference for the Secret Service. I've heard rumblings that POTUS will be his replacement. If that's the case, only a few will know that POTUS will be speaking. If there is a leak in our system, someone will know that the President will be speaking that day."

"What you're saying without saying it, is that if only a few know that POTUS is speaking, who could tell him there might be a problem with the agency protecting him at that speech? That would be those who are aware of a problem. In other words, you or me." Matt sat back in his chair and looked at Glenn for a long moment.

"We have to talk to the President before that speech happens. Any ideas on how that's going to work?" Matt said.

"Sure. All you have to do is figure it out. After all, I'm supposed to be planning my retirement party. Your only problem is you're in hiding and recovering from a gunshot wound. So, it makes more sense that you call the President. Right?" Glenn chuckled.

"I do have an idea and involves something that happened five years ago. There was a major player in an operation years ago that you might recall, it was called Descendent. That is the only person I know who has a get-out-of-jail-free card and a straight-through call to POTUS anytime they want one."

"I want to ask how you have access to that person, but I don't care. And you're right, POTUS would listen to that person. I don't know how you make that happen, but I'm assuming that you can put that call through today. The one-day conference is next Tuesday. Today being Friday, we don't have much time."

"I'll call today, but you know how these things work. There may be a delay between her call and POTUS. Especially if the reason she's calling, she has to make clear to the gatekeepers, and they decide not to put her through. She'll need a good reason to call him and yet one that is not clear to those monitoring his communication. Sometimes he takes his calls. If by some miracle, that happens, she will get a chance to tell him our concerns. But if he doesn't listen, or doesn't believe her, I don't know where that leaves us."

"Dead, that's where."

Matt stared at Glenn. He was not as interested in the food anymore.

"Since I'm not sure we're going to get another chance to see each other, let me try to put through a call in a few minutes. But first, I have to hit the head, be right back."

Matt hobbled to the men's room. He wanted to trust Glenn. They had always been good friends and the only way he would know if what Glenn said was right, he'd have to make a call no one tracked. That would entail a phone with no connection to him.

He entered the men's room, hoping that he wouldn't be the only one there. He was in luck. A man was washing his hands at the sink. He pulled out a paper towel, took a pen from his pocket, and wrote the word phone, question mark, on the paper towel. He handed the paper towel to the man. For a minute, the man looked at the message, sized up Matt, and reluctantly handed over his phone. He stood off to the side and waited for Matt to use the phone.

Matt silently mouthed the words, "Thanks." He made a motion that he was going to step out in the hall. Matt pulled out his wallet and set it on the sink so the man would know he was coming back.

He pulled out his other phone and got Katie's number. He hoped she'd take a call from an unknown number.

The call stopped ringing, and there was silence on the other end.

"Katie, this is Matt. I borrowed a phone. Listen, I think I know why I was a target in the garage."

"Go on."

"A lot of other former Secret Service agents have disappeared.

Especially those who worked with POTUS when he was Vice President. There could be a hit going down on the President of the United States. Can you use your get-out-of jail-free-card and call him?"

Katie was quiet for a long moment. "Are you sure?"

"Yes. I'm going to make a couple of phone calls to back up what I just heard. But I want to know, would you make that call?"

Matt waited through the quiet on the other end of the line.

"Make the calls. Call back in an hour. Huff is very close to us. Dan is with me, and we think that we have slipped his surveillance. It doesn't mean much since we both know how good he is. The faster we can make this happen, the better it could be because who knows if I'll be here by the end of the day."

"I guess I could say the same thing. I'll call you back in an hour." Matt ended the call.

He stepped back into the restroom and handed back the phone, again mouthed thanks, and picked up his wallet. He used the facilities and realized the guy was gone. Funny, he didn't hear him leave. What was that his mom used to say, angels unawares? He reached down to adjust the ankle holster on the gun his dad had sent to his apartment. At least he was armed.

He stepped back in the hall, and a man emerged from the side door of the kitchen, but he was not a waiter. In his hand was a Glock with a suppressor. Matt grabbed his ankle gun.

"GUN!" Matt yelled loudly. Looking beyond the gunman, Matt saw Glenn duck under the table as he drew his weapon. The gunman fired, and Matt also fired at close range, hitting him in the shoulder. He went down but swung around to shoot. Matt kicked hard with his uninjured leg and sent the Glock flying. Matt pointed his gun at the shooter.

"Don't move."

The shooter lay still, blood pouring from his shoulder wound.

There was a towel on the rack next to the kitchen door, and Matt grabbed it. Leaning down, he pulled both of the gunman's wrists back and wound the towel around them, and tied it. It was not secure, but it was going to have to do.

Screams continued from the restaurant. Gunshots directed Matt's attention. Glenn hunched under the table and then shot at a man in a hoodie. The shooter sprang back out the front door. People screamed and ran out.

"Glenn, you okay?"

"Yes, clear."

"Off duty policeman, don't shoot." A man stood with his hands raised.

"Shield number, District?

"46702, District 7."

"Approach, please, can you secure the shooter?"

"Yes." The man pulled a set of cuffs from the back of his pants and moved toward Matt.

He bent down and put on the cuffs and stuffed the towel hard into the bleeding wound.

Matt leaned into him to whisper.

"Undercover. Homeland. I have to go. Can you handle the scene?" Both could hear sirens roaring outside. The man nodded.

Glenn joined him, and they exited out the kitchen and walked under trees away from the restaurant.

"I didn't lose my tail," Glenn said.

"Ya think?" Matt answered.

"We need to split up. Call me on this cell when you are clear," Matt handed Glenn a burner phone. Glenn took off under cover of the trees, dodging and weaving, Matt heard him calling for an Uber on the cell he had given him.

Around the corner, a man on a bike pulled one of those pet trailers, a large one, which was empty. He frantically waved the biker over to his position under the trees. The man looked confused but stopped at the curb near Matt.

"Can I help you?"

"I can't explain, but this is an emergency. I am a federal agent. This is going to sound strange, but can I get in your pet carrier? I need to get out of the area."

The man smiled. "You with "We Prank You?"

"Can't say, but I have a Franklin for your trouble."

"Climb in."

For the second time in three days, Matt crammed himself into a small uncomfortable space. He pulled the Velcro windows shut.

"I'm good, where are we going?"

"To my doggie daycare, about ten blocks. That work for you?"

"Yes, perfect. Thanks."

Matt's mind was racing. He would borrow another phone and call Katie. He heard a lot of police sirens. They would call it a robbery gone south.

Whoever was pulling these strings appeared connected and powerful.

# CHAPTER THIRTY-THREE

"Thanks, Don, appreciate all the tips on local history. I will try and catch your next history talk at the Tumwater Historical Society." Katie ended the call, and reverently sipped her coffee. At least her inner woman had been restored with a great shrimp salad at Steamboat Betty's and a cup of perfectly brewed coffee.

"Looks like what the school group shared with us is a known local mystery. My contact, Don Crosby, confirmed there was a break-in at the Tumwater City Municipal Hall in 1927. The records stolen were never recovered. No one knew if there were important documents stolen or not."

"You think we lead with the break-in and ask them to share what's in the diary? We need to know what they know, but most important, what they want," Dan said.

"Time for true confessions. My mom homeschooled me through the eighth grade. I understand these homeschoolers. They are freethinkers, and they like to problem-solve. We let them tell us what they know, how they have figured this out so far, and we give them an assignment. That way, we look like we know more than them when we don't."

"And you know that how?"

"I always wondered why my mom was so smart. She told me later when I was in college that she pretended to know all the answers when she was homeschooling me. So, when I found the solutions, she could always say, "Yes, you discovered some good things." She told me she knew I pushed harder to find answers when she laid out the problem, but no solution. I learned more that way."

"Sounds like your mom knew you pretty well. Um, did you wear like those long, jean jumpers when you homeschooled?"

"No. And my mom didn't either. Get that out of your head. Homeschoolers are not weird, colleges love them, and employers find them to be more productive on the job."

"I was joking."

"Statistics don't lie."

Katie peeked over at him, his irritating movie star grin in place.

"Do you have home school perfume, so they know you are one of them?"

Katie threw her empty coffee container at him, but his reflexes were too good, she missed.

"Hey, stop with the death glare, will you? You're scaring Lucky."

Her phone vibrated an unknown number. She answered and waited for someone to speak. Dan looked at her questioningly as Katie turned to the window, speaking quietly. She disconnected.

"Matt has asked me to do something. Can't explain to you, but he will call back in an hour to let me know." Dan's smile disappeared. He pointed.

"Is this the Grange Hall?"

"Yes. It looks like some of the students are in the parking lot. Time for a meet and greet."

Dan pulled in the lot, and Katie turned to Ellie, who was wagging her tail, anticipating a chance to get out.

"Dan, can you let her out to go to the bathroom and I will check out the group."

189

Katie hopped out and approached what she figured must be a mom in the parking lot.

"Hi, my name is Katie Parson. We are here to meet with some homeschoolers regarding a history class?"

"Yes. My name is Beverly Young, and this is my daughter Sandy. She's a member of the class that asked you to come down. We're excited to begin this project."

Dan let Ellie back in the truck and caught up with them.

The building, a Washington State Grange Hall, had a plaque on the outside wall stating in 1913 it was a grade school. Interestingly, it was being used as a school again. A foyer area that held a kitchen with an open counter area was the entryway and off to the side, a bathroom. Double doors opened into a large meeting room that held benches and tables, with a podium upfront. It looked like table seating would hold about twenty- four. As they entered, students filtered in and sat at the tables.

"Mr. Wendall, this is Katie Parson and her associate," said Mrs. Young.

Wendall was much different than Katie had assumed. Katie pegged him at about fifty, slightly graying, glasses about five foot eleven. He was dressed more formally in slacks, button-down shirt, and a sports jacket. He gave off a professional kind of impression. Bureaucrat maybe, Olympia, was the capital, so perhaps he worked for the State of Washington and was volunteering to teach this history class.

"We're glad you are willing to take on our case." He addressed the class. "Everyone, please take a seat."

Katie listened as Mr. Wendall droned on about the case and what they knew, mostly what he sent in the email. He finished and turned to Katie expectantly.

"Thanks, Mr. Wendall. I'd like to introduce my associate, Dan

Beck. I'm sure you all are wondering a little about how private investigators do their job. A usual private investigation case involves finding someone, or delivering a summons, or doing a background search. Why do you want to solve this ninety-year-old mystery?"

"Daniella, do you want to explain to the detectives about your great-grandma's diary?"

A girl who looked to be about sixteen stood.

"Hi, my name is Daniella Reynolds. Last summer, my family cleaned out an old house that's stood on our property for years. One of the things we found in the attic was a box of books, including an old diary from my great-grandmother. I read the diary and shared it with my parents. We believe that part of the property that my great-grandmother, Bell Dawson, owned, was stolen from her by a local businessman, Finn Erickson, and later sold to the city of Tumwater. We want to show for the record that my great-grandma owned this property, and now her heirs are due the payment for it. We have to prove that a local businessman took the deed and falsified it. That means finding the stolen documents. We have clues to where they are and are looking to hire you both to track down the documents."

"What information do you have that can lead us to the documents," asked Dan.

"In my great-grandma's diary, she refers to a man who was her lawyer at the time who helped settle her husband's estate. During the settlement process, he discovered that her husband owned another piece of property. From his position in the court, he knew that the city of Tumwater was interested in buying that property. The lawyer insisted on bringing the legal documents to the Municipal City Hall for safekeeping. However, just a day after removing the documents from my great-grandmother, there was a break-in at City Hall, and those papers went missing. She mentions the name of the lawyer,

Gunnar Ericson, who was a cousin to the businessman, Finn. We are hoping to be able to find the documents with his heirs. We have found doing a little research on our own, that the lawyer's family still lives in town, and has a small museum located in the legal offices of his heirs. We want to see if the documents are located in the museum and how to get access to them. That's where we felt we needed help."

"Thanks, Daniella. This is when we, as the private investigators, tell you we can either take your case or not. If you give me a moment to discuss this with my associate, we will be right back with you." Katie motioned to Dan to accompanying her out in the foyer area.

"What you think?" Katie asked.

"Ding, Ding, I think we have a winner. The only question is, how do we charge them for this case. I like the idea of taking this on a contingency."

"I agree. We get ten percent of the client's recovery, if they recover nothing, no charge. I have a contract in my purse. I need to add your name." They returned to the classroom.

"We have consulted and agreed to charge on a contingency basis. What that means, if our client, Daniella, recuperates some profit from the case, we will charge ten percent of what you recover. If nothing is recovered, we receive nothing for our work. I suppose sometimes it could be said we are more motivated to work harder if we only get paid if there is a recovery. What do you guys say, you want to pay us by the hour, or on a contingency? We do have a contract, and Daniella will need to sign it, or her parents if you are under 18?" Katie looked questionably at her.

"I just had my birthday last week, and I am 18, so I can sign. I would love for you to work on a contingency basis." She looked around the room for agreement.

"All in favor, we work on contingency raise your hand," Dan said. All hands went up, except for Mr. Wendall. Hmmm.

DEADLY PURSUER

"Great, Daniella, if you will come and sign, we will start today. Usually, we will get back to you within 48 hours for an update on what we have found. We will need your contact info."

"Excuse me, but I feel that the parents will want me to be the contact person." Mr. Wendall said.

"Sorry, but we have to work with the person we have under contract. Daniella, can you report what we find to the class and Mr. Wendall?" Katie asked.

"Yes, I will do that," Daniella said.

"Good, that's a go. We will get the lawyer's office and museum address from you, Daniella?" Dan asked.

"Yes, I have all the information for you in this packet," She said.

"Great, we will be back to you with an update soon. It was great meeting you all, and just so you all know, I homeschooled too." Katie smiled.

Dan and Katie moved out to the foyer area, and Daniella followed with the packet. Mr. Wendall excused himself from the class and also accompanied them.

"I appreciate your enthusiasm Daniella for this project, but I think the parents in the class are going to want me also to sign the contract." He said a little too intensely for Katie.

"Sorry, no can do. Daniella's family would be the ones to profit from this recovery of property, so only she can sign the contract, as it's a financial gain. We will call her parents and verify this is okay before we get started." Dan said smoothly in his business voice. Something about his six-foot-one muscular frame and the way he said it, made Katie smile inwardly.

"Well, as long as Daniella lets me know immediately any results, I think the parents can live with that." Mr. Wendall said a bit too quickly.

Dan's smile was slight, and Katie noticed he had his professional

193

"I'm not a guy you mess with" look about him when he took Daniella's arm so she could sign the contract on a nearby counter. Mr. Wendall reluctantly went back to the classroom.

"Just to cover our bases, can you call your parents, so we are all on the same page about this?" Katie asked.

"Sure, but I already know all about it, we have talked about this as a family forever."

Dan and Katie let her make her call, and she handed over the phone to Katie.

"Hi, this is Katie Parson, Private Investigations. Am I speaking to Mrs. Reynolds?"

"Yes, you are."

"Great, I want to confirm that if Daniella signs this contract for us to work on a contingency basis, which if we recover information leading to the recovery of property or funds, that myself and my associate Dan Beck will receive a total of 10% of said recovery? Is that okay with you, Mrs. Reynolds, if Daniella signs this contract, knowing that it is legally binding?"

"Yes, we can sign on the copy she brings home to us too. We are very excited about what you might find. Thanks for taking the time for the job. Many of the families are excited that our class can participate with you in investigating a crime that took place here in our town so many years ago." Mrs. Reynolds said.

"You are welcome. We only hope we can find some information that will be helpful to you all." Katie handed the phone back to Daniella.

"Bye, Mom, tell you later what happens."

Katie handed Daniella the two contracts, both for Daniella to sign, and one for Katie and Dan to keep. Dan extended his hand, and Daniella delightedly shook it, Katie's as well.

Once back in the truck, Katie opened the packet and put the

lawyer's office address, on the East Side of Olympia, into her phone.

"Hey, did the Wendall guy strike you like a little bit eager to get all the information?" Dan asked.

"You bet he did. Let's find it first. You up to scoping this place out as long as we are here in Olympia?" Katie asked.

"Sure, that works."

"Coffee, first, though, take a left, and we'll hit the coffee stand."

"There are three coffee stands?"

"Oh, yeah, the first one, the other two are nasty."

"Great to have a coffee snob on location."

Katie practiced her lesser death glare in his direction and put the GPS on the speaker.

After they had coffee in hand, in a few minutes, they pulled up to about a block away from the lawyer's office that housed the museum. The morning rain had made a mess of the parking lot, mud puddles everywhere.

Katie grabbed her kit. She pulled on a brunette wig, straighter than her curly mop. She put on some black-rimmed glasses that screamed nerd and wiped off her lipstick. The no-makeup look made her look more innocent. A neat gray yarn beanie matched with her corduroy thrift jacket was just enough business casual to give the impression she was a working girl. To get information from people, it helped if you looked the part.

"Hey see that mud puddle? You need to rub some mud on your license plate in case we get into some trouble doing this. Both front and back, and put a piece of paper on your dash over the VIN. You never know what satellites are looking at you."

Dan popped out of the car and grabbed a handful of mud from the grassy bank that bordered the parking lot and covered the license plates. He found a rag in the backseat to wipe off his hands before climbing back in the cab. He pulled out, and thirty seconds later, eased into a parking spot in the lot next to the building.

"Is this the oddest house/office you have ever seen?" Katie asked Dan as they pulled up.

The grayish building looked foreboding and uninviting.

"I'll wait outside while you go meet the vampire, I mean the lawyer who works here." Dan grinned.

Katie wrinkled her nose at him, but secretly she wished Dan was going in with her. There was something about this whole case that bothered her. But if there was stolen property from years ago, at today's property value, it could be worth a lot. Ten percent of several million dollars in property value was a considerable paycheck.

"Since this is a teensy, weensy scary for you, if you hear screaming, don't try and come in, just call the police." Katie intoned sarcastically.

That movie star grin in place, Dan inclined his head toward the creepy looking double door.

# CHAPTER THIRTY-FOUR

Terrell Huff felt his phone vibrate. A text was coming through from the Secretary of State.

> The gun was used in defense of an attempted assault four years ago by a local private investigator, Katie Parson. Ballistics test the same for the bullet you sent as being from this gun. No other information. No knowledge if the current owner is the same as the registered owner.

Terrell immediately googled Katie Parson and found her website, which included her office location, email, and phone. The phone was probably a voice mail account, but the address to her office was listed.

He called the phone number. Voice mail picked up, and he listened intently to her voice.

"Yes, I am interested in speaking to you about my missing daughter. She has been missing for a week. My wife and I, and the police have been unable to locate her. I want to meet you to hire you to help us find her. Please give me a callback. I can meet with you at your office location anytime that is convenient for you. Please call or text this number."

A woman and he had seen a woman in the satellite picture. Was she the same? And why had she helped the agents by shooting him? She would tell him. He would clean up any loose ends and kill her. A shiver of pleasure rolled over him. Some killings were pleasant, and this one would be all that.

Terrell immediately left for the office location. He would set up and be ready to surprise her even if she didn't respond. He would have a woman associate also call, much more non-threatening, requesting a meet up at her office.

He formed a gun with his hand and smiling he pretended to shoot it. "Goodbye, Katie Parson."

Another text came through.

> It is set up for POTUS to be at the Secret Service event next week. You need to wrap up and get to DC. Advise when targets eliminated.

Terrell waited in anger. He always controlled his emotions, and yet this man irritated him. He would love to see the look on his face when he eliminated him. He allowed the anticipation of that to play in his mind.

> Expect elimination today—Will report when on the way to DC.

In his search this morning, nothing out of the ordinary stood out, and the car appeared abandoned. He would check with his drone operator and leave for Katie Parson's office.

No new information on Matt Dunn's location had surfaced. His associate reported Jim Dunn headed back to the Airbnb. But no sightings of his son. He couldn't hide forever, Dunn would show up, and at that vulnerable moment, he would disappear.

Soon, deliciously soon.

# CHAPTER THIRTY-FIVE

Katie approached the door to the office/museum, formulating a cover story. She carried a briefcase Dan had in his truck. Acting, in the course of an investigation, was second nature, but she wished she'd practiced her cover on Dan for believability.

The door creaked.

It seemed a little darker inside than most offices. Old paintings on the wall leaned to a décor that felt like Katie had stepped back in time forty years. One entire wall was a glass case filled with old newspaper articles, books, and historical documents. To fit the mood, a little old lady sat primly at a desk in the corner of the room. At first, Katie thought she was a mannikin. She sort-of cracked a strange smile. Creepy.

"Can I help you?"

"Yes, I am writing an article for an online historical group and was directed to this office as a place to research information for the city of Tumwater? Am I in the right place?"

"Why yes, thank you so much for thinking about us. As you can see by our wall display, we have a small collection of historical documents for the city of Tumwater. Please feel free to take a look at what we have on display."

"Thank you so much for your hospitality." Katie gushed. "Um, I hate to bother you, but a couple of days ago, I found a little abandoned kitten. I brought him down with me as I do my research and was wondering if I could get a little bit of water to give to him? He is in my truck."

"Oh, of course. Would you like to bring the kitten in?"

"Yes, I would love to, if that's not too much trouble? He is very lovable and cute."

Katie had guessed right; the little old lady was a cat person.

When Katie went back out to the truck, Dan was leaned back in the seat with Lucky on his chest.

"Give me Lucky. He's my ticket in."

"Must be a little old lady in there."

How did he always know these things? Supernatural PI mojo?

The old door creaked again.

"Oh, he's so cute," the strange little lady burbled.

"Would you like to hold him? Unfortunately, his mom was run over by a car. I heard him crying and found him."

"He is just precious," the little old lady held him in her lap, petting him. Lucky did his part and purred.

"My name is Lucinda Parks," Katie eased smoothly into her fake id.

"Oh, I'm Ida Olson, pleased to meet you. You know, I can take him into the kitchen in the back and get him some cream?"

"That would be so nice of you, thanks so much." Katie schmoozed.

Beaming, Ida carried Lucky out of the room. As soon as she left, Katie began to search the room visually, noting the security camera above Ida's desk pointed at the glass case loaded with old news articles that possibly would be helpful to their investigation. Stepping close to check the documents, from what she could see, most everything seemed to be simple historical information and pictures. One thing that caught her attention was an old leather box in the corner of the locked case. The box had a padlock. Interesting. Wouldn't that be a nifty hiding place, in plain sight? Katie wondered how she could get into the glass case. She grabbed a latex glove from her pocket and pulled it on under her jacket.

Slipping behind Ida's desk and she eased out her front drawer. As she suspected, there was a set of keys, one of which was a small key that looked to fit the glass display case. Katie grabbed the keyring to see if it opened the case. She stood in front of the lock to shield what she was doing from the camera. None of the keys on the ring fit the lock. She walked over and pretending to get a tissue from Ida's desktop, put the keys back in her desk drawer.

Katie stood in the room and looked carefully at everything in the room. The security camera mounted above Ida's desk was placed to view out in the room, so she was sure it did not capture her theft of the keys and replacement. In one corner of the room, there was an old earthenware vase sitting on top of a little end table. Katie walked over to it and picked it up, pretending to look at it closer and shook it—a slightly jingling sound. Hiding it in front of her to avoid being picked up on camera, she tipped the vase upside down, and two small keys fell out. She carefully replaced the vase.

"Lucky do your best in there," Katie whispered.

Using one of the small keys, Katie slipped it into the lock and twisted. The case did not open. She switched to the other key, and the case swung open. Instantly Katie went to the locked leather box and tried the first key. The little lock dropped open, and Katie lifted the lid.

She saw the logo of the City of Tumwater on some documents in the box. Without waiting to read them, she lifted them carefully out and slid them inside her briefcase. She closed the box and locked it. A black streak raced by her from the kitchen area. Lucky had escaped, which wasn't lucky for Katie. She didn't have time to lock the case as Ida was coming down the hallway. She leaned back against it and heard it click shut.

"He's fast," Ida said as she slowly hobbled from the kitchen area.

"Yes, he is. The cream probably energizes him. Can I ask you, are there any more historical documents than the ones in the case?"

"No dear, that's all we have. We're just a small historical depository. Have you tried the state library?"

"Yes, I've been there and have looked at some of the things. Is there any way I can look closer at some of the things inside the case?"

A shadow seemed to cross Ida's face.

"No, dear. These are all private documents and fragile. We don't share them with anyone. But you are welcome to look at all of them through the glass. I'm sure there's nothing that you will find that you can't see from the outside of the case."

Lucky made another break toward the kitchen.

"That little rascal. I'll get him." Katie said.

"Oh, no, I can't let you back to our private office. He's such a cute ball of fur. I'll get him. Just a minute."

As she tottered back into the kitchen, Katie slipped closer to the vase and dropped the keys into it. Ida appeared carrying Lucky, who was squirming in her arms.

"I will take him back to my vehicle. Thank you so much for letting me look at your case and the documents."

"Documents?"

"I mean the newspaper articles and things in the display case," Katie said quickly.

"Of course. Come back at any time."

Her tone seemed colder. Katie collected a squirming Lucky and backed out of the office. She almost sprinted to the truck. The security camera mounted above Ida's desk would show her as she opened the locked leather box and removed the documents. But considering Ida's age, the security tapes might not be reviewed for a week or so. There were no security cameras out front, and with mud on the license plates, she and her cohort in crime Dan could escape without a trace. If she had five-fingered the actual stolen documents from long ago, no one would search for them, as they proved a crime had been committed.

Best to make a quick retreat and search for gold.

# CHAPTER THIRTY-SIX

Matt Dunn found people at the doggie daycare who were happy to let him use their phone for a few minutes. He called Katie.

"Hey, Katie. I met with a close friend of mine who served with me on the detail for the vice president six years ago. He told me many of the people in the Secret Service that we worked with are missing or dead. Our Vice President is very sick and is dying. Because of his illness, POTUS is scheduled to take his place speaking next week at the Secret Service conference. Both of us think this is when there will be an assassination attempt by Terrell Huff. The missing and dead Secret Service men would be those who would notice differences in his detail and alert POTUS. Their absence makes an opening to take him out.

"We need you to call the President. Add me to the call, and I will fill him in on what I know. He will take a call from you. The biggest miracle would be if he answers personally, and you don't have to go through gatekeepers. Look, I'm on the run, and if we don't do this now, it may not happen."

Katie was silent.

"You there?"

"Okay," Katie spoke in a whisper.

"Years ago, he gave me his card. I memorized the number, even though I never thought I would use it. I'm going to put you on hold and call him. When he is on the line, I'll add you to the call. If there are gatekeepers or he doesn't answer, I'll get back on the line with you. I have to do this little thing. I have to pray, so give me a minute, okay?"

"And while you're at it, say a prayer for my friend Glenn. They came after him today, and we both got away."

Katie covered the phone and kept Matt on the line.

"Dan, please drive. There is a park next to Capitol Lake, just down the road. Please pull in there. I have to make a phone call. Listen, while I'm doing that, you got gloves? Could you look in the briefcase and see if there is anything that relates to our case?" Dan looked thoughtful as he drove.

Katie got out of the truck and walked toward the lake until she was alone. Staring out to the lake, she prayed quietly.

"Going to put you on hold for a minute. I'll make it a three-way if POTUS picks up." Next, she dialed a number from memory. The number went through.

"This is Winston Baxter. I am unavailable; please leave a message."

"Mr. President, I'm sorry to bother you, but the nature of my call is very urgent. My name is Katie Parson. You will remember me from a Secret Service field operation some five years ago called Descendent. At that time, you told me if I ever needed anything that I could call you. If you are able, please call me back." Katie completed the call, and Matt came back on the line.

"Left a message. Have to see what happens. I'll be back to you soon, I hope."

Katie looked back at Dan's truck. Dan had let Ellie out to go to the bathroom, and Lucky was exploring under her watchful eye. Katie caught his eye, and her look caused him to call Ellie and scoop up Lucky. She got back into the truck and accepted Lucky onto her lap.

"I called the big guy," Katie said.

"So, do you think the President of the United States is going to call back? I know this is a little awkward, but I am ready to be on the team to protect you, no problem. Umm, just my usual hourly rate?"

"Dan. Right, of course, while I'm talking to the *President of the United States,* I'll ask if the government can fund my protection." Katie's answer dripped sarcasm.

"Thanks, girl. Just hoping it's not on the government rate program."

"You are going there?"

"Just kidding. Well, not totally kidding, but if the government is going to pay someone, it might as well be me, right?" Dan chuckled.

Katie practiced her death glare. Dan tried to hide a smile as he petted Ellie.

Katie's phone vibrated earlier, so she checked her voicemail. A male who requested a skip trace was the first message. He wanted to meet at her office. Next, a woman also asked to meet at her office to do some background checks. She would have to fit them in somehow.

"We seem to have struck gold, and I mean real gold." Dan read from one of the snatched articles from the case, an old newspaper article from the Morning Olympian.

"OBITUARY Jim "Skookum" Dawson, a former miner on the Klondike Trail, passed away December 1, 1920. Jim is best known for his tales of the California and Alaska Gold Rush days. Skookum mined in the California Gold Rush in 1855 when he was fifteen years old. He made a good nest egg and moved to the Northwest to become a logger where he married his wife Martha, and settled in Tumwater in 1865. In his forties, Skookum left for the Klondike Goldfields in 1896. It's believed he came home in 1899 with a small fortune in gold.

He is survived by his son, Timothy Dawson, Timothy's wife Bell, and their children, Grace, Lizzie, and Janice. Jim used to regale the neighbors with tales of burying his fortune in gold on his property in Tumwater, as he didn't trust banks. Skookum spent most of his life prospecting gold. He settled in Tumwater, but Skookum never let go of his tale of buried treasure. Timothy, his son, said no wealth ever existed. Rest in peace, Jim, your treasure is in heaven now. But that's not all. Listen to these articles."

"OBITUARY: Timothy Dawson, husband, and father, passed away suddenly on February 5, 1924, from a logging accident. He was a good provider for his family. His widow Bell, and her three children live at the family home in Tumwater. Services will be conducted at the Methodist Church in Tumwater on February 9th at 2 pm. A potluck will follow the service.

The *Morning Olympian*, June 1, 1928, **The City of Tumwater Buys Land for Water Facility**. The land sits next to the old family home of the local miner of record, Skookum Jim, who was reputed to have buried his treasure of gold from the Klondike Gold Rush on his family property. No gold was found, but many folks around town did search for it. Richard Benson, the former owner, and lawyer in the city, only laughed when asked if there was buried treasure on the property. However, when the city began construction, the land appeared to have been thoroughly excavated before the town broke ground. The facility will be built in one year.

"Buried gold?" Katie asked.

"Not on the property sold to the city for the water facility. Even if Benson stole it, the property would have long since been owned by the City of Tumwater by adverse possession laws. But maybe, Daniella and her family don't know about the buried gold. Our only stake in this is if we could find it. It might be worth a fortune. Interesting twist, huh?" Dan said.

"Life is often way weirder than fiction. Okay, so any ideas about how we find buried treasure? It doesn't seem like Daniella's family has any idea about that, so where would we look?"

"Me great-grandpa be a pirate, I know about buried treasure, har har."

"Why am I not surprised? Okay, Black Dan, how do we find it?"

"Matey, you need to think like a pirate. Or, in this case, you have to think like a miner. Old Skookum Jim was a miner, and one thing you can know about miners is that they're very precise about the land. If he did bury his treasure, he would've bought land like he would've bought a claim. If we could find a record of land owned by Skookum Jim, or even find relatives of his at the time, we might be able to find where he would have put the gold."

"This is fascinating, but it's not something we can follow up today. It's going to take some time to unravel a little bit of history. And some time with the family to figure out the locations of any other properties nearby. There are a couple of people who want to meet me at my office, and you need to get back to see your mom. Ricky texted me a while ago to say he thought there was still a drone in the neighborhood of Ellie's house. It looks like Terrel Huff is still surveilling us there.

"Why don't you take me back to your place? I will get the Explorer and meet some potential clients at my office. You can see your mom and will meet up after that. If I hear back from the President or Matt or anyone, I'll let you know."

"That works. Stay in the Explorer. No one can trace that to you."

Dan reached over and turned on his country music. Katie frowned at him.

"Mojo, Katie, girl, mojo."

# CHAPTER THIRTY-SEVEN

The last couple of days spent with Dan made Katie felt a little uncertain on her own. In the previous five years, she watched out for herself. Katie learned long ago as a private investigator that no job was worth her life. If a job tended to be dangerous, she didn't take it, unless she arranged backup. Having a man of Dan's skills working with her gave her courage. Maybe, Dan would like to share a business? That kernel of thought was something she would explore later. But today it was back to just her, and fear crouched at the door of her mind. At least she had Ellie, and there was some comfort in that. Although watching her curled up in the seat with Lucky cuddled on top of her, she did not seem like a fierce police dog. But Katie knew her history, in her police career, Ellie had apprehended over 50 suspects.

On her way to the office, Katie remembered this might be the weekend she was supposed to serve her time at the storage facility. Every couple of months, she staffed the head office to pay for her office space rent. She called the owner.

"Storage Solutions, this is Bill, can I help you?"

"Hey, Bill, Katie Parsons. Am I supposed to be on duty this weekend? I will be there soon to see some clients, but I couldn't remember if my turn is this weekend or next."

"Let me look at the schedule. Not this weekend, next. You have a schedule conflict?"

"No, no worries. I can do it, I would have had a conflict this weekend, so I'm glad I'm not on until next week. I have some clients coming today, and I will be there soon."

"If you are on the road, you might want to take the back way. There is a semi that turned over in the northbound lanes of Interstate Five, and it's a mess."

"Ugly! Thanks for the tip. I will do that. Bye."

Katie could see that traffic was already beginning to stack up. She took the next exit off the freeway and went the back way. Thankfully Katie found a quick stop grocery and got coffee creamer and her mainstay, a burrito in the deli section. Nothing like the burrito she got from her favorite taco truck, but when traffic was this bad, she had to make adjustments. She wolfed it down in the Explorer and fed and watered both Lucky and Ellie in the vehicle. Lucky promptly curled up on the seat, like eating took up all his energy. Cats were so mellow.

"Come on, Ellie." Ellie popped out right away and found a grassy spot to do her business. At least traveling with two animals had worked out okay. From her viewpoint one street over, she could see Storage Solutions, since the only thing between was two large industrial parking areas. On a whim, she got Ellie back in the Explorer and pulled out her spotting scope from her kit bag. Her phone rang.

"Hey Katie, this is Bill again at Storage Solutions. There is a guy here a couple of minutes ago. He wanted me to open your office so he could wait there. I told him I didn't have a key even though I did because I didn't think you wanted him to be in there without you. Did you want me to unlock the door for him?"

Katie looked across the parking area to see a car parked down the aisle way from her office. To her practiced eye, it looked like a rental. Something was not quite right about that.

"Hey Bill, was it a gray sedan?"

"Yep, not sure where he parked, but after I told him he'd have to wait for you, he left our office."

"Thanks, Bill, that's okay, don't worry about it. I'll let him in when I get there."

Katie didn't tell Bill she was nearby because she wanted to check out the client first. She reached over and pulled on her Mariners cap and a pair of sunglasses. She scanned the parking lot of the storage facility with her spotting scope until she saw the sedan.

Adrenaline shot through her. The man in the car looked like an older man, but there was something odd about his appearance. His hair was gray, but he had darker beard stubble. She scanned the other side of the facility, on the L shape from her office. A second vehicle waited there. A woman in it had a spotting scope pointed right at Katie. They were looking at each other, and the woman reached for a phone. Sweat broke out on Katie's forehead.

She jumped in the Explorer and drove toward Highway 99. Katie saw the gray sedan speed out from the storage facility. Maybe he didn't know the traffic situation on the freeway? She prayed he didn't. Katie raced to the old highway, but the overflow from the interstate slowed travel. She weaved in traffic, trying to get as far as she could from the man who chased her.

Frantically she called Dan Beck.

"Katie, you miss me already?"

"Huff was waiting with someone at my office. He must've gotten the ballistic information because that would've given him my office location. I've been made. He's behind me in a rental vehicle and has a woman in another car. There's a chance I can lose them in traffic, but not a good one. You have any ideas?"

"Where are you?"

"Old 99, North of Tukwila, headed to the Waterfront."

"Katie, listen to me. He's not going to care who he takes out along with you. Do whatever you have to do, stay ahead of them. If he can't get a good shot at you, he's not going to take one. I'm calling Ricky. Go to Vine and First, there is a parking lot there. I'll have Ricky meet you. I'm on my way, but I'm at least an hour and a half out. In traffic, you're at least an hour out too. Stay calm and ahead of him. You can do this. Ricky will know where you can hide."

"I called in some help from an Army Ranger buddy of mine, Prey, who currently lives in Alaska and has a plane. He is of the caliber of Terrell Huff. Occasionally the CIA calls him in on black ops. He is flying into the Boeing Field, ETA, two hours. We'll both come to wherever Ricky has you. Stay off the phone and watch your driving."

"Tell Ricky I'm in a gray Explorer."

"Okay, call me back when you're close. Be careful." He disconnected.

Katie's stomach turned over, and she felt like the swallowed burrito had crept into the back of her throat. All she wanted to do was keep her eyes glued on the rearview mirror, but she couldn't. She had to drive like a maniac to get away from the monster that tracked her.

*Lord, help me.*

In her training at FLETC, Katie had taken several defensive driving classes. She considered herself a good driver, but no driving course gave tips on what to do when being pursued by a murderous assassin. Katie focused on the road ahead and weaved crazily through traffic. If she drew the attention of the police, that wouldn't be a good thing. Pulled over, Katie would be a sitting duck for a man of Huff's skill. She saw the sedan far behind her, but it was getting dark, and soon she wouldn't be able to distinguish his car. Her eyes flicked to the traffic ahead as Katie raced to get to the location Dan had mentioned. She saw the woman's car stuck in a non- moving lane, but Huff's car tracked her relentlessly.

She knew Ricky had many friends who would be able to move her around in the city. Huff was good, but the advantage was they were local. Huff had associates also, but she hoped none as resourceful as Ricky.

Katie raced through city streets and caught a break when she went through a yellow light but saw that Huff several cars back had been forced to stop. The parking lot was in the distance. She was going to make it, park, and get out before he could catch up, and she could only hope Ricky was waiting. She hit redial to call Dan.

"I'm almost to the parking lot. Are you talking to Ricky?"

"Go to the North end, he's there, and he has a parking pass to put on the dash of the car. He'll get you out of there. I will be there soon as I can."

Katie swung into the parking lot at the North end. Ricky leaned up against a pole. She jerked the car into a slot and grabbed her kit bag. She tossed a sleeping Lucky in it and clipped on Ellie's leash.

"Hey, Girl." Ricky handed her a pass, which she threw on the dash and locked the car.

They took off toward the Waterfront. Ricky moved them at an unhurried pace. In a few seconds, a car pulled up, and Ricky pushed Katie toward the open door. She slid in the back with her kit bag and grabbed Ellie's leash. Ricky hopped in next to her, and the car took off. Katie looked for her little mirror in her purse. Without turning around, she held it up behind her, frantically looking for the Ford rental that carried Huff. She saw it and saw he was searching, suddenly he turned in their direction.

"He's behind us!"

Katie took note of the driver in the car, a flashy guy who probably did things she didn't want to know. She would say he was a "bad" man. The kind of man you stayed away from on the street, but at the moment, a rescuer. He tore down an alley, wrenched a couple of weird turns, and popped out on the waterfront. Ricky opened the door and grabbed Katie's arm and pulled her with him, along with Ellie. They ran, and Ricky directed her into a bar. Ellie raised a few eyebrows, but Ricky smiled his way along, and said, "Service dog," to anyone in their proximity.

He led her down a hallway toward the women's restroom.

"Dan told me about the guy. Here's the deal. I have a few girlfriends in the restroom. These are the girlfriends you see when you're Sally. For the next couple of hours, you're going to be 'in the life.' The best way for you to hide in the city is to walk a track like these ladies. They're going to help you. They have clothes for you, makeup, and they will take you with them. This guy is not going to look for you there." Ricky pulled her close to him and looked directly in her eyes.

"Katie, pay attention to what they do. They'll watch out for you a little bit, but you're going to have to act like you know what you're doing. You've seen what they do. I'm going to stay here and meet Dan, and I'll give him the dog. Give me your bag too."

"Be careful; there is a little kitty in the bag." Katie opened the bag and let him look in.

"Girl, you need to travel lighter." But his eyes smiled, even though both of them were tense.

Katie impulsively hugged him. He held her a moment, and Katie clung to him. She pushed away and said shakily, "Thanks, I owe you big."

"No charge." She felt the electricity between them as he stared into her eyes.

"Ellie, obey Ricky." She handed over the leash. Ellie looked a little concerned, but she was well trained. Ellie knew if Katie handed Ricky the leash, she needed to go with him.

One longing look passed between Katie and Ricky before Katie turned into the bathroom.

Ricky was right. Katie did know how prostitutes acted because she had walked streets near them, but not on their "track." It was the route they used to advertise who they were to anyone who wanted their services. Huff would never look for her among prostitutes on the street. Hiding in plain sight in the city appeared to be her only hope until she could lose Huff. It didn't change how crazy everything seemed.

Fear choked her. Her grandma's voice came into her head, reading a long-ago Bible story of Rahab, a woman who lived as a prostitute, and how she trusted the God of Israel. Good to remember. She opened the door and read suspicion in the women's eyes who stared at her.

She would become one of them if she wanted to stay alive.

# CHAPTER THIRTY-EIGHT

"Girl, you need help. Nobody is looking to take *you* for a ride." Said a girl who looked the friendliest. "I'm Star. I'll help you with your face." She pulled out her makeup bag and motioned for Katie to come to her.

"So, Ricky says there's something sweet in it for us to help you. You got the sweet stuff, girl?" A woman sidled up to Katie, but her tone was aggressive and her manner the same.

"Listen, I am paying Ricky later, I got nothing, not even a purse on me. Whatever he told you, yeah, you are going to get it. But *I* don't have it, Ricky does. He ever let any of you down?" Katie's tone was rough.

"Lay off, Vett. You know what Ricky said!" said Star.

If she showed weakness, these girls would take her apart. She had seen women on the street attack each other over drugs, a john, or even because they looked at another woman like they wanted what she had. Every day on the street, they were often hurt physically and suffered emotional destruction. They weren't safe, but if Ricky had them in the room, it was because they were the toughest. She was going to have to play a part, and they needed to believe she could do it. Otherwise, she would be spotted immediately and targeted.

"You gonna need these." The girl Star had called Vett handed Katie some jeans, with lots of holes in them. Some black underwear that would show through the holes paired with a white lacy top, nothing too showy, just enough to suggest the obvious.

Something about the last woman, a girl really, that caught Katie's attention.

"Got some shoes, but I need them back. You get them to Ricky, OK? I'm Raven." She handed Katie some name brand tennis shoes. Women on the street walked all day, and they did not walk a track like in the Hollywood version with tight shorts or high heels. You couldn't keep up wearing high heels. Besides, that Hollywood version wasn't the real-life they lived. The difference? Their lives were ugly, filled with drugs, terror, and uncertainty. They hurt every moment, and the hard look in those women's eyes was brutal. Even their names were street names, Star, Vett, and Raven.

Numbly Katie stripped down to put on the clothes. She wanted to sniff them to see if they were clean, but she knew better. As soon as her clothes hit the floor, the girls grabbed for them. Katie stuffed her cell phone in a back pocket.

Star and Vett both smelled repugnant and decent at the same time. Body odor covered with huge amounts of cologne. Their hands especially were filthy, and when they opened their mouths, there were few teeth. These women were heavy drug users, and Ricky would supply them to get them to help Katie.

Raven was a little different. First, she could only be, even with all the makeup, maybe sixteen. Most all were old enough to be legal, but if you looked younger, that was a bonus. Even though her hard exterior, there was something about her that made Katie sense she wanted to help Ricky, not just for the drugs. Katie had a friend, Shelly, who rescued prostitutes who tried to leave the life. It was a hard and lengthy process, one which few chose. But maybe this girl could be one. When this was over, she would reach out. She had to pay back in some way, and she could perhaps help Raven.

"Sit on the counter girl, we'll make you pretty," Star said.

With her back to the mirror, Katie could only feel the girls putting on the makeup. It seemed to take forever, layer upon layer. Star stepped back finally.

"Take a look, Girlie, what you think?"

Katie didn't recognize herself from the caked-on makeup.

"Not enough." Vett proclaimed, and she added black eyeliner, foundation, and blush.

Katie knew no one would recognize the woman looking back from the mirror. Now the girls pulled out a brush and teased up Katie's curls a bit. Red lipstick finished the look.

"Put your hands on the counter," Raven said.

Raven painted one hand with nail polish, Vett the other. Bright purple.

"Keep your mouth closed girl, you got teeth, and that means you are new. You'll get eat up if you open your mouth." Katie understood her comment because most street people had few or diseased teeth from drug use.

"Let's go," said Vett.

The girls filed out of the restroom, and Katie stayed close to Star, who seemed to be the leader. They left the bar, and the girls began to fan out along the street. A couple staked out their territory on the corner and just stood, smoking and smiling. Star turned to Katie.

"Keep moving, honey. Someone slows down, get on your phone, act like you are busy. You might want to walk a track between us. Don't get in anybody's car. Motion one of us over."

That was all she got in the way of instruction. She walked fast, and she didn't look at cars that passed her. She moved from girl to girl, smiling at them and always in motion. She had a couple of vehicles follow her, and she led them to the other girls. Soon there were only a couple of girls still on the street. A vice patrol did a drive-by, and everyone got on their phones, looking very busy. Katie's phone rang. The ID was unknown. Matt? Nervously she connected.

"Katie, I need you in Washington, DC. We need to make a personal connection to the President." Said Matt Dunn.

"Why? I mean, how is my being there going to make him listen to me. He hasn't called back. Maybe he doesn't think what I did five years ago matters now. It was a chance we took, but so far it hasn't paid off. I can't think my being there makes any difference. Besides, I'm less than one step ahead of Huff. I'm not sure I could even get to the airport to find my way to DC in one piece."

"Katie, someone is managing POTUS's phone. I spent five years with him. I know he would call. We have to get you in front of him if we are going to stop an assassination. Listen, this is your country. I know you don't know this yet, but the Vice President just died. My Secret Service friend told me, and the world will know in five minutes. Do you know anything about succession to the Presidency?"

"Well, usually it's the Vice President and, um the Secretary of State?"

"No, it's the Speaker of the House, the President pro tempore of the Senate, then the Secretary of State, and after him, the Secretary of the Treasury."

"Thanks for the history lesson, but right now I'm trying to stay alive, and I can't even tell you where I am and what I'm doing, because it's beyond description."

Katie noticed a car with a window partially rolled down kept pace with her. She couldn't see the driver.

"Hey girl, get off your phone!" the driver called out. She couldn't tell if he was old or young. He held out a hundred-dollar bill. She started moving faster, her goal to reach Vett on the nearest corner.

Vett ran and jumped in front of Katie and snatched at the bill, but it disappeared fast.

"I got what you want, Billy" She cooed in the window. Turning, she snarled to Katie, "Get OUT—this is my man!"

The transformation to vicious was instantaneous. Vett did whatever it took to survive, and the man meant money.

"CAT fight! Ladies, there is enough of me!" Came the laughing voice from the inside the Mercedes. Katie could only see a hand with lots of rings and jewels.

Vett didn't wait. She opened the door and jumped in, and Katie waved them on.

"Lots of room here, girl, you can join us?" the voice called out to her. The car began to move slowly away.

"Katie, are you working on the street?"

"Matt, I'm trying to stay alive. Huff was literally on my tail when my friend got me protection on the street. He is not looking for me here. Trust me."

"Katie, he has to know you play a role. By now, there is some video that Homeland has somewhere that shows a homeless woman near the parking garage. He will know you can play a street role. He followed you to near to where you are now. He is going to look at everyone, which includes prostitutes. Get out now! I have your location. I'm calling a cab." He disconnected.

Fear consumed Katie as the same gray sedan cruised a block away. Matt was right. He'd see through the makeup because that is what he did. She saw him as he searched each woman's face.

# CHAPTER THIRTY-NINE
## MATT DUNN

"Dan. What were you thinking? She is on the street, Huff will know. He will find her." Matt yelled.

"What do you mean? Ricky, our contact, stashed her in a way no one would look for her. I just met up with him and picked up her dog."

"He stashed her as a prostitute. I just got off the phone with Katie. Maybe he thought that no one would look for her that way, but Huff knows she has played a homeless woman. If she is downtown, he will look for her in any role. He will find her."

Dan cursed.

"I am calling Ricky. He can get to her."

"I called a cab. I got her location from her phone. They were five minutes out."

"Matt, Huff knows Katie's gun was used in a self-defense case about four years ago, and a police officer who is a friend told me that the information about that case was accessed recently. The ballistics test on the gun that shot Huff and Katie's gun would match. But to know that information and know who Katie was, he would have to have Homeland intervene to pull the ballistics report. Do you know how to find out who did that?"

"That all plays into why Homeland wanted to know if I used a different gun at the scene. They took my Glock, but Katie fired too, and she must have hit Huff. There is a connection at Homeland that is feeding information to Huff. I knew there was a smoking gun, but until now I didn't know where to look. I am going to need the name and contact information of your friend as soon as Katie is safe. Huff knows she shot him, and now he can recognize her. No one has ever stopped him. Get her and get to DC. Huff will come here, for the business he will be called on to do. She will be safer here."

"Ok, I have an Army buddy with a private plane. He is here too."

"Dan, we can't just be muddying the water with anyone else."

"He is a retired Ranger who moonlights for the Agency. A sniper of rare talent, his codename is Prey."

Matt paused.

"One of the few in the known world who could go head to head with Huff. Call me when you have her."

"My buddy will fly us to DC."

"If she lives. If you pray, now would be a good time." Matt disconnected.

# CHAPTER FORTY

Katie kept moving. She didn't hurry as she headed down the street to Raven. Someone touched her arm. She jumped and looked into magic brown eyes.

"Hey, Katie, I didn't mean to scare you. Got a tip to get you off the street."

"Too late, Ricky, he's in the gray sedan behind you. I don't think we can get off the street in time."

Ricky leaned into Katie, and he turned toward the street. The sedan was almost on top of them, and the window rolled down.

Ricky threw his arm around Katie and began to hustle her down the street. Several things happened at once. Raven ran to Ricky and Katie.

"GUN!" Raven screamed.

An SUV roared down the street on the opposite side, aiming at the sedan. Ricky threw Katie down as they tried to avoid the shooter. At the last minute, he threw himself on her.

Time seemed to stop as Katie heard the soft pop of the suppressor. She felt the impact of the bullet hitting Ricky.

She screamed.

A loud crash as an SUV hit the sedan head-on. Katie rolled over and pulled Ricky down beside her.

"Ricky," Katie sobbed.

He stared at Katie, and she could see the bullet had gone through his back to his chest. He was bleeding out.

"Listen to me," Katie said as she leaned close to his face. His eyes fastened on her. "Remember, all that talk about getting married? Remember when I told you had to know Jesus, for us to get married? He laid down his life for everyone. He said to me, to you, to everyone, "Whoever calls on the name of the Lord will be saved." He is calling to you Ricky, do you hear him?"

"Yeah, I hear Him," Ricky whispered.

"Do you believe in Him?"

"Yeah."

Wonderous joy filled his eyes. In the next precious seconds, Ricky's face lit with supernatural peace. Then slowly before her eyes, the light of life slipped gently away, and his grip on her hand grew limp. One moment alive, believing in the Savior of his soul, the next face to face with Him. Home in the arms of Jesus.

She heard Huff jump out of the sedan, and the click of a gun forced her to lift her eyes from Ricky's face to Terrell Huff as he pointed a gun at her from a few feet away. She would see Ricky now and waited for the impact of the bullet that would send her to him.

A man dressed in camo gear crashed into Huff and sent the gun flying. He tossed Huff from him.

The men circled each other, and Huff pulled a wicked-looking knife.

"You know Terrell, I have always wanted to meet you. They call me Prey, maybe you've heard?"

Katie saw a look, almost fear, pass over Huff's face, he sneered.

"You think you are somebody? You are nothing, nobody."

They circled and got closer.

Sirens screamed closer, forcing Huff to step back behind the wrecked sedan. A car pulled out from the opposite side of the road, and Huff ran to it.

Dan's truck slammed to a stop next to Katie, and he ran to her and Ricky.

"Katie, we have to get out of here now!"

"Dan, I can't leave him."

Dan reached over and touched Ricky's neck to check for a pulse.

"He's gone. This is a lot of blood. Are you hit?" Dan gently grabbed her shoulders.

"No, it's all Ricky's blood," she sobbed.

The man who had confronted Huff moved close. "Dan, we have to go."

"Katie, this is my friend, Prey."

"I won't leave Ricky."

"Katie, when the police come, there will be too many questions. We'll take him with us. You will be able to say goodbye in the way you need to. I promise."

Dan gently put his arms around Katie and carried her to his truck.

Ellie barked furiously as Dan set her on the back seat next to Ellie. Dan and Prey lifted Ricky into the bed of the truck, inside the canopy. They both jumped back in the truck, and Dan drove away from the scene in a different direction, slowly as to not draw attention from the approaching police.

Ellie was all over Katie, licking her and barking. "Ellie, sit."

"Katie," Dan lowered his voice, he spoke calmly and slowly, "You're sure you didn't get hit?"

"No, I'm alright. Ricky—this is all Ricky's blood. He—" she sobbed, "He took my bullet. I was supposed to die, and he—". Katie buried her head into Ellie. Her sobs echoed in the cab.

Dan's friend reached to pat her shoulder, and Ellie showed her teeth growling.

Dan pounded the steering wheel in frustration.

"Prey, can you call in a clean-up? They need to get your rental SUV out of there. Tell them to meet us at Boeing Field. Your plane is there?"

"Yeah, it's an updated Piper Meridian turboprop, an M500. I'll call in a cleanup. Someone owes me a favor."

In a low voice, Prey spoke on the phone.

Loud noises like a trolley car or big rig truck rushed by them. The sound seemed to burst through her shock.

*Lord, why did Ricky die?*

She heard a tiny sound, and Ellie was scratching at her bag at her feet. She opened the bag, and Lucky peered out. Katie picked him up and held him close. His rough tongue found her cheek, and she buried her face in his little body. Waves of grief rolled over her. Ellie protectively hovered as she alternated, licking Katie and Lucky. Katie's eyes closed as she tried to blot out everything as she focused on the motion of the truck. The video played in her mind of Ricky's violent death. She remembered the joy as it transformed his face from fear to joy. Safe forever, gone from her. The grief began to roll over her again—her fault.

"We're here. I see the crew. Prey, can you direct?"

The man beside her jumped out. Dan came around to her side and opened the door.

"Katie?" He held her in his arms. She wrenched out sobs and couldn't stop them.

He held her for a while; she didn't know how long, but finally, he looked into her eyes.

"Katie, listen. It had nothing to do with you. Do you believe that?"

"Before he died, I asked him to believe in Jesus. I saw the joy on his face. But he should have never been there, I—"

"Katie, there is a verse sometimes quoted about men in battle. 'There is no greater love than to lay down one's life for one's friends.' Don't take away Ricky's sacrifice. He laid down his life for you. He chose it. Soldiers are willing to make that sacrifice for the man next to them. Ricky was a soldier in this battle, and he gave his life for you. That is love beyond what we understand. We'll all die someday, and God knows that day. Our names are written in the Book of Life. Ricky's name was written there a moment before he went home to Jesus."

Dan spoke the truth, but her heart ached.

"He was my friend." Katie fell back against Dan, and sobs shook her.

"Dan, she needs to get changed, the plane is being fueled, we have to go." Prey stood by the truck.

Slowly Katie sat up and wiped tears from her face with the back of her sleeve. Dan handed her the kit bag he must have retrieved from Ricky when he picked up Ellie. Lucky lay curled on the seat next to Ellie

"There's a woman's restroom just over there," Prey pointed out.

"Stay, girl," Katie said to Ellie and walked toward the bathroom. She gritted her teeth as she felt a wave of nausea wash over her. She wasn't going to throw up in front of them. She got through the door and ran for the stall. Over, and over she heaved. Finally done, she shut the stall door and peeled off the clothes given her by the prostitutes. She grabbed clean jeans and a sweater out of her go-bag.

She started to throw the bloody clothes away but realized that wasn't a good idea. She pulled the plastic garbage sack out of the trash container and put the bloody clothes in it.

The face she saw in the mirror couldn't be her. A mask of black smeared make-up and puffy eyes stared back at her. She stuck her face under a spigot in the sink and let the warm water flow over her for a few minutes. She wanted to wash away the horror of the last hour. Wearily she pulled out a little makeup kit with makeup remover and cleaned her face. A clean face looked back at her, and she stood there a minute. She knew she should put makeup back on, but had no heart for it. She ran a brush over her curls and grabbed her go-bag and the plastic sack. One last look in the mirror. Her sister would have said she looked like a truck had run her over, and she would be right.

"Showtime," Katie said to her reflection. She stepped out to find the plane and saw Dan.

"What will happen to—to—Ricky?"

"He will be treated respectfully. We have a crew of people here who will take care of him. When we get back, we will have a service for him. I promise you." Dan's look was compassionate.

"Ok," Katie took a deep breath, "What about Ellie and Lucky?"

"Did you say your mom could take care of them? Can you call her? I can have a friend deliver them."

Katie nodded. She was going to have to pretend to her mom, the one person who always knew if there was something wrong, that there was nothing wrong. She dialed a number.

"Dad? I need you guys to look out for Ellie a couple of days. And there is a little kitty named Lucky too. Can you?"

"Katie, we can. Are you safe?"

Katie looked at Dan.

"Yeah, I'm safe. I'll be home in a couple of days. Thanks so much."

"Take care, Katie, we love you. Call me when you can."

"I will, Dad, thanks. I love you." Katie disconnected.

She handed Dan the bag with the bloody clothes, and he took it over to some people who were near his truck.

As she got into the plane, she thought of Terrell Huff. Anger began to work through the grief in her. She knew one thing, the man who killed Ricky was no longer the hunter.

He was the hunted.

# CHAPTER FORTY-ONE

Katie was thankful for her kit bag as she had the clothes she needed for a short trip. Anything else she needed, she could buy in Washington DC. Katie buckled in next to Dan in the two seats behind the pilot's seat, as Dan's friend Prey pre-flighted the plane. Once buckled in, she leaned over, head in her hands.

Dan leaned over, "We have to talk."

"I can't."

Dan was quiet. Katie seemed to be in another world as the plane taxied for takeoff. They were in the air, and she felt like she was going to be sick again.

"I'm going to throw up, is there a bag?"

Dan grabbed a bag from under his seat and quickly handed it over. Katie heaved. It seemed as if every burrito she'd eaten in the last two days came up. After a few minutes, Dan handed her a napkin. She wiped her mouth and stuffed it inside the bag.

"Sorry," Katie said as he handed him the barf bag.

Dan grimaced as he gingerly took the bag, unbuckled, and rummaged behind his seat for a plastic sack to stash it. She heard him gag a little. Despite the strain of the day, a ghost of a smile tugged at her mouth. She tried to imagine the Jurassic Park actor, touching a bag full of vomit. She giggled.

Dan buckled his seat and looked over at her.

"Really?"

Wiping the smile off, "I'm sorry, I don't hand vomit bags to people every day.

Dan turned in his seat and looked at her, and she could tell he had something to say.

"Katie, I've been in a war, and a couple of my friends died. I know you don't want to talk about Ricky, but stuffing those emotions makes it worse. We've got a four-hour flight to Lincoln, Nebraska, where we refuel. Can you talk to me about Ricky? After all the psycho-babble from military counselors on this, I think all the guys I've known who lost friends in the war said what made it easier was to talk about the person. Ricky died today. Tell me about him, what he meant to you. It hurts, but it helps."

For a long moment, Katie looked at Dan. "Okay." She leaned back in her seat, closed her eyes.

"I know that you knew him too. I think I met him about three years ago. I, in my homeless, "Sally," disguise getting a meal at the mission. Ricky sat down next to me and started talking like he knew me. He ignored my "Sally" persona. Ricky said a few people told him I wanted to meet him. We made a deal. He would sell me an untraceable cell phone. After that, we met at coffee shops. Sometimes when I needed help on a case, or when I needed someone to listen to a conversation, he would do that. I guess you could say our worlds were miles apart. You know what it's like when you work alone. But there's that one person that you can talk to, someone you could tell what's happening, and they 'get' you."

"We talked, we flirted, we drank coffee together. Sometimes I wouldn't see Ricky for a month and sometimes I would see him every day. He was like a magic feel-better potion."

Dan leaned toward her.

"Did you know anything about his past life? I've known Ricky longer than you, and maybe what you didn't know he was a recovering addict. He's probably been clean for six years. In the last couple of months, something happened, and Ricky relapsed. I talked to him about it. I told him I could help him get treatment. You know as well as I do that addicts have to decide when it comes to recovery."

"Ricky wanted to be there, but he knew he wasn't. He told me he hated his life, and he hated oxycodone. I told him I'd help him. We both knew that Pastor Chuck in the mission would've helped him. But he stayed away from people when he was high. So, if you hadn't seen much of him in the last couple of months, it was because he didn't want people to see that he'd relapsed."

"Last week, we talked, and I was worried. Ricky said a few things about not wanting to be here. I told him that God loved him. A few days later, I saw him downtown, and he was high. That was a few days before all this mess started with Huff. You have to know that Ricky was desperate to stop using, but he didn't know if he could do it. Maybe he was thinking about overdosing. Maybe his friendship with you kept him from doing that. I don't know. Ricky liked helping you, and he told me that."

Katie opened her eyes and smiled.

"You think his life was cut short. Maybe he believed what he did was the only answer to his life. I believe Ricky knew what he was doing. God allows divine appointments, and sometimes they aren't the kind of appointments we want to have. It doesn't make it any easier."

Tears poured down Katie's cheeks. She grabbed tissues from her bag.

"I knew something was up with him. I didn't want to think it was drugs."

Dan reached over to his bag and pulled out a small New

Testament. He opened it, shuffled pages, and handed it to her, his finger on Psalm Twenty-Seven.

Katie silently read verses thirteen and fourteen.

"I would have lost heart, unless I believed that I would see the goodness of the Lord in the land of the living. Wait on the Lord; be of good courage, and He shall strengthen your heart, wait I say on the Lord."

"We always lose heart, but seeing God's goodness, we can let Him strengthen us," Dan said.

Katie sat still, letting the words wash over her. After some time, she gave Dan back the New Testament with a teary smile.

"Thanks."

"No worries."

Katie leaned into her seat and stared out the window, seeing nothing. When she thought of Ricky, she felt an emptiness, like a hunger she couldn't fix. A man gave his life for her. It didn't matter he was an addict, or he lived on the edge of criminality. She loved him as a friend, and the ache in her heart for that friendship lost would always be a part of her life. She hungered for the old church she attended growing up. God seemed so real there, while the Bible and Brews Bible study didn't seem to cut it when it came to knowing God. She would make some life changes. Ricky had changed her, and she wanted to make her life count when it came to people. Knowing about God and letting Him be seen in her life were two separate things. She hadn't thought about it much, but she would now.

*Ricky, my friend, I will never forget you.* She turned her face to the window and sobbed.

A while passed, and Dan pulled out his phone to check the time. Katie could see his phone and realized they had about two hours to go to the refuel.

"We've got business to take care of," Prey announced from the seat in front of them.

Katie made a face behind his back.

"I saw that," he said.

"You have eyes behind your head?"

"It's a requirement for special forces," He deadpanned.

"Right, I knew that." Katie arched an eyebrow.

"Couple things to bring you up to speed. Some friends took care of the wrecked SUV at the scene, and they heard on the police radio that the ladies told the cops that someone got hurt, but people took him to the hospital. There wasn't a body, which meant there wasn't a crime, so after a while, they cleared out."

"We will refuel in Lincoln and have a conference call with your friend from Homeland, Matt Dunn. From there, we go to get set up in DC." Prey explained.

Katie wondered for a moment how Prey was so well informed, how he knew Matt's name. Scary man.

"But what can we do if the President won't talk to us, how can we get a message to him?" Katie asked Prey.

"Washington, DC, is like a sieve. Nothing is secret. We're on our own. But the smaller the group, the more flexible we are. Trust is what we have, and it's enough."

"Did you learn that in special forces too?"

"No, my mom taught me that. She's a special force all her own."

Katie smiled. Her mom was all that.

# CHAPTER FORTY-TWO

As they waited to refuel in Lincoln, Dan and Katie decided to put through a conference call to Jim Dunn. He quickly added Matt to the group.

"Matt, you are on the phone with Katie, Dan, and a friend of Dan's, Prey," Jim Dunn announced when the call connected.

"Sit rep on what we have. All the media focus is to cover the death of the Vice President. It would seem reasonable for the President to cancel his speech to the Secret Service. But as far as my friend Glenn Richter can see, since he is still on the active roster for Secret Service, it's still on POTUS's schedule. Huff is probably on the way to DC, and an assassination attempt could take place at this function. Since the Vice President's casket will be on display at the Capitol, there is some downtime for the President as all the media is there. The pitch will be made to him to go forward. It makes sense, and from what I know of the President, he will want to thank the men who have guarded the Vice President so that this speech will be a 'go' for him."

"Matt, are you saying there is no straight-through communication that can reach the President? I have contacts." Prey asked.

"So does Dad. The gatekeepers are intense at this time with the death of the Vice, and more importantly, we don't know who we can trust. There is a full leak of all information coming out of Homeland Security. I did some careful digging, and the request for information about the ballistics report regarding the shooting in the garage, and Katie's gun, came from channels that lead back to the Speaker of the House. Any operation authorized by Homeland Security to provide additional protection for the President at this time would more than likely be denied."

"Can that digging be traced back to you?" Prey leaned forward, focused on Matt's answer.

"No, I have a techie friend who tracked down the email from the Seattle Police Department. He just said it went to an email box for the Speaker of the House's driver, which is odd. I guess you could say that's another way of saying it went directly to the Speaker of the House without there being formal channels."

"Sounds like he didn't want there to be a "there-there." Prey's gray eyes seemed colder.

"Stating the obvious, the President hasn't called me back," Katie said.

"I have an idea, it's a little bit crazy, but unless someone has a better one, we have to get a message to the President. The most important part of the message is that it has to be off the information grid. Once that's done, if we have no response from the President, we are on our own."

"So, what is this ingenious method to get a message to the President?" Katie asked.

"I'm still working on that, but I have a line on how to do it. I had an out-of-car experience this week. The experience brought to mind something I knew from being on the Secret Service detail to the President when he was the Vice. The president's dog Lion had a standing appointment to be groomed once a week. There is an opportunity to attach a message to Lion's collar when he gets groomed, which, as far as I know, is scheduled to happen Monday. I will take care of that."

"I have to ask, how did you come up with the dog idea?" Dan said

"Let's just say I had a transportation problem the other day, and the solution inspired me."

"You *are* going to tell us that story later." Katie chuckled.

"How soon will we land at Ronald Reagan Airport?"

"Will be ready to roll out of the airport at 1730 hours," Prey replied.

"Do you have accommodations in Alexandria?

"Affirmative." Said Prey.

"I think it's important to note that things are going to get more intense. Because we can't use most of our connections to the government, this is going to be an outside-the-box operation. Which means we won't have any backup."

"Matt, you will have all the backup of my company. Just let me know what you need." Jim Dunn firmly entered the conversation.

"Thanks, Dad, it's nice to know we have some professionals helping. Please put Tyrone Johnsen on that team. I will message you guys a layout of the building as much as I know. The location is a new training facility for the Secret Service, just built in Alexandria. The President's speech, as far as Glenn knows, will take place in the outside auditorium. Which means a sniper with Huff's skills could be utilized. We'll use some electronic mapping data of the area to plan where a sniper's nest would be located. I'm going to leave that up to you, Prey, as that is your expertise."

"I have a friend who's a contractor with the Defense Department and wouldn't think it odd if I asked for information on a protection plan for that new facility. He'll probably think of it as an opportunity for business. I'll give him a call, and you guys see if you can come up with some possible locations that Huff might use. My contractor friend should be able to get back to me by the time we are in Alexandria." Matt continued.

"Let's connect at 1830 hours in Alexandria for a planning meeting." Matt disconnected.

"Wheels up in 25 minutes," Prey said.

Katie was frantically typing on her phone.

"Okay, listen, I have an Uber eats that can deliver food and, most importantly, coffee, in 20 minutes, you guys in?"

"You are not ordering girl-food, right?" Dan asked.

Katie death glared at him. Prey observed the standoff.

"I eat any gender of food." Prey chimed in.

Katie threw him a grateful look.

"Surprise me," Dan said carefully.

Katie turned away to order. "Do you have quiche on the menu, yeah we'll take three orders of that. Mocha Breve, and two black drip coffees. Thanks." Feminine food on the menu, Katie smiled wickedly.

The food arrived. Without a beat, Prey pulled his wallet out and paid for it. A dangerous man who also was flush. Something to keep in her girl-brain. He was not hard on the eyes, either. Dan appeared as soon as the food arrived. He reached for a container.

Dan stared at the quiche for a moment, but Prey dived in.

"I love Quiche, all protein, low carb," Prey said between mouthfuls. They stood around the plane and devoured the food. Prey stepped near Katie to do his pre-flight.

Katie avoided eye contact with Dan as she savored her Mocha. Dan headed to the restroom.

"You mind if we have a chat?" Prey said.

This man was not asking. Dan's friend was a dangerous man, but someone she wanted on her side.

"Sure," she said a little nervously.

"Do you find Dan irritating?"

It was not anything Katie expected, and she laughed. "On occasion," with a wry smile.

He bent down and pulled up one of his pant legs to a spot above the knee.

"Do you know what that is?"

"A gunshot wound."

"Yeah, Dan pulled me out of a firefight in Iraq. No way he should have even tried, but he got there and carried me to the Medivac helo. No matter how many favors he asks me, there is no way I can repay that."

"Understood."

"Just wanted you to know we have a connection. What you ladies call your BFF?"

Katie smiled. "And?"

"I heard your heart-to-heart with him. And that's all good. But you have to be feeling some strong hate right now toward Huff. I imagine you are thinking that when we get to DC, you are wanting to be on the end of things that make sure he pays for killing your friend?"

It was a question, and Katie looked down. She had tried to tamp down the rage at this man who took the life of her friend. But Prey knew.

"When we get there, there is one mission objective. Save the president. If Huff gets away, while no one wants that, the President must live. If your focus is the President, you are on the team, if not, you're off."

Katie looked at him.

"He is a psychopath. Killing your friend made no difference to him, nor would it make any difference to him to kill you. If you think by killing him, you will feel better. You won't. Your friend is gone.

Accept he is gone. Be glad you knew him. If by some miracle, we can pull off saving the President, I will go after Huff. It doesn't mean I will find him. Are you going to be okay if he is in the wind?"

"I do hate him. I know in my mind that trying to get revenge is not going to make any difference. I am sorting that out. I will let God take his vengeance on this man because it will happen. I'm not emotionally where I need to be, Prey, but I will not go after him. You seem to know a lot about Huff. Have you encountered him before?"

"I can neither affirm nor deny."

"So that's a yes. What do you know?"

There was a long moment that Prey appraised Katie, a look that made her uncomfortable.

"He's not just a paid assassin. He's a serial killer. In many of his targeted kills over the years, there have been unsolved murders in the same area. His MO is to leave no evidence, no real similarity to the murders, no trophies taken. But in every incidence of a hired kill attributed to him, there are murders. We know he kills for pleasure. This man is wickedness walking."

"As to my experience with his history, I cannot say. I am retired from the Rangers, but I am called in to work an off-the-book operation. Let's say for conversation, that Huff has been a project of a certain agency for many years. I have worked with that agency and know of him from that arena."

Katie gave Prey a thoughtful look. Finally, she asked, "Do you have a real name?"

Without a beat, he said, "Everyone usually does. For your safety, call me Prey. By the way, Dan's not always irritating. You might like him after a while. Anything going on there I should know about?"

"Oh, so besides being an all-around bad guy to mess with, you are a relationship counselor on the side?" Katie raised an eyebrow.

"Hey, he's my buddy, what can I say."

"Even though I don't know you at all, I should spill like we're besties?"

"I did save your life." Prey leaned in with a slow smile.

Katie made a face at him. "I always think men are more interested in gossip than women. Fine. We haven't always got along. But I know he is one of the best private investigators in Seattle. We are currently working on a case together. Except for the country music, I like him, mostly. Being a private investigator means you work alone, but when you can share information with someone and throw ideas around, it can give you enough insight to find the answer you need. Time will tell if we keep sharing cases."

"Your turn, what did he tell you about me?"

Prey gave the sign to indicate his lips were sealed.

"I spill, and you don't? Don't pull that super-secret black-ops stuff. I told you things."

Prey leaned in close, and she could smell his aftershave. He was scary, and Katie wanted to take a step back, but she held her ground

"Dan and I are BFF's. Would you spill on your BFF?" Prey said in his measured, dangerous tone. He grinned and walked back to the plane.

Dan walked over to Katie and looked at Prey's retreating backside.

"You make a friend?"

"He's an interesting man."

"He tends to be irritating."

Katie stifled a giggle. "I didn't notice."

Prey returned from his last flight check. "Time to climb, folks."

# CHAPTER FORTY-THREE

The Speaker of the House checked the phone in the car. At this time tomorrow, he could be the President of the United States, and he worked to focus on the last few details of the plan because he couldn't allow the emotion of reaching his goal to cloud his thinking. There would be time to bask in his power soon.

By now, he should have had a situation report. He tapped on the window of his driver. The driver passed him a cell phone in a plastic bag. It annoyed him to have to ask for information. His asset should have reported any completions promptly. Even if there seemed to be a connection to his boss, he intended to make this asset disappear. Isn't that why there was a CIA? He would be in charge. A few words said personally where no taping was present would take care of this man. Again, he needed there to be no loose ends, no ties back to him. This asset had too much baggage and knew more than he should. Accidents happened, and he would make sure the moment he was sworn in, a termination order would find the asset when he did not expect it. That would give him the leverage he needed. But beyond influence? This asset, the most dangerous assassin in the world, could not be allowed to live.

He texted.

Report?

There was a pause, which irritated him. The timetable was in motion, and so far, the asset had not been punctual.

> Completed assignment on the companion to the
> woman. Her connection is severed. Will complete the
> woman after Assignment Oval. No danger of
> contamination or leak.

Good, that at least was done. There had been no press coverage of the death, but he didn't care. If the asset said it was finished, he didn't need explanations. Besides, he would have to verify completion to get paid. So, at this point, he could afford his involvement to be distant. The text continued.

> Presently on route to Culpeper Regional Airport.
> Rendezvous in Alexandria with the team in three hours.
> Will proceed to Assignment Oval location in early AM
> for a status check. Assumed that the first incomplete
> will remain in the local state, the site with relative
> verified. Completion after RED operation.

At this point, the asset seemed to have covered all the bases. There were loose ends, but the lack of concern by the asset assured the Speaker that these were unimportant. But was that true? If his boss concurred, he needed to pay attention to that inconsistency. Already he had seen how much leniency his boss gave to this asset.

If the boss didn't want to be questioned about this asset, he would be suspect if he raised concerns. At this stage, playing dumb had served him with a reputation of not being smart enough to think of a different plan than the one the boss fed him. He understood he was to go to the White House, accept the mantle of President until the boss had eliminated one other between him and the Office of President, then as a good soldier. He would step down due to feigned illness. But that wouldn't happen. He had carefully fostered a relationship with the director of the CIA. He would call in favors.

He made a decision. Until asked, he would not give a bad report about any uncompleted assignments. Time was short, and now all the planning of the past few months must not be distracted by a few trivial details. No information meant there were no problems, and that message counted in the final days. His work at maintaining the façade of the menial soldier, loyal to the man leading this operation was complete. Only he knew of his deception. While he did not trust his boss, he had also made arrangements there. Surprises were unfortunate for those who didn't plan for them.

His hand shook a little as he handed the phone to his driver. He took a deep breath and steadied himself as his driver turned to respond.

"Thank you, Mr. Speaker."

Soon, thank you, *Mr. President.*

# CHAPTER FORTY-FOUR

Terrell Huff breathed deep. The Fool had not asked him to verify his kill, which would have been difficult since there wasn't a body. He surmised that Homeland or someone had a cleanup crew remove it. If Homeland removed the body, he would verify it through channels. In two days, that wouldn't matter. The President of the United States would be dead, and his boss would become President.

He celebrated the win that he had killed the woman's companion. He walked through the kill in his mind. Sadness. No trophy photo. Prey, the interrupter, had interfered. He would now replace what he interrupted, and the trophy for him would speak for two. He leaned back, hands behind his head, eyes closed, and savored how he would destroy this man.

Finally, let go of his reverie, and thought about the man killed. While he couldn't prove this was the man at the hospital, there was no reason to believe that he wasn't. That would make sense why another assassin named Prey would show up. The man killed had some connection and had called this man to help. But with his death, the man Prey would no longer be in play. He would know no details and would fade back to where he came. Alaska. He already knew of Prey's home location, and he licked his lips. He liked hunting there.

The woman could not be a connection. A local private

investigator, and while her link to homeland security agents was not in evidence, it was unimportant now as her partner had been eliminated.

In a week, he would return for a short stay in Seattle and erase her small part in this drama. For a moment, his finger caressed his phone. He wanted to look, to see his accomplishments. But not yet, his mouth watered in anticipation.

He had failed to mention to the Fool, the appearance of Prey. No need, the connection had been severed. For the first time in many years, his breathing quickened, and even though he planned to kill Prey, he unconsciously bit at his lip. He had heard of Prey's reputation and that his skill as a warrior. And for once, he was glad he had not had to prove his skills superior yet. Prey would take some careful planning to terminate, but once done, even his abilities would be rendered useless.

He needed to go to the location in Alexandria and complete his set up for Tuesday's RED operation. Just thinking about the plan brought a sense of accomplishment. He'd spent the better part of the month securing the location and preparing his shot, and he felt supremely confident in this. Making a long-distance kill shot required a lot of planning, a lot of information in the correct weapon. He had procured a .338 Lapua and an excellent spotting scope to view the damage he intended to inflict.

His associate had assured him that Matt was with the elder Dunn in Washington state, which meant they were neutralized for now. He would not interfere with the Assignment Oval.

Overthinking slowed his process down. He would take care of loose ends in perfect timing. The Fool had not asked about them because Huff's reputation had stifled any concerns.

He allowed one last sweep in his mind, and the only thing that kept showing up was the readiness of the man Prey. No matter, he swept him aside. No one had bested him in hand to hand, and this man wouldn't have done it. If he met him again, he would be prepared, and whether he took him out by stealth or not, it did not matter. That man would not bother or interfere with him again. He'd do him for free in Alaska, the perfect vacation.

# CHAPTER FORTY-FIVE

The men moved about the house, always on the phone and talked. She drank coffee and nibbled at the breakfast someone made at five this morning, now an hour old in the comfortable kitchen of the three-bedroom rambler in the outskirts of Alexandria. Prey's explanation of his ability to use the house indicated to Katie that it was a safe house used in connection with some shadowy operations, owned by a corporation, not traceable. For her, that only contributed to Prey's dangerous man status.

She listened to the men in the room. They all knew the desperate nature of the plan they devised. Save the life of the president, but do it without involving the Secret Service, who would look on them as conspirators. Search for and find the man who planned to kill the President. A man who had eluded all national and international law enforcement for over twenty years. Was it impossible? Maybe they believed it because the alternative was unacceptable.

"Katie, you with us?" Dan asked.

"Yeah, I zoned for a minute."

Katie saw Dan and Prey exchange a look.

"Wait—I'm exhausted, but all of you are the same. Matt is supposed to be lying flat somewhere, resting his leg, and none of us have had much sleep in the last few days. It doesn't matter. If we cannot find a way to save the President, we face a future that we cannot imagine. So please, let's get done what we need to get done. Worry about the toll it has taken on all of us when this is over."

Prey's look was speculative, and Dan nodded in agreement.

"Katie is right. We have to get through the plan. This is Tyrone Johnsen. He is security from my dad's company. And this is Tommy." Matt explained.

Katie looked at the teen, standing in front of Matt. What was a child doing here?

"Tommy looks young. Just so happens he is an IT wizard and is working off community service time for hacking Homeland. He took a week's vacation for me, so he is off-the-books. He will do things that most normal people couldn't."

Matt continued, "Right now, Huff thinks I'm in Washington State. My brother happens to be my look-alike in real life. He flew in a private plane and is now limping around with my dad. For anyone who didn't know us well, they would assume I'm there. That means we have some small advantage over whoever is running Terrell Huff. He probably reported from his associates in Washington state, that I am not in the picture here in DC. The incident with Glenn was reported, but my presence there was not noted, and it appears they were only there for Glenn."

"Matt, any idea who is running Huff? You and Glenn have a theory?" Prey asked.

Matt looked over at Glenn Richter. "You want to bring everyone up-to-date?"

"There is a succession to the Presidency if the President dies in office. Everyone knows that the Vice President is next in line. As everyone knows, he died this week. Next in line is the Speaker of the House of Representatives, after him, the President pro tempore of the Senate, then the Secretary of State. If the President is taken out, it's the Speaker of the House who takes over for the President. Matt has indicated there is a line of information leaks coming from the Speaker's office that point to knowledge of the attack on him and his partner in Seattle. That indicates that the Speaker is involved in an operation to kill the President. But we don't think the conspiracy stops there."

"But if the President is killed, he's the successor? How can there be more people involved beyond him?" Dan asked.

"Because if something also happened to the Speaker, the President pro tempore of the Senate would be next, but what most people don't know is that he is too ill to assume the office. After him is the Secretary of State who is overseas at a sensitive North Korean Summit. Just a historical note, during Kennedy's assassination, his Secretary of State was also overseas. If something were to happen to the Secretary overseas, the next man to assume the presidency would be a disaster to this nation of incalculable proportions."

"Who is next in line?" Prey asked.

"The Secretary of Treasury."

Prey leaned forward his face grim, "Grigory Volkov."

Matt continued, "Years ago Volkov's CIA connections supposedly uncovered a plot to kill Vice President Baxter. When he became the President, Volkov was on the President's shortlist for a cabinet position, especially since he had been working his way up the ladder in the Treasury Department from a lot of retirements and "unexpected" deaths. People were opposed to his appointment, but the President felt he owed him something."

"However," he said, looking at Katie, "he has long been suspected to be a Russian operative by those in the intelligence community."

The room went quiet.

"I get that, and it's a concern, but aren't you counting out the Secret Service?" Dan asked.

"Many of the men who served President Baxter on his Vice President detail a few years back are all dead except Matt and me, and we have both escaped recent attempts on our lives. Some of these men retired but died not long after that retirement, so their deaths went unnoticed except by old friends like myself. Additionally, the new detail assigned to POTUS has seen almost a complete do-over in the last year and a half. New men who appear competent, but who lean heavily on management to guide their protection since they do not have experience in the field. The Secret Service has a new director, and he is unknown to many. He either owes someone politically for his appointment and is taking orders from that person, or lacks any knowledge about a plan to put the President in harm's way."

"If I did believe all of this was a bunch of crazy coincidences, that belief ended when someone tried to take me out last week. There are few experienced agents enough to have their antenna's up on POTUS's speech at the new Secret Service training building. Who would think an assassination could take place in the house of the people who protect the President? It's brilliant. It's unexpected, and with the loss of the Vice President, the world's media is focused on preparation for his state funeral. I have never been a conspiracy theorist. I'm not one now, but I believe I can see this train coming," Glenn's face was a stern mask.

"We are on the same page. I compared notes with Prey last night after we arrived, and we have a logistical op plan. Partly logical, partly not. Every electronic device, including drones and cameras, will be everywhere. That makes it necessary to appear differently on camera or hidden since we all are known to Huff. We don't want him blowing the whistle to his team leaders if he saw any of us. There are a few things that work in our favor. Here's a skeleton plan," Matt explained.

"Glenn attends the event. He hasn't retired yet, and he is an invitee. He will be our eyes there. He will give indications of changes in the event and any signals he sees."

Matt reached down to a package at his feet. "Cell phones with wireless buds are here too. If you see anything at your assigned locations, constantly update everyone." Text if you can't talk, when you call, conference. Everyone clear on communication?"

"Dan, you have the least exposure on face recognition. We have something that will alter that recognition even more. Prey will update you on that. You will be hunting a sniper's nest, using the coordinates Prey obtained. Both of you will be searching in a specific area that could target the platform from where POTUS will be speaking."

"Katie has seen Huff several times and, as such, will be a spotter in the area, but in a way, he won't be able to see you."

Katie looked at him. "And how am I invisible, a new black ops secret?"

"Oh, better than that." Matt grinned. "I'm sending you in a new concealment vehicle that I used this week. Katie, you will be traveling in a bicycle dog carrier, powered by Tyrone as he is searching for Huff. Fortunately for us, there is a dog park near this building. The area is crawling with folks bringing their dogs to exercise there. You will have a spotting scope and complete concealment inside the carrier."

"Thank goodness for advanced technology," Katie said dryly.

"We have drones and have tapped into a few local cameras feeds due to my dad's company. I will be here, monitoring all those with Tommy, and coordinating efforts in the field. I wish I could be out there, but dragging my leg is too obvious, and someone has to coordinate. Feedback anyone?"

"What do we do when we find him?" Katie asked.

An uncomfortable silence.

"He and I have a conversation to finish," said Prey.

As she looked over the room, it was clear his ability to end that conversation was plain to the men in the room.

*Would they find him in time?*

# CHAPTER FORTY-SIX
## MATT DUNN

Larabell, a Labradoodle in need of grooming, had come their way via a quick transaction on Craigslist. Now all they had to do introduce Larabell to Lion. That included teaching spycraft to Tommy.

"Tommy, the key is to get the note on Lion just under her chin. A little bit of superglue, and stick it in her fur. The President loves to scratch her there so that he will feel the note. Lion should be coming out when you are going in, so let Larabell go, and she will hopefully do her duty, run up to Lion and sniff. When she does, get that note where it needs to be."

"Okay," Tommy said doubtfully. "Not sure how this will go. What if the Secret Service guy gets in the way?"

"Fall, pretend you sprained your ankle. These guys are trained to lend a hand. They will help you. Take the opportunity to pet Lion while you have the chance and attach the note. Get it done."

Tommy hitched his loose jeans up and jammed on his ballcap lower on his head to perhaps cover a nervous twitch. He headed into the shop with Larabell. Matt could see the Secret Service vehicle parked in the lot. One agent was probably in with Lion, the other in the car. It all seemed reasonable, and he remembered having had the duty once. He scrunched down in the seat and pretended to check his phone.

Slow minutes passed. The shop door opened, and a Secret Service guy came out with Lion and marched to the car. Matt again busied himself with his phone. They pulled out, and a few minutes later, Tommy came out without Larabell.

"Dude, the deed is done," Tommy said, grinning.

"No trouble?"

"Nope, Lion came over to sniff Larabell, and I petted him and attached the note. No one noticed. I gave the lady cash for the grooming and a fake name and number. I guess they have a new dog to keep now. Some lady gushed over her, so I don't feel bad. She's a nice dog. They'll find her a home."

Matt was pleased. The operation had gone off without a snag so far. The only hitch remained if the President didn't have time to pet his dog. Once again, they would have struck out on getting word to him that an assassination attempt was going down tomorrow.

Matt texted the team.

Operation Pet accomplished. Sit-rep?

A text came from Katie.

Lots of activity near the dog park. Cars that seem to be government issue, men who are subtly patrolling the area. A little old lady tried to look in my carrier. Tyrone tried to repel her with a line that his dog bites. But that didn't work. So, he smacked her hand with a dog toy. She might have been an agent, but after she hit Tyrone with her walking stick, we figured a normal old lady.

Matt knew Katie's humor was intentional to lighten the stress load.

Dan checked in for himself and Prey.

We have made progress, eliminated three buildings in
the strike zone—about twenty to go. Public Works
uniforms worked as we have routinely checked street
lights with no attention on us.

Glenn was watching the monitors while Matt and Tommy had
their mission.

Nothing unusual had been on monitors yet. Traffic and some
pedestrians. All moving, nothing suspicious. Matt sent a group text.

Thanks all, sit-rep every 2 hours or if suspicious
activity.

Matt chewed on his pen. No visuals on Huff, and even though
they had eliminated some buildings as possible sniper nests, they
would not get through all twenty buildings before tomorrow. Luck
or *something* would have to happen to find it. He was sure Huff had
already checked his position early this morning, and maybe they had
missed him. Next, he would turn Tommy loose with a drone to give
them overhead vision capacity. Not sure if someone would shut
down his drone, but Tommy looked the part of a kid checking out
his toy. An eye in the sky could cut their search time in half.

As he drove back to the house, he scanned the sky for small drones
from under his baseball cap bill. He spotted a few—Homeland
Security by way of Secret Service preparing for a visit from POTUS.
His sunglasses and cap covered his searching eyes, but the hair on the
back of his arms raised as he watched the electronic eyes cover him—
time to get back and not draw any attention.

He could not afford to lose this game of hide-and-seek.

# CHAPTER FORTY-SEVEN

Huff lay down in his shooting position on the roof. He looked through the rifle scope to where POTUS would stand—a white spot marked on the stage for the podium about 800 yards from his position. Crystal clear.

An hour before execution time tomorrow, he would be in place to test the wind, sight where POTUS would stand, and calculate how much movement the man usually made during the speech. Huff had studied previous addresses, and POTUS often stayed close to his teleprompters. But whether he did this time or not, Huff was confident he would make the shot.

On his way to his sniper nest this morning, he noticed Homeland Security personnel patrolled the area. His excuse from their scrutiny rested on the security contractor badge stuck on his jacket. Because the death of VPOTUS had required many agents to return to DC for added security at the Capitol, it made sense to the bean counters to pay for additional contracted protection for the President. He loved the irony.

His handler had made arrangements, so no one questioned his approach. He fingered his contractor badge and carried his workman's bag confidently. Both the disassembled gun and spotting scope fit comfortably inside.

Rehearsal time. Steady breaths. Half out, hold, and squeeze between the heartbeats. Put the gun down and roll left to the spotting scope. Verify the President was down. Fluid motion, and all things he had done many times. He would proceed to the next target when confirmed.

He disassembled the weapon and stored it in the cardboard box left on the roof for him. He noted the container with the pop-up canopy. His plan included using it as an HVAC construction ruse. A few "Keep Out" signs placed around it kept the curious away while the pop up insured no satellite pictures of a shooter on the roof. The HVAC signs were a plausible excuse for the canopy conveniently located over a few air vents on the roof near the edge.

He would walk the area near his sniper nest in the morning. If any word had leaked of an attack on POTUS, an operative could be in the area. Since the government was a sieve of information, no one was impervious to information leaks. Even though his handlers had held this plan closely, if he walked the area, he would spot them. And if necessary, he would remove them. Spies were a part of the game. His plan? Always be prepared. Perfection was not the rule when it came to government action, which is why they hired him. Perfection was *his* rule.

He carried a small air gun with a dart dipped in succinylcholine. It was his preferred method to kill as it was a neuromuscular paralytic drug, and paralyzed all muscles in the body, the critical muscle being the lungs. He had seen it asphyxiate a person in less than a minute. The drug was fast-acting and metabolized in the body as untraceable, unremarkable body chemicals. Death was agonizing because the victim remained awake, but that was a quiet bonus. Coroners always listed a heart attack as the cause of death. His followup demanded he approached the victim, pulled out the dart, and inject in the same dart hole a killing dose. On several occasions, he pretended to yell in panic for those around to call 911. Chaos always surrounded the person who had collapsed, which made it easy for him to disappear. No one had ever remembered him, and he was never the person who called 911. The key to using this method meant his targets died a death that appeared to be from natural causes.

He would check for suspicious personnel, and look for anything that might slow his escape. He went over his timetable for the removal of the second target. Traffic could be the only problem, but with a motorcycle, he had ensured that he would have the mobility needed. He would strap his bag on the storage rack he had installed on the cycle. One small stop in an adjacent park for a pickup and change, and he would be on schedule to go north to DC and remove the Fool.

Even with traffic, the trip from Alexandria would be a maximum of fifty minutes. It would be at least an hour from the time the President would be declared dead, to mobilize the government heads to bring the Speaker of the House to the White House to swear him in as the new president. Plenty of time to get in position. Only the Speaker would not make it to the swearing-in; he would die of a heart attack en route. The heads of state would be forced to go through the list of those who replace the president. With the Secretary of State out of town and the President of the Senate ill, eventually, they would call upon the Secretary of the Treasury to take up the mantle of President. That plan would all fall into place shortly after he killed POTUS tomorrow at 10 AM.

His associates would place a plastic tent over a fire hydrant with a sign stating "Maintenance Service" on the route from The Speaker's office to the White House. The driver knew to lower the window when they arrived at the appointed hydrant. He chose the air gun with the dart for his removal method, which would be in his bag. Once he stuck the Fool with the dart, the driver would pull over, and motion for help. Huff would enter the car, remove the dart, administer a killing dose, and the world stage would change forever in a matter of minutes.

His plan accounted for foreseeable variables. He hesitated when Prey popped into his mind. He realized his subconscious was warning him of this man. Prey had prevented the killing of the woman. If some unknown variable had placed this man here in Alexandria, he would carefully look for him on his morning reconnaissance stroll. He was not a superstitious man, but he trusted his premonitions, and he was edgy. Prey had triggered his survival instincts. However, whenever he felt doubt in his skills, he had a remedy for that doubt.

He pulled out his phone and inserted a micro SD card from his wallet. He tapped to the storage files. He scrolled through picture after picture of his kills. Some paid, some not. He had never been close to being caught. And each of these targets had been eliminated. He lingered over the ones he had done for free. It took a while to page through the 217 pictures, but he savored them. Trophies.

He would make his most crucial kills tomorrow and would begin a life of legitimacy. The beauty of it all? No one would know, and no one could stop him. And if Prey tried, he would just become another picture on his SD card. Reluctantly he pulled the card from his phone, deleted the temporary storage files, and put the card away in his wallet.

He smiled. Prey was nothing, a nobody.

# CHAPTER FORTY-EIGHT

Katie was scanning the crowd of walkers with her spotting scope. For a couple of hours, she had been at it, and her back cramped from the carrier. The urgency to find Huff tugged at her. But so far, she had come up empty in her search, as had the whole team.

Her eyes focused on a walker. Something seemed familiar about this man's stride. All she could see was his back. His pace pulled her gaze toward him as he walked through the crowd. Purposeful and intense, he moved through people like a knife. Before she could speak and alert the team she has seen something, he was gone. Was it Huff? Quickly she texted.

> I think I saw something. I only saw the back of a man walking, but I have noticed that walk before, in the parking garage in Seattle. Five seconds ago. We can't take the dog carrier after him. What should we do?

> Matt: Where are you?

> Katie: Old Town North, the end of Montgomery St.

> Matt: It's within range of the Secret Service building amphitheater. Logical for him to be there. Katie, how unsure are you?

Katie: Really? No idea. I almost didn't say anything. But it was *familiar*.

Dan: Katie has a great Spidey sense.

Matt: Stay sharp, I'm sending the kid in with his drone, Huff's never seen him. He has the best chance of getting pictures of nearby buildings.

Katie waited as they circled on the bike. She was constricted in the dog carrier, even if it was for a large dog. However, her biggest problem at the moment came from an insistent bladder.

Her every sense was on high alert. Perhaps Huff had circled behind them? Like a cat, she twisted in the carrier and put the spotting scope up to the tiny hole in the back. Nothing. Just a few folks strolled in the busy lunchtime crowd. She breathed deeply; adrenaline flowed through her bloodstream. It was going to take the kid at least five minutes to get in position and if it was Huff, he had disappeared. Minutes dragged by as they waited for an update.

Katie spoke in a low tone to Tyrone. "Hey, we need to do more than circle the block, we are going to get noticed. Take a left to the end of the road and go into Tide Lock Park. We make ourselves obvious if we hang here. People walk dogs in the park."

"Copy that."

Katie squirmed in the carrier.

"And I need a bathroom break. Pull under some trees, and I will hop out."

Tyrone grunted in return. If he approved or disapproved, he would never say. A definite improvement over Dan who would have run a non-stop commentary on the best of country music. Gag. As uncomfortable as the carrier was, at least it was a country-music-free space.

She felt Tyrone pull over and noticed the carrier darkened, likely under shady trees. Carefully she looked out. Tyrone dismounted the bike and put his considerable bulk behind the door of the carrier. A tree blocked the view from the front. The man knew his stuff. She half fell, half crawled out and stood up — no one in sight. The park sign pointed to the restrooms ahead. She signaled to Tyrone and headed that way.

Two women speed-walked past her. Pretending to read her phone, she kept her head down. When she washed her hands, she tossed the paper towel in the garbage, but something unusual caught her eye. A clear plastic bag that looked like it held clothes. She pulled gloves from her pocket and plucked the bag out. It was tied shut, but she unraveled it.

Woman's clothes, a wig, glasses, and running shoes; the kind of clothes a woman might wear in the business area near the park. Why would this be in the garbage? She laid out the garments and snapped three or four pictures. Her ears were tuned to listen for incoming occupants, so when she heard footsteps, she grabbed the bag, tied it, and put it back in the trash. She slid off her gloves and put them back in her pocket. Her eyes scanned left and right as she left the building. An older woman approached the entrance. Katie held her phone in a reading position in front of her face and pretended to focus on the screen as she trudged back toward Tyrone.

What if the contents of the bag were a getaway outfit? Or one used to approach the area in disguise? It would be interesting to find out the trash removal schedule for this park. Could trash be collected only twice a week? Something stored temporarily in the garbage was ingenious. Either way, Huff dressed as a woman would be doubly hard to identify if you were looking for a man. It could be significant. At the least, she could check the local garbage schedule and peruse nearby bathrooms. Besides, it provided an excuse for a continued ride in the carrier.

Was a bathroom break the lucky clue? She didn't believe in coincidence. She had seen so often in her job as a PI that God seemed to be in the little pieces of partial answers that later added up to the whole picture. They had nothing, but maybe this was a small piece to the puzzle. They were running out of time.

# CHAPTER FORTY-NINE
## 10 PM Alexandria

"We have debriefed on everything, but so far, Katie's possible sighting and bathroom info are all we have. Tomorrow at ten AM, the President speaks, and we have no idea where Huff will take his shot to kill POTUS. Ideas, anyone?" Matt said tensely.

Katie looked around the room. These men were better trained than she. They knew the military protocol, and yet, they lacked street smarts.

"One thing we do know, Huff thinks outside the box. We sent a message to the President; I left a voice mail. Any chance that either of those things got through? Matt, did you leave a backdoor way for the President to let you know he got the message?"

Matt was silent.

"Oh, so you did. No need to say it, we get it. But you haven't heard back. Otherwise, you would be sitting here with a mysterious smile. Let's say; the note did get through. But for whatever reason, maybe security, President Baxter is not going to respond. So, for just a moment, think. If the President does know, how can we help *him* locate Huff? Maybe it's not about us taking Huff out, what if we draw Huff into the open? We stop playing by the rule book and set up our own rules?"

"Wonder Woman. Girl, you are a country song looking to

happen." Dan burst out into the tune from *Jolene*. "Katie, Katie, please don't take my man just because you can!"

Katie sighed loudly.

"Listening." Prey tried to hide a smile.

"The playbook is that we are hiding, not letting Huff know we are here and that we are hunting him. But what if we do let him know? The speech is set at 10 AM. What would the normal sniper do, say at 7 AM?" Katie asked.

"Reconnaissance, check the perimeter of the operation." Prey responded.

"He would be looking for what, exactly?"

"People who would stop him, people who would blow the assignment."

"Us? Right?"

Prey narrowed his eyes.

"What if we wander the streets, near where we have focused on a possible location. We flush Huff out, and follow him to his sniper nest?"

"We stand out in the open and let a world-class assassin take a shot at us?" Matt asked incredulously.

"No, we make mistakes. We try not to be obvious, or Huff gets it's a trap. Hopefully, he'll see us looking for him and slip away. It throws him off his game. Set the Kid up with three drones going at once, anything to spot Huff seeing us, trying to follow us. I think one thing we all know. We are not going to find him before 10 AM; We are not going to find him unless we do something different. What is the one thing this man loves to do? Kill. So, we give him a chance to do the thing he loves doing. Why wouldn't he take the chance? The only carrot we have is us."

Prey leaned forward.

"Last night, when all you were sleeping, I studied what's known about Huff's techniques. One thing that has been consistent with political assassinations attributed to him, most of his victims died of heart attacks. That would point to a drug called Succinylcholine, sometimes just called "Suc." It paralyzes the victim, specifically the victim's lungs. The victim can't breathe. A full dose can kill in under a minute. But it has to be injected."

"He got that close to all his victims? Close enough to inject them with a syringe?" Dan asked.

"I would assume. Maybe Huff used an air gun with a dart. There would be enough of the drug to begin the process, but maybe not enough to kill. He'd have to get close enough when the victim collapsed to inject a killing dose."

"And no one ever saw him do that?"

"He sets up his assassinations. He makes sure no cameras work in the area of his kill. Wasn't that true about Seattle? Before the incident, lots of videos, but during his mission, which is part of his MO, there is no video of his kill. He hasn't been caught for twenty years because he is that good."

"So, we look for Huff, and he has a dart gun that can kill us in less than a minute, and we do what, let him pick one of us off? Maybe this is a bad idea," Katie said.

Prey responded. "When I challenged Huff on the street in Seattle after he had killed Katie's friend, he looked off base for a second. He didn't expect to see me, and he recognized my name, one that has made the circles in black ops. I showed up unexpectedly in Seattle. His antennas are up; he would look for *me*."

"So, we let him kill you?" Dan asked in mock innocence.

"Yeah, that's about it."

"Do we have a better plan?" Katie asked weakly.

"There is not an antidote for Suc, but if you ventilate the victim, in ten minutes the dose, would wear off and I could breathe on my own. As long as I'm on oxygen, I don't die. If I draw him out and he hits me with a dart, someone will need to spook him away from injecting me. A medic gets me ventilated, and everyone else follows Huff. We'd want to do it about 8:45 AM, close enough to his need to get to his sniper position, but not time enough to administer a killing dose to me before he gets in place to take his shot. Besides, he will trust the Suc to take me out because no one would know I would need to be ventilated to live." Prey explained.

"We're going to need a Medic with intubation experience and the equipment close enough to get to me within 20-30 seconds. After intubation, in ten minutes, I would be recovered and in twenty minutes ready to move. But he wouldn't know that, and *we* would know the location of his sniper nest."

"How do we stop him from injecting you if he decides to kill you? He will get to you in less than five seconds with a syringe. We can't shoot him in a crowd, and we have no way of proving if we do shoot him that he intended to shoot the President." Katie asked.

"We use a weapon that doesn't look like a weapon," Dan said.

"Care to elaborate?" Matt asked.

"I played baseball in college, had a few offers for professional ball. My fastball was about 85 MPH; sometimes, I got up to 90. I decided on a military career as baseball was iffy at best. So, instead of a gun, I have a few baseballs in my pocket. I hit Huff in the head with one, and ring his bell. Happens so fast no one knows what happened, no sound and nothing bloody like a shot or a knife. Except Huff has a huge headache, he knows he was attacked, and he gets out of there."

Katie stared at Dan. "I know someone has to say this. So I will. What if you miss?"

"Moi? Katie-girl, that is not going to happen. Prey, you trust me?"

Prey looked thoughtful. "It could work."

"I can get the technician there, with the right equipment. I'll make a call," Matt said.

Katie sensed the intensity in the room, but as she looked at the men, their faces revealed something.

Hope.

# CHAPTER FIFTY

At four AM, Katie couldn't sleep, so she crept into the kitchen and made a cup of coffee. She bent to search for some half and half in the fridge, and when she stood, she noticed Dan leaning against the counter.

"Hey partner, you didn't use all the cream, did ya?"

"Saved you a dab."

Dan shuffled over to the Keurig and started his cup. He looked at Katie. "So those dark circles mean you didn't sleep."

Katie sipped her coffee. "I guess I would feel better if I didn't have this great idea that might get Prey killed."

"Don't worry about Prey. He is a hard man to kill. Matt seems to have all the connections to make sure he won't die, and honestly, none of us had any better ideas. Speaking of Matt, he let me get my phone out of phone jail to check any texts, and I have some info on our case, the history mystery."

Katie tilted her head, "Do tell."

"I reached out to my connections. I have a friend who is a geologist at the Department of Natural Resources in Olympia. He specializes in minerals, and has a little handy dandy machine that can locate gold."

"And you were going to tell me about this when?"

"When some world-class assassin was not trying to kill the President or us."

Katie stifled a smile and raised an eyebrow.

"So?"

Dan reached into his pocket and pulled out the phone. He tapped on a text message.

I found GOLD. Call me.

"Whoa doggies, did you call?"

"Slow down. I read this message like last night at midnight, and its 4:10 AM, That's why we're talking about it. I had to tell *my* partner about the development in our case. We should pair up today, as we're about to be rich. I'll watch your six, you watch mine, and let's get back to the other Washington in one piece so we can collect our commission!"

Something warm seemed to spring from her insides, and it wasn't hot coffee. Katie stared at him a minute and impulsively hugged him.

"I know what you are doing. You're distracting me. It won't work, but thanks."

Dan flashed her that movie-star grin. He wasn't a bad guy. They had connection, not chemistry, exactly, but a bond. Partners. She liked that idea going forward. Who knew beyond that?

"No country music at all today, and don't hum it either."

"Moi? Katie, girl, we are all business today. Mojo will be needed when we get close to the gold."

Matt appeared at the door, "Coffee? And Dan, sorry, but I need to confiscate your cell again. We can't have people tracing us to this location."

Right behind, Matt, Tyrone, and Prey came looking for coffee. Prey nodded pleasantly, but Tyrone looked dangerous. Without a word, Katie handed him a cup, and his scowl slightly improved. The man had no sense of humor at all.

"Hey, Katie and I are going to pair up today," Dan explained.

"That works. Tyrone, you and the kid, are with me."

Tyrone grabbed out bacon and eggs from the fridge and started breakfast. No one got in his way.

"Fifteen minutes, and we will debrief and head out. I have some intel to share."

Prey grabbed some gluten-free English muffins from the freezer. Katie was surprised but gave him a thumbs-up as she grabbed one for the toaster. Prey gave her his slow smile. Her BFF would say good-looking men surrounded her. But would they all make it through the day? Katie leaned on the counter and prayed silently for God's protection and Huff's capture.

Katie carried her bacon and eggs into the living room. Matt started the sit-rep.

"We have enough info from discreet inquires by Prey and drone reconnaissance to narrow things down to four buildings where Huff might set up. Prey will position himself in the center of those buildings, and the medic will be within 20 steps of him at all times.

Katie and Dan will be on the north side, Tyrone, myself, and the Kid will be on the south side. A few men from my dad's security team will be scattered throughout, spotting if they can. It's 4:45 now. We want to be in position by 6:00. Please utilize the clothing we have to minimize your identification from facial recognition. Dan, you will find an assortment of baseballs in a pile. Glenn will be on-site to give us updates about the President and his speech. Keep your earbuds in and relay *any information,* no matter how trivial. We will have only one chance to stop this, so let's keep alert. If any of you are praying people, you might want to do that." Matt added.

Tyrone cleared his throat, "I would like to pray."

The group was silent, and Katie felt the shock she supposed the rest of the team did, as Tyrone did not seem the praying type.

"Lord, keep everyone safe and keep our President protected from harm. Help us to stop this man. Amen."

For a moment, there was a quiet, a silence that Katie leaned into like a deep breath.

Almost as if a signal was given, everyone headed to the pile of clothes, glasses, sunglasses, and hats displayed on the counter. Katie had her bag of things she used, but she pulled out a large sun hat that kept her face from being seen. It had a matching bag, and she put a few things in it, water bottle. Dan stopped beside her and dumped three baseballs into it. She glanced questioningly at him.

"What? I can't be walking around with those in my hand. Just stay close."

Most took cars to the area, but Prey went on a motorcycle. They all parked in different areas near the target zone. Dan and Katie began to stroll, they bought coffee from a local stand and sipped it casually like they were on a date. Prey was about a block away, for all purposes a homeless man asleep on a bench. There was no need for him to advertise his presence yet, so he created a position in the center of the designated area.

She saw Tyrone and Matt sitting separately on benches looking at their phones along the street about a block from them, two blocks from Prey.

"How are you doing?" Dan asked as they walked.

Katie knew his question referred to Ricky. "I woke up every hour wondering what I could have done differently to save him. I feel like all of this is so unreal. Last week the biggest thing I was worried about was Ellie pooping on the carpet. Being overwhelmed? That would be understating my life right now."

"Not sure, but I think Corrie Ten Boom once said something like, "To realize the worth of the anchor, we need to feel the wrath of the storm." He didn't elaborate, but Katie pondered his words. Sometimes it was better to think about the bigger picture than the storm that waged inside of her. There would come a day that she would talk to God about Ricky, and perhaps she would understand better.

They continued to walk and sip coffee, checking the time, and listening to their phones. Every few minutes, people checked in, but there were no sightings of Huff.

Dan checked his phone, "Prey just texted that someone is checking him out. It's early yet, only eight. Should we go over there?"

"Hey, he is sitting up. Dan, he's looking at someone. Can you see it? Oh, dear God, its Fred Lindley! Fred is supposed to be dead in Huff's book. If he sees him, it will spook Huff. We have to get to him."

Katie felt Dan's hand squeezing her arm. "Wait!" He whispered fiercely, "Look at Fred. He's standing there, out in the open. He is doing the same thing Prey is trying to do, draw Huff out!"

"He knows Huff can't resist killing him because he thought he already did. How did Fred know we were here?"

Both Katie and Dan heard Matt in their ears, "That's on me, the old guy played me. He called and said he felt so far away from the action and wanted to know our op. So, I told him, I had no idea he was in Alexandria and planned on sacrificing himself. Dan, Katie, get to Fred, see if you can get him out of there. Prey, sit up, make yourself known. It's 8:25. Huff is near, I can feel him."

Katie walked fast toward Fred, who saw her but did not smile. His eyes were drawn to the left of Katie, and she followed his gaze. An old veteran in a wheelchair waving a flag with a sign that read "Homeless Vet, Please Help" was parked next to one of the buildings. *Huff!*

He moved his hand to behind the sign and raised a metal tube that had a small spring action on it. He smiled, and waved the flag with one hand at Fred and released a dart from the air gun with the other. It hit Fred in the neck, and he went down. Katie ran toward Fred, her eyes glued on Huff.

Prey charged Huff, who in no hurry calmly loaded the air gun and shot Prey twenty feet away in the neck. Almost in one motion, Prey pulled out the dart and threw it down, and he stumbled and landed hard on the pavement fifteen feet from Huff, who was rising out of the wheelchair. Huff hesitated for a mini-second, his gaze swept the area as he saw Dan and Tyrone storm through the crowded sidewalk. He turned the chair, activated the auto mechanism, and glided swiftly into one of the closest buildings.

"I have Fred. I'm going to drag him to Prey. Where is the medic, they both need help *now!*"

"Katie, he will find you. Stay with them. Stay calm. Dan, Tyrone, can you see Huff?"

"Can't see him. He went down between two buildings and must have gone into one of them." Dan panted. "Tyrone, I'm taking the one on the left, you got the one on the right."

Tyrone grunted a reply, and both men disappeared into a building.

Katie reached under Fred's arms and leaning back with all her weight, and she dragged him to Prey. He was dead weight, yet in panicked fear, he would die, she propelled him forward. As she reached him, the medic arrived and began to prepare Prey.

"Listen, I know you didn't plan for this, but both of them have to be intubated, they both have been darted!"

Medics train for an emergency, but this was not the plan. A flicker of doubt passed over the man's face, and then he pulled out a second tube from his medical bag.

He started on Fred first, threading the tube down his throat.

Seconds passed as he struggled to get the tube in place.

"He's going to intubate you both, hang on Prey," Katie leaned down and spoke in Prey's ear and squeezed his hand. His eyes were wide open, and Katie could only pray the medic could do the unexpected.

"Hold this tube up, please," the medic instructed Katie, and he hooked the other end to the machine and turned it on. Katie could see Fred's chest rise as the oxygen machine pumped in the air. The medic was already pushing a tube down Prey's throat, struggling as seconds passed. Soon Prey would asphyxiate. The medic didn't panic, but in a hard motion, shoved the tube. He must have got it in place as he connected it to another port on the machine and turned it on. Prey's chest began to rise and fall.

Katie searched the area for any other of Huff's associates who might try and take them out. She recognized two men from Jim Dunn's team, who approached her, and she relaxed. Body-builder types like Tyrone, she was confident they could repel any attack.

The color seemed to come back into Fred's face. They were still both rigid. The plan worked, Huff had exposed himself, and now Dan and Tyrone hunted him.

Her hands trembled as she squeezed both Fred and Prey's hands, willing them to keep breathing and begin to move. Where was Huff? Would he use his dart gun on Dan or Tyrone? Fear gripped Katie in waves.

*God, please help them.*

# CHAPTER FIFTY-ONE

Dan pulled his gun from his shoulder holster and kept his hand on it under his jacket. Every corner in the building, he looked and pulled back quickly. He saw nothing, no wheelchair, just women and a few men were walking the halls. There were rooms all along the corridor, but if Huff had entered one, Dan wouldn't know. Huff had to get to the roof, to get in place for his shot.

"Matt, listen, I can't see him, but he has to be on the way to one of the roofs here. I can see that the two buildings Tyrone and I are in are connected on the second floor. There is a walkway from one to the next. I'm going to take the elevator to the roof, or as close as I can get, to check there first. Tyrone, if he came in this building, he might be in yours now because of the walkway."

"Copy that," Tyrone responded.

Dan found the elevator and hit the button to the top floor, number four. He breathed deeply to catch his breath as the elevator made its slow rise. It stopped on the third floor, and a woman entered. Either Dan's demeanor or his hand in his jacket alerted her to something strange going on. She moved to the door nervously and started tapping on her phone. Looking over her shoulder, Dan read her text.

Call security. There is a weird guy in the elevator. I
think he has a gun.

Dan had no time to reassure the woman he was in pursuit of a
deadly hitman, so there was no need to call security. When the
elevator opened, the woman burst out and ran for the nearest room.

Dan looked toward the end of the hallway and saw the "STAIRS"
sign. He sprinted and wondered how fast it would take for the
security in the building to get to him. He entered the staircase and
started his climb. The door behind him opened, and two plainclothes
security type looked his way.

"Hey guys, I'm with Homeland Security, we have a possible
sniper on the roof."

Both men looked at each other first, and one responded, "We can
check that out, but you are going to have to come with us."

"Matt, you catch that, these guys do not believe I'm with
Homeland. Can you patch into someone and make that happen?"

Both men moved toward Dan, who turned and bounded up the
stairs.

"Listen, I can get verification. The President of the United States
is just a few buildings away speaking today. There's a man who is
going to try and shoot him," Dan huffed as he climbed the stairs to
the roof.

Now both men were rushing after him and as he came up to the
door to the roof. He pulled it, hoping it was unlocked. Locked. He
turned to face the men.

"Dan put me on speakerphone," Matt yelled in his ear.

"This is Matt Dunn, Special Agent with Homeland Security. This
man is undercover. Stand Down now. Your supervisor will text you
to leave the area."

Both men lunged for Dan, who kicked one in the shoulder,

knocking him down the stairs as the other tackled him. Dan pulled his gun and pressed it against the man's temple as they struggled on the stair landing.

The man went stiff, and Dan growled, "Stand up, hands on your head."

His partner was moving but slowly on the landing below.

Unbelievably the man below pulled a gun and aimed at Dan. His only course of action, Dan stepped behind the man with his hands raised. With no remorse, the man below fired into his partner, who slumped in front of Dan.

Dan fell with him and shot at the man below who slid deliberately down the stairs.

"Matt, these guys are not regular security, they must be with Huff! The talkative one just shot his partner and is leaving the scene. The roof door is locked, and I'll try and pick it to get on the roof. I need someone to watch my back. These guys are serious."

"Copy that Dan, I can't send Tyrone because Huff might not be on the roof where you are, he might be across the way. Sending one of dad's guys your way."

"How are Prey and Fred? Sit-rep?"

"Katie is with them, and another one of dad's men is there too. The medic is working on both, but we don't know yet."

Dan listened. The man below who had shot his partner was gone. Either he had escaped out a door, or he was waiting for Dan to try and get to the roof. No time, he pulled his lock set from his pocket and leaned down to pick the lock of the door to the roof. The hair on the back of his neck stood on end as he tried to work the lock and keep eyes out for an attack from the man below. Katie was right. His lock picking skills were rusty. He heard a click and pulled the door slowly open. Cautiously he stuck his head out for a second and pulled back. No one in sight, but Huff was ingenious at hiding. One thing

Dan had not seen was the wheelchair, which made him wonder if he was in the right building. Huff would have had to ditch it.

Not wanting to alert Huff, he texted Matt.

On the roof, beginning search.

Copy. Tyrone report.

No response. Tyrone was a soldier, and he knew the importance of communication. Something had happened. Dan crept out the door and, leading with his Glock, looked both ways. He eased over to one edge of the roof, careful to follow HVAC exhaust tubes and not expose himself to fire. He looked at the building across the way. Through the window of the stairwell, Dan saw Tyrone was one floor below the roof, engaged with a combatant. The man was good because Dan wasn't sure Tyrone was getting the best of the struggle. Suddenly Tyrone head-butted his attacker, and the man stepped into Tyrone's hard left. As he watched the man slid to the floor, Dan figured the left hook put him out cold. Tyrone disappeared from Dan's view, probably headed to the roof. Nothing to do now but a painstaking slow search of the roof. Dan saw no one. He felt his phone vibrate; Tyrone checked in with a text.

Tyrone: Ran into a slight problem. Roof is not only locked but barred. If Huff is there, I cannot access it from below. He had two men guarding the roof, believe he is on the roof in this building.

Matt: Tyrone, did you say *had* two men guarding the roof?

Tyrone: Affirmative, both down.

Matt: Copy that, Dan, can you go to assist Tyrone?

Dan: Yes. There was one injured man below me. He is still active. I will work my way to Tyrone.

Matt: Katie report on Prey and Fred.

Katie: Both are breathing. Prey stirred about 30 seconds ago. I think he might be coming out of it. Fred is still breathing oxygen, but not moving.

Matt: Good. Stay with them and alert. Four armed men with Huff could be more.

Dan looked over to the adjoining roof. He saw a pop-up tent in the far corner, with some construction tape around it. A guy was working under the tent. Huff?

Dan: Matt, on the other rooftop, is a pop-up tent with construction tape. One man working under it. Possible Huff, too far to see.

Matt: Glenn just alerted me to a schedule change. The president will be speaking in the next 20 minutes. No way for us to know there had been a change, but typical to presidential schedule. We have to get to the roof and speed up our intervention. President is going to be under a temporary overhead cover. Possibly due to the forecast of rain or potential safety concern by Secret Service. Might slow down Huff's shot, but he will still take it. Report as soon as on the roof.

Dan ran, praying that man with the gun below him was not waiting for him. He crept down the first set of stairs and looked down. Nothing. With his weapon out, it was less noticeable to take the empty stairwell, so he raced, looking below him. At the bottom, another text was coming through from Katie.

Prey is up and moving toward the building Tyrone is in,
Fred is stirring.

Dan holstered his gun. He would have to cross the $2^{nd}$-floor walkway to get to the building next door. Waving a gun was not going to get him there unnoticed. He sprinted across the skyway, not caring if he drew attention.

They had minutes to get through a barred steel door. If they couldn't, Huff would kill the President of the United States.

# CHAPTER FIFTY-TWO

Katie squeezed Fred's hand and felt him squeeze back. He began moving his legs and arms.

"Is it safe to remove the bag and tube?" she asked the medic.

Prey had indicated to the medic to remove his bag and left five minutes ago. She watched him move toward the building. Being older, Fred had responded by movement only a minute ago.

"Let me recheck his vitals."

Fred motioned to remove the bag, and the medic held up one finger. He checked BP and pulse and removed it.

Katie helped Fred to sit up and tightly held his hand.

Fred searched her face. "You know?"

Katie reached the phone in her pocket and showed Fred she was muting her sound.

"I didn't until this morning. You were standing there, and Huff was dressed as an older man. I had this feeling in the back of my mind that on that first day in the garage, he reminded me of someone. I never made the connection until today. He's your son?"

Fred grimaced.

"Many years ago, I was working for the CIA. I was involved in an operation that was a sting for a Russian spy. Her code name was Alla. When it was over, she was allowed to defect. She chose not to.

Because of her choice, I could not help her. Survival must have been difficult for her. She was pregnant with our child, but I did not know it until years later. She hated me for the betrayal. And she raised our son to be a trained killer, one who she knew someday as an agent I would be called on to track. When he had begun his career, Interpol hunted him as did other police agencies. She contacted me through an unknown source and told me that he was our son. She sent pictures. I could not deny the resemblance, and the date of birth was obvious. Her revenge? Weaponize my son as someone I would have to hunt, all the while knowing I was his father."

"I followed his crimes. I knew more about him than any agency. I retired, and yet consulted often as an expert when new kills were attributed to him. I came today to stop him."

"Does he know?"

"I don't know. His mother knew one day I might find him, and she hoped he would kill me. She might have heard that he killed my brother, thinking it was me. I imagine in her mind that it would be her greatest revenge. She would tell him the story of my betrayal, and they would rejoice over my death."

"I asked Matt about his plan. I knew if Terrell saw me, his ego would force him to take me out. I was supposed to be dead. If I was alive, he had failed. He would try to kill me, and that would slow him down. Perhaps enough for you all to stop him. I trusted the same methodology to save Prey could be used to save me. If not, I have lived a long life. One in the last fifteen years has been rich and full of love thanks to your family and my dear wife, Marilyn. It was a risk I needed to take for our country."

Fred's eyes narrowed. "Where is he?"

"We think he is on the roof of the middle building. The roof door is barred shut, and Prey and Dan are trying to secure entry."

Katie unmuted the phone and texted Matt.

> Fred is conscious. We are available to help.

> Glad to hear he is okay; tell Fred he can explain later
> his surprise visit. Waiting on Tyrone, Dan, and Prey to
> check-in.

"He is not your fault or responsibility. Everyone makes their own choices Fred, he chose the life his mother encouraged him to choose, but he could have gone a different route." Katie said.

Fred shook his head sadly. A text was coming from Matt.

> Someone knocked down Tommy's drone with an
> electronic attack. We don't have eyes in the sky. Katie,
> can you get in a position to see the roof of the building
> Huff is on? Glenn says POTUS has arrived at the
> location and will be moving to the stage in a few
> minutes. Tommy is trying to get his backup drone in the
> sky. We are trying to get visual.

"Can you walk?" Katie asked Fred.

"Just help me up."

"I think we are okay now if you want to go," Katie told the medic.

"I am here for the duration of this operation. Matt saved my life a while back, and I owe him more than I can say. Lead the way."

Katie looked at him, "You're former Homeland?"

"Affirmative."

"I guess only us former government agents are qualified to save POTUS. Let's hope we can stop Huff in time."

Katie and the medic helped Fred to stand, and each took his arm, moving back from the building. She hoped to get a visual of the roof as she pulled the spotting scope out of her bag. Katie was well aware that would put them in Huff's range, but they all stood to lose a President and were willing to give the ultimate sacrifice to save him.

Her phone rang.

"There is no way to get through the door," Dan said. "Prey is going down one floor and will free climb to the roof. Tyrone and I are going to cover his approach, best if everyone there did too. The time frame on POTUS speaking?"

"Glenn says five minutes to the podium," Matt said.

Katie was scanning with her spotting scope. "I can *see a gun!* He has a stand near the edge, and he is sighting the rifle."

"I just told Glenn. He's trying to get through security, but no one believes him." Matt said.

Katie saw Prey free climbing up the side of the wall away from the point of the gun.

"I'm out of range, and he knows it, but I'm going to fire at him. Maybe it will rattle him or bring police," Dan said.

Dan fired five times. The gun remained where it was.

No one spoke. Katie's mouth was dry, and she gripped Fred's hand hard.

"He is at the podium." Matt murmured.

Katie saw a puff of smoke.

"He fired!"

"THE PRESIDENT IS DOWN!" Matt yelled. "The President went down, and they collapsed the cover over him and the agents with him. Glenn says they are saying the rain cover collapsed and hit the President and injured him. They are keeping it over him as they carry him to Cadillac One. There are no photos." Matt said.

There were no words from anyone.

"Too soon." Prey spoke quietly.

"Get Huff," Matt yelled.

Katie could see that Prey had almost reached the roof, but now Huff's exit plan was in place. He had thrown over a retractable ladder and was repelling down the building rapidly to the sidewalk. He threw a smoke bomb to the ground about halfway down and landed in the smoke cover. Dan and Tyrone could not shoot for fear of hitting innocents. People were scattering and screaming from the smoke, and someone yelled, "Fire!"

He must have thrown two or three more smoke bombs as the entire area was filling with smoke — no chance of seeing him.

Katie could see that Prey had reached the roof and had grabbed the rope ladder to repel down into the smoke.

"Glenn just said he was close enough to Secret Service agents to hear them calling for the Speaker of the House to come to the Situation Room. He'll be the next target for Huff. We have to get to DC. If he were assassinated next, Grigory Volkov would be the in line to be President of the United States. Prey, where are you?" Matt asked urgently.

"I'm," coughing, "In the smoke. Look for him. Huff will have changed his appearance."

"He'll head for the Park," Katie said.

People were running from the smoke, and there was mass confusion. Katie searched those who ran away, but no one resembled Huff.

A block away, a bus stopped at a bus stop. The wheelchair ramp was extended, and an older woman in a wheelchair accessed the ramp. *The wheelchair!*

"Look for a wheelchair."

The bus began to head toward the park.

"Get to your vehicles. Prey head to DC, get in position to warn or help the Speaker of the House."

Katie saw something on the sidewalk. It was the dart Prey had pulled out of his neck earlier. She found a plastic Ziplock in her purse and stuffed it inside.

Prey sprinted to his motorcycle.

She googled breaking news. "The President has been injured in a collapse of a rain cover. He is being transported to Walter Reed Hospital."

It had begun.

# PART THREE

# DIVINE APPOINTMENTS

# CHAPTER FIFTY-THREE

Katie helped Fred to the car, and Dan ran to them.

"Hey Fred, nice, you can join the party. You okay?" Dan said.

"Yes, thanks to Katie."

"I'm on route to the WH, no idea if I can get there in time. Matt, I noticed a lot of Homeland guys all over Huff's location. Who's covering the Speaker?" Prey asked.

There seemed to be a slight delay in Matt's response.

"Secret Service will be alerted to cover the Speaker."

"We are almost at Tide Lock Park, we'll report back in a few minutes," Katie said.

Katie glanced at Fred. He had a faraway look, mostly sad.

Looking at Dan, Fred asked, "Why did Prey say "too soon?"

Dan threw the car in gear and delayed answering as he navigated traffic to the park.

"The timing of the shot fired and when the President went down. It was almost simultaneous. At that distance, there would be a delay of less than a second.

"Head to a women's restroom, he's dressed as an old lady in a wheelchair," Katie said. "Fred, please stay in the car." She looked at Fred, "You carrying?"

"He's here."

Instantly Dan and Katie's eyes swept the grounds, "Where? Where?" Katie spoke slowly.

"Not where anyone can see him. But he is here. He set us up, specifically you, Katie. He knows what you found. He left it there for you. He can't stand the fact that you shot him. And that you stole something private from him. He is waiting for you to come." said Fred.

Katie shivered involuntarily.

"Fred, you mean because I shot him in the garage?"

"No. Maybe a little of that." Fred said wearily.

"What did I take from him?" Katie asked.

"The agency file on him suggests strongly that he, like other serial killers, takes a trophy from his victims," Fred explained.

"But he is not a serial killer. He is an assassin, and he kills for money."

"I think what Fred is saying, is that he also kills for the pleasure. He is addicted to watching someone die." Dan said as he visually searched all around them, looking for movement anywhere.

"In areas where paid assassinations occur, there are unsolved murders at the same time. It is believed that Huff is a serial killer, too," Fred added.

"But he can't take something from his victims? Isn't that why the agencies have consulted with you over the years? The crime scenes are pristine. There is not a speck of DNA, nothing to identify the killer. He never uses the same gun, varies his methods, and as far as they know, and you've told me, nothing's taken from the body?" Katie's voice held the puzzlement she felt.

"We think he takes a picture. He keeps an album of his kills. When he was in the room with my brother who was dying, one of the agents said the older woman took a picture of him. He wanted a picture of your friend, Ricky. You stole that from him by taking him away. It was his sense of accomplishment and enjoyment. It's very personal to him, and he sees you as the reason he doesn't have that enjoyment. He is here because he knew you would come and he planned to kill you. That I am here is a bonus. That Dan is here, means he gets an extra treat. Dan, drive away, now. We will not beat him at his game. Not when he has planned this. The only way to beat him is to plan as he does. He has a mission yet, and he will go to it and plan another day for us. We must plan for him. Go, or we will all die here. Fight another day."

Just ahead of them, the bus pulled away from the stop for the park. Near the restroom, they could see a wheelchair parked nearby.

The wisdom of an old spy had spoken, and they all knew to confront a killer as deadly as Huff, they would need more than the raw courage that filled them today. They would need wisdom. Both Katie and Dan holstered their weapons. Dan backed the car up. Then he turned the car around and drove away

They left because to stay meant death.

# CHAPTER FIFTY-FOUR

He had killed the President of the United States. Years from now, this day would still be infamous. The "Unknown Shooter" would have been searched for and never found. He gloried not only in his expertise and planning to do something that few men in the world could have done, perhaps he was the only one who could have done it. Not only had he done the impossible, but he had also escaped, maybe even the most significant achievement—the best in the world. No one would ever dispute that now.

He saw them leave. Pity, he had such plans for the woman, but no matter. She would die, perhaps slowly now because he still had one enjoyable "paying" job left to do. He ran to the motorcycle stashed in the brush. Stupid, they were all so unintelligent. He had plenty of time to get through traffic and to his kill spot. He would enjoy this one so much, and then he would stalk the girl. A matter of time and he enjoyed the hunt.

# CHAPTER FIFTY-FIVE

Katie furiously texted Matt Dunn.

> Get me on a helicopter to where you think the Speaker
> of the House will be. Huff will be prepared for Prey. I
> have seen Huff more times than anyone. By the time
> Prey locates Huff, it will be too late. No one can identify
> him as I can. You know that. Get me there.

There was a pause. Was he checking with someone?

> Get to the roof of the building next to the one Huff used.
> Your transport will be there in five minutes.

"Dan, take me back to town. I'm coordinating something for
Matt that is on a need to know basis."

Dan gave her a look, Fred remained still. Katie closed her eyes.
*God help.*

# CHAPTER FIFTY-SIX

Traffic was lighter than he had thought, and he eased through it in the motorcycle. He parked the cycle in a spot that had been marked with an "Official Parking Only" sign. From the storage area behind his seat, he pulled a cover that said, "District of Columbia Public Works." No one would bother the cycle, and he would leave unnoticed.

He was in contact with his associate, who advised him the Speaker was on the move and near the target. He heard a helicopter and noticed it landed nearby. Lots of confusion as the government panicked. He could see the car now, approaching slowly in traffic. He withdrew the dart gun from the purse, part of his disguise as a woman.

Like clockwork, the car pulled next to the hydrant, and stopped, a window went down and sighting the Speaker in the car, he quickly dispatched the dart. The surprise on the Speaker's face made him smile in anticipation. The Speaker slumped, but Huff was on the move to approach the door, his syringe in his hand. He had soaked the dart in Suc, and at the Speaker's age, it was enough to kill. But he would make sure.

# CHAPTER FIFTY-SEVEN

Katie sprinted from the helo. She had seen the official government limo from the air, and Matt had explained it carried the Speaker. She slowed to a walk and searched the crowd walking in front of her.

She saw Huff, dressed like a woman only five feet away. She saw him looking at Prey and realized he recognized Prey looking for him in the crowd. He was arming his dart gun again, lifting it toward Prey.

Katie felt in her purse for the dart she had picked up from the sidewalk. The one Huff had dropped in the street. She had noticed when she picked it up. It still glistened with the drug Suc. Not enough to kill maybe, but she prayed sufficient enough to stun.

She leaped and drove the dart into Huff's neck. He stiffened and fell. Prey glided to her through the crowd.

Prey pulled out the dart Katie had used.

"Was this used on Fred or me?"

Katie pointed to him. He put it in his pocket.

Prey leaned down to the paralyzed Huff.

"Sorry ole boy. The dart you used on me still had a little Suc left on it. Not enough to kill you, just enough to paralyze you for a minute." Prey spoke slowly.

Katie watched as he reached down and pried out of Huff's hand the syringe he had intended to inject into the Speaker. He held it in front of Huff's frozen gaze and injected him.

# CHAPTER FIFTY-EIGHT

Prey's face remained in front of him. Then a wave of unbelievable pain started a crescendo in his chest as he couldn't breathe. He wanted to close his eyes, but he could not. NO! No one could do this to him! The woman, the woman, did this, he would kill her. How could his mind work so correctly, and his body not move? He was better than them. He was the best! His chest was roaring for air, agony inconceivable.

The man stared. "Now, you know how it feels, what you have done to others."

Terror.

The woman's face entered his vision.

"My friend, Dan, would say you deserve to hear some words. And even though I know Jesus died for you too, you killed my friend. But because Jesus died for all, I will say it. Jesus came into the world to save sinners. He came to save you, even though you are not worth saving. But for that matter, neither am I. Ask Him to save you. He is the only one who can. Not from death, but from what is beyond."

The woman's face in front of him faded away.

# CHAPTER FIFTY-NINE

Katie's phone vibrated, a text from Matt.

> Team, please go to the safe house and wait. Don't
> contact anyone. I will update everyone there.

When she arrived with Prey via a quick helo ride, Katie went into the kitchen to make coffee. No one followed her, the quiet in the house heavy. In a few minutes, she heard someone else arrive, and Tyrone slipped quietly into the kitchen and searched for a cup in the cupboard.

She carried her cup into the living room, where someone had turned on the news.

"At this time, there is no report on the President. He's at Walter Reed Hospital with unknown injuries. We will update his condition as soon as there is information."

Every channel was carrying the news, and yet there was nothing of substance being reported.

"I'm going to make some sandwiches," Katie announced. She wasn't hungry, but it was lunchtime.

Time seemed to creep by. She made piles of sandwiches, probably way too many. But she couldn't stop. It helped to have busy hands because her mind was numb. A great sense of loss seemed to descend over her.

Her phone vibrated again, Matt.

In route. Ten.

He would have news, knowing more at this point seemed a good thing. Huff wouldn't have missed, and yet.

Prey seemed to think there was something to the timing of the shot. Maybe. A ray of hope tried to find its way to her heart.

"Are you feeding an army that I don't know about?" Dan asked as he came into the kitchen.

"My mom always makes piles of food when bad things happen. It's apparently, hereditary. Have at them. Someone has to eat all this." Katie tried to smile.

Dan grabbed a plate and piled it high.

"So, you're hungry? All this doesn't bother you?"

"Yep, hungry. Learned in the military if food is available, better eat it, as you don't know when you will eat next. Maybe it taught me to think about what's in front of me, and worry about what I can't change later."

"Are you giving me advice?"

"Only if you want it." Dan smiled. It was a pleasant smile and warmed her heart a little.

Katie piled a sandwich on a plate, threw on some grapes, and grabbed a glass of water to bring to Fred.

When she approached him, he waved her off.

"Dan says we have to eat now," ignoring his protest she handed him the plate and glass and went back into the kitchen to grab one for herself.

Tyrone was filling a plate high. Food did seem to help, something she would have to tell her mom about if she got back to the real Washington soon.

She heard the front door open. There was some murmuring. Matt

Dunn and Glenn Richter walked into the kitchen.

"I heard there was the food?" Matt said quietly.

"Help yourself." Katie looked at him, questioningly.

"Give me a minute Katie, and I will be updating everyone." He didn't look at Katie, and she wondered about that. He was not a man she would like to play poker with because he didn't give anything away in his demeanor, and she could not read sadness or anything in his facial expression.

Katie went back into the living room with her plate and tried to eat. Finally, she just sipped her coffee as everything tasted like sawdust. The news suddenly showed a screen that said, "BREAKING NEWS." She braced herself for what would come.

Matt came into the room and stood silently, holding his plate.

"We have news that the President is uninjured from the collapse of the tent covering as he was addressing a gathering of the Secret Service staff. He will be broadcasting from the Oval Office in a few minutes. Please stand by as we bring you the President of the United States."

Katie was sipping her coffee and almost choked on it as she sucked in a deep gulp of air.

"What—what just happened?"

"My fellow Americans. Our nation has undergone some tremendous loss in the past few days with the death of Vice President Jones. I am sorry to say that it is not the only loss. This morning the Speaker of the House suffered a heart attack and passed away. The loss to this nation is great, and we are working to overcome the enormous loss of these two great men. I wanted to assure the nation we will continue to operate at the highest ability we can. But considering these losses, I felt it was important to reassure the nation I am working tirelessly to lead the nation at this time. We ask that you continue to pray for these families. My cabinet and I will be working to make sure we keep American strong and safe during this transition time, and we ask for your prayers. Thank you."

The camera cut to a reporter with a news alert about the Speaker of the House.

All eyes turned to Matt, and he looked at his phone.

He took a call, "Yes, Mr. President, we are here. You are on speakerphone Sir."

"I know you all have been in the dark about the happenings of the past hour. It was necessary to keep the information as secure as possible to protect our country. I wish to thank each of you, especially Katie, as you seem to have a propensity to protect the Baxter family."

Relief and a deep thankfulness washed over her.

"As you all are aware, there was an attempt on my life. You all are required to sign a non-disclosure document that will be delivered in a few minutes to your location. Matt, please brief your team with the information you receive from the Homeland Security team that will be arriving. However, that said, I wanted you all to know my thanks for your part in this operation personally, and that a secret ceremony to honor your heroism will be held to distinguish your efforts. Thank you all." The phone disconnected.

Almost immediately, they heard doors slamming outside, and Katie peeked out the window to see two black SUVs with very intimidating looking men exiting the vehicles. Non-disclosure documents were a serious business. Matt went to the door and greeted the agents as they entered.

"My name is Jeff Whitman. I am here today to receive from each of you, a signature. It is my understanding the President explained this need."

No one spoke as each signed a document handed them by the agents. Jeff Whitman gave Matt an envelope. After the papers were collected, the Homeland agents left the way they came.

Matt quietly pulled a page from the envelope and read it.

Finally, he looked up.

"What I am authorized to tell you all is what you have seen on the news. The Secretary of State is dead. His death is recorded as a heart attack. Any other explanation is not applicable at this time. There was a bystander near the Secretary's car who also suffered a heart attack. The FBI recovered the body of the bystander as there was concern this person was a known criminal. We do know the FBI has identified this person as the terrorist known as Terrell Huff. DNA evidence is being sought, and we will keep you informed as we know. This information isn't on the news and is included in the statement you all signed to keep confidential. You'll see news sometime today the Secretary of the Treasury has resigned his position to return to Russia for personal family reasons. His resignation is immediate, and his travel plans are also immediate. Again, this information is confidential, although this news will be released to the news agencies within a few days."

"Is that it? He gets away with an attempt to kill the President?" Katie asked.

Matt looked at her. It was a look that she would always remember as saying everything, even though his mouth remained closed. Some things cannot be said, and she understood that justice would find its way to that man, as did everyone in the room.

It took a day to wrap things up in Alexandria, and it seemed that Prey had exited in his plane, requiring Katie and Dan to fly commercial to Seattle. She was glad the government picked up the cost for that. She understood why Fred was not on the plane, and that he had to do a blood test for a DNA match while in DC.

During the downtime before they left DC, she asked Matt why he was in the parking garage. His explanation was cut short by his need to keep the operation confidential. Still, he briefly said

Homeland had received intel that a Chinese diplomat was involved in espionage and could be a potential target. They'd been sent to observe the diplomat when attacked by Huff. He believed as Katie did, the intel was only a ruse to get both agents to the garage so that Huff could take them out.

When she returned to Seattle, she was happy to collect Ellie and Lucky from her parents, although she could tell that her mom was having second thoughts about giving up Lucky. He was an adorable kitten, but Ellie was attached, and there was no separating them.

She received a text from Ellie's owners that they wouldn't be returning to Seattle but had decided to live in Hawaii permanently. They asked if she wanted to keep Ellie and she sent a text back that she'd be happy to keep her. Also, they asked if she would stay in the house until it sold, as they did not want any vandalism. They would not be selling the house for six months, and Katie breathed a sigh of relief that she had a home for a while.

A few days after arriving home, she watched a news report that stated the Secretary of the Treasury had resigned to take care of ill family members. Two days after that, another news report that barely contained any information at all explained that a small plane carrying the former Secretary of Treasury went down and crashed at an unknown location just after it left the airport in Alaska. The airplane's destination was Russia. No details and no follow-up news. The long arm of justice scored a victory.

# CHAPTER SIXTY

"When is your friend meeting us at the property?" Katie asked.

"A little antsy, Girl? I already said 10:00 AM." Dan raised an eyebrow.

"Well, he might have changed it, just checking."

"Dreaming of money filling your pockets? Yeah, I got that."

"Hey, by the way, what happened to Prey?"

"He flew back to Alaska, no words as to what happened. I think some classified stuff went on."

"Speaking of what happened, what was the deal with Fred?"

Katie paused. "He's been a patriot all his life. They don't make them like him anymore. He will be fine."

Dan sent a sideways glance her way. Katie could see he didn't believe her explanation, but she let it go.

Katie's phone vibrated. A text from Daniella Reynolds, their client, on this case.

> Hi Katie. I wanted to give you a heads up about
> something another girl in our history class, Becki
> Baxter, told me. We both have had our DNA tested and
> like to compare notes on our family trees. Becki's
> uncle, Mr. Wendall, is our teacher for this class and we

found out something interesting. Becki had a cousin a couple of generations back, he was an Erickson, like the family that we thought swindled my great-grandma. Also, on that family tree is Mr. Wendall. So please don't share any information with him. We believe he had a personal reason for teaching our history class when he found out we were researching information on the historical break-in at Tumwater City Hall.

Katie typed a response.

Thanks for that heads up. As a practice, we never share confidential information with anyone but our client. We hope to be able to give you an update today on our findings.

"You're going to find this interesting. I knew there was something fishy about that Mr. Wendall," Katie said before she read Dan the text.

"Elementary, my dear Katie," Dan grinned.

Pulling up to the property, Katie saw an official State of Washington vehicle parked.

Dan approached his friend and stretched out his hand. "Rick, this is my partner, Katie Parson. I would say give us the whole scoop, but I think we want the short version of 'There's gold in them thar hills!'"

Rick chuckled. "I hear you. Step right this way. He picked up a machine about the size of a small suitcase. It had a wand attached, and he pulled it off the device and marched to an old fireplace, still standing on the property. The house had long since disintegrated, but the bricks were partially upright, and the rest were in a heap. He waved the wand over the old bricks, and the dials on the machine went wild.

"Looks like your old miner didn't trust anyone. He took the ore and made it into bricks and used the bricks to make a fireplace. The gold was hidden in plain sight in the house, but no one knew. This old homestead has always been at the back of the property owned by the family. No one knew the bricks contained gold."

"Creative and not where anyone would look. How much gold are we talking about?"

"My professional opinion would be at least four million. The bricks will be assayed and the ore removed, that will be the official answer."

Katie stared. She barely stopped herself from dancing or jumping up and down. Dan had his movie-star grin going and said, "Katie, at ten percent, we are looking at $400,000. Keep the partnership, open our agency?"

Katie gave him a stern look. "No country music will be played in the office. I refuse to chase potential clients away by forcing them to listen to the lyrics of "Momma went to prison." Besides, there will be an espresso machine that will be in *my* office."

Dan switched to a tough negotiator mode. "I get a vending machine in my office, and I get Lucky."

"No way Jose, Lucky is not your cat. He may come to the office to visit you, and you will have visiting residential time allowed."

"You are a hard woman Katie Parson." But the twinkle in Dan's eyes softened his words.

As they walked back to the car, "We need to let the family know of the findings and explain how the contingency fee works." Katie reminded Dan. They both smiled, this was going to be financially significant for them, and they were partners. A small joy spread from her insides to a smile on the outside.

# CHAPTER SIXTY-ONE

"Let not your heart be troubled; you believe in God, believe also in Me. In My Father's house are many mansions; if it were not so, I would have told you. I go to prepare a place for you. And if I go and prepare a place for you, I will come again and receive you to Myself; that where I am there you may be also." Pastor Chuck shared the familiar passage from the book of John.

Katie found that passage comforting as they gathered to show their respect for Ricky. Now he would live in a mansion, not on the streets. Now he would be with Jesus and never worry about scoring drugs or food.

After they got back from Washington DC, she had got a call from the manager of the coffee shop downtown, Dancing in The Rain. She said that Ricky had a small cubbyhole storage room that they allowed him to use on the alley side of the shop. He kept people from scavenging in their dumpster, and in exchange, they had let him sleep in a five by seven unused storage room. It was his home. When they heard the news he had died, the manager checked the room. Not much in it, but Katie's business card was stuck on the door with a tack. She called Katie to see if she wanted any of Ricky's things.

As she viewed the room, a sadness washed over her at how little Ricky owned in the way of material things. Yet his personality had

309

been so full of life and friendship for those he lived with on the streets of Seattle.

Dan had kept his promise to provide a service for Ricky, and Ricky's urn was centered on the front table in the group area at the mission. She was a bit in awe of how many people had shown up to pay their respects. The crowd at the Mission was people from the street, people who knew Ricky and loved him too. Star, Vett, and Raven were all there, and Katie had talked to Star about her friend's program for prostitutes. Star wanted to meet her, and she wanted to try and get out of the life. And so it went, good things happened even though her friend was gone.

Katie's tears spilled down her face. She would see Ricky again someday when it was her time to go home to Jesus.

Dan's phone went off. He pulled it out, and his smile disappeared.

"What?" Katie asked. Dan leaned over and let Katie read the text from Prey.

> I ran into trouble when I got to Alaska. Bring Katie.
> Come in a week, if possible.

Dan was already on his phone, and she looked at her new partner with a sense of camaraderie and maybe something more.

Why did trouble find her like a bee found pollen? But this time, she knew she was not alone. Her God had saved the President of the United States, given her a tiny kitten named Lucky, a good business partner, and God was here with her in a way she had never known before. Trouble was ahead, but He would go before them again, and she knew it as well as she knew it rained in Seattle.

## THE END

# Author's Note

A writer needs a reader, not only to read what they write but to find in that writing a "home" a moment in time that takes the reader to a different, more exciting place. For myself, that is a suspense-filled journey that is thrilling and full of mystery. I hope that as a reader of *Deadly Pursuer*, you found that journey, and I hope you got to know Katie and Dan.

I want to thank you so much for reading the book, and if you enjoyed it, please take a moment to leave a review on Amazon. Reviews are the lifeblood of writers. Leaving a review helps me keep telling those thrilling stories that always have a sense of the inspirational genre as well. To learn more about my writing, please visit me at www.sastacy.com.

Now please turn the page for a preview of Book Two, *Deadly Intentions*, in the Parson Investigation Series. Look for this Book Two by September 2020!

# DEADLY INTENTIONS

## ONE-*Deadly Intentions*

His captor hit him again in his low back with the cold steel muzzle of the Glock.

"Pick up the pace, Ranger." His tone of voice low and almost casual.

For the umpteenth time, Dan Beck cursed his lack of attention, thinking this assignment was the usual skip trace of a runaway girl. The location of the job in a remote town in Eastern Washington had been the only unfamiliar part of this job. He figured on finding this skip hidden with a girlfriend's or boyfriend's family in the remote town. Picking up a trail from there would be easy. The ease of the job caused him to relax his general awareness of his surroundings. That inattention allowed the man at the gas station to move too close behind him. Dan was taken by surprise when he turned a stun gun on him. He regained consciousness in the back of a car, his hands zip-tied behind him.

The past 20 minutes of marching through a private field, brought Dan's senses to high alert. This man knew Dan was ex-Army Ranger, and his handling of Dan identified him as a professional. The skip trace job that lured Dan from the security of his stomping grounds in Seattle, from the safety of a good private investigation company that he co-owned with his business partner Katie Parson, would have been engineered by this man. This march to a very remote area outside a small town did not presuppose a return trip for Dan. That and the persistent prodding of the Glock.

They entered a small forested area of pine trees before a meadow opened into a strange view. PVC pipe stuck out of the ground every 10-12 feet in three rows that were about twenty feet apart. The hair on the back of Dan's head rose. He took a deep breath and grimly hurried forward before he could be struck again.

He captor marched him to the end of the first row, and Dan saw a pipe protruded from a cement tank, similar to a septic tank. The cement round lid was lying next to the opening for the tank-like container. Dan could see very little of the inside of the tank but noticed a rope ladder descending into it. He felt the cold muzzle against his back and stiffened, waiting for the shot. Instead, he felt his captor cut the zip ties.

"Climb down." He could fight, but the muzzle against his back meant he would lose.

He climbed down the ladder, and when he hit the floor watched as it disappeared out of the tank. The light from the overhead opening illuminated a bucket in one corner, and two cases of water, and a couple of boxes of granola bars in the other corner.

"In a couple of weeks, I will be back. If you can tell me everything about Prey, you get to live. Otherwise, you die here. Up to you."

Then the light in the small ten-foot cement tank disappeared as the lid slammed into the opening. Now only an inch of light barely shone into the darkness from the breathing pipe. Silence.

He squatted and put his head in his hands.

"Lord, don't let Katie find me." His fear of this place was not as desperate as the fear of his friend joining him in one of the other tanks.

# TWO-Deadly Intentions

For the fourth time, private investigator Katie Parson called her business partner to hear Dan Beck's phone go straight to voicemail. Yesterday Dan left to investigate a skip trace on a missing girl. The clues lead to a small town in Eastern Washington. While it seemed to be a routine case, Dan always checked in with her to give her details since they operated as a team. But he had not checked in with her last night, and he was not answering his phone. Usually, Katie wouldn't have been too concerned about that. But an hour ago she picked up someone following her. An advantage of having a former Army Ranger as your business partner included having a six-foot-one dangerous man at your side. With Dan missing and an unknown person on her tail, Katie's red flags were flying.

It was time to find out if the person who followed her was a pro. If not, it could be someone trying to make contact with her on the quiet, not unusual in her line of work. Katie drove to the mall, parked her car close to the inside coffee shop. No matter how dangerous things got, coffee made life better. Maybe that was just because she lived near Seattle, the home of everything coffee. More likely, the savoring moment over a hot Americano gave her a moment to pause and think about her cases as she tossed details in her mind. Today she used it as an opportunity to see if her follower would make an appearance in the mall.

She paid for her Americano and found a table to sit and read the news on her phone. In a few minutes, the same man she had seen earlier, about five feet ten inches tall, dressed in high-end outdoor wear with a Seahawks ballcap wandered purposefully into the mall area near the coffee shop. She observed him without seeming to look his way. She turned the flash off her phone camera, and when he pretended to study the menu of the coffee shop, she took a picture.

Katie felt fear tingle at the base of her spine. For the last couple weeks, she loved the pleasantness of not being solo in her business. The beginning of their partnership happened when she and a small group of men, including Dan Beck, had taken the assignment of stopping a conspiracy to kill the President of the United States. That assignment had changed all their lives. The bonding over saving each other's lives had led Dan and Katie to create a private investigation agency.

*Lord, I don't know what to do. Please show me what this all means. I know I'm new at asking You to help, but put me on the right track. Be with Dan. I used to do this by myself, but Lord, please send someone to help.*

"Hey, Katie, right?"

Startled, Katie watched as a man slipped into the other chair at her table.

"Do I know you?"

He slid across the table to her a business card that said "For Hire" and a telephone number. Tight tee shirt over a muscled frame, tattoos, pierced ear, and scar on his cheek told a story of a man who knew his way around tough places.

"I've heard about you. You are that guy who "might be" a private investigator without a license, and you are "for hire."

"Let's say you're right about that. Leaving the mall just now, I noticed you don't have your usual muscle guy with you, and you have a tail. So, if you need him to go away, I can do that."

Katie looked at him steadily for a moment. Not her first choice for help, but something substantial about this man stood out to her. That and she had just prayed. God, did you send him?

"So, For Hire, anyone ever tell you that you were an answer to prayer?"

"I don't network with God usually, but if that works for you, no problem."

"I'm going to lose this tail. Can you pick me up at the Macy's exit door on the opposite side of the mall in ten minutes?"

"Yeah." He slid out of the chair, and Katie stood up with him and walked straight down the mall to the large opening to Macy's.

In the woman's department, she selected a few items of clothing and carried them to a dressing room. A master at changing her appearance, Katie turned her reversible hoodie inside out. She pulled on a beanie from a pocket and a pair of glasses. A little tight getting her unruly curls tamed inside the beanie, but when she left the area, and she looked different than when she entered. Katie left the clothes in the booth and exited the dressing room on the opposite side. She ducked between clothes racks until she found her way to the outside exit to meet her ride. In space beside the door was the usual rack of umbrellas, there to borrow and bring back. Katie grabbed one, opened it. It would cover her exit from security cameras.

As she stepped out of the door, a black Subaru pulled up next to her, and "For Hire" beckoned for her to jump in. Katie hopped in the back to avoid notice again from cameras.

"Can you circle the parking lot? I want to see if he goes back to my car."

Slinking low into the seat, Katie observed as they passed her parked car, the same man in the mall seemed to be loitering nearby. Her misdirection in the mall had given him the slip, but he guessed she would return to her car. Interesting. She watched as he returned to a parked vehicle nearby that had a sticker in the window of a local rental company. Now things were getting even more intriguing. The person following her seemed to be someone from out of town, definitely a professional.

She called Dan again. Voicemail. Katie liked to think that not a lot of things spooked her in her short years of being a private investigator. However, it was that street-smart experience that caused her to be cautious. She clicked on the app of her phone to see Dan Beck's location. His last position, she noted, seemed to be near Hatton, a remote unincorporated town. Why would he turn his phone off?

"Can you take me to my office?"

"Sure."

"Do you need an address?"

"Nope. I know where your office is. Sent a lady there last month who needed the kind of help you guys provide."

"Hmmm." This man was a mystery, but oddly one she felt she could trust. That gut feeling had not failed her in the six years of needing to read people in this business. On the approach to her office, she noticed two occupied cars parked within sight of the building, but in places that were usually vacant.

"Hey, can you go past the building? I think I've picked up a couple of watchers here too. By the way, For Hire, do you have a name?"

"Tip Monte."

"Tip?"

My mom used to say I sent her over her tipping point. The name stuck."

Katie hid a smile. She had a feeling this man sent a lot of people over their tipping point.

"Tip, you are hired. I do need some muscle. Dan is missing, and people are following me. I don't know what this means, but I need help, and I think God sent you."

Tip grunted and gave her a skeptical sideways look.

"I'm not cheap."

"The good ones never are. I need to get to a garage that houses some equipment we keep for emergencies. You up for a road trip?"

"Whatever, I always carry an extra bag in my car."

*Where are you, Dan Beck? I'm coming.*

S. A. Stacy's life-long love of writing found her writing freelance as well as raising a family, which included hosting a local weekly radio show for six years. She has been the featured speaker at women's conferences and taught workshops for both Washington state and regional homeschooling conferences. She taught writing classes, where she instructed her students that combining their passion for life with writing could turn an assignment into a lifelong adventure!

Her Thriller series begins with *Deadly Pursuer*, Book One in Katie Parson Investigations. *Deadly Pursuer* was a semi-finalist in the 2019 American Christian Fiction Genesis Contest, Thriller-Mystery-Suspense category.

She lives in the Pacific Northwest with her husband Mike, and their Australian Shepherd, Buck. Spending time with her children and grandchildren and gardening in the Northwest are her favorite activities. The Zucchini Chronicles, a writing sideline, is a testimony to her ability to grow far more zucchini than she can deposit on the unwilling porches of her friends!

She finds hope in a cherished Bible verse.

I John 5:11, "And this is the testimony: that God has given us eternal life, and this life is in His Son." NKJV

For more news about upcoming books in the Parson Investigation Series and other publications and information, please visit her website at sastacy.com.

Made in the USA
Monee, IL
23 December 2020

55400521R00194